Hunter Prepares

"For two dollars more, you can watch me work," the gunsmith said. "Take the secret back to—well, to wherever you're going back to. I'll even tell you stories. It's nice to have somebody to talk to while I work."

Adam Hunter paused. "I guess I'll have to put that pleasure off until I come back for the gun," he said finally. "But I don't think I'd better be unarmed right now. Do you think—"

"Oh, you can take this one until I'm finished. I don't believe it'll disappoint you. Yours will be ready Tuesday, unless you'd like a bit of engraving on the frame—a marshal's badge, maybe?"

Hunter stiffened, staring at the blank eyeglasses. "Now, why would you think that?" he asked.

Cox shrugged. "Oh, just an idea." He smiled a directionless smile. "I heard a voice like yours once, and its owner was a marshal. Was it you?"

Hunter hesitated, then managed a laugh. "No." He took two silver dollars from his pocket and laid them on the counter. "This ought to cover fixing my Colt."

Cox felt for the coins, then rolled them nimbly between his fingers. "Oh, I'd trust you, Mr. Hunter," he said. "Just as I do with the pistol. Don't forget to load it."

Praise for *MANHUNT*
by Wayne Barton and Stan Williams

"Catering both to the Western buff and mystery fan, *Manhunt* is well worth the price for a few hours entertainment."

—*Topeka Capital-Journal*

"Plenty of action and suspense in this novel that combines the best elements of the classic Western and the classic detective yarn—all of it seasoned with sound and believable characters. Barton and Williams surely are a pair to ride the river with. I look forward to their next collaboration."

—T. V. Olsen, author of *The Burning Sky*

"Equal parts classic Western and classic whodunit, *Manhunt* is a page-turner spurred to full gallop. Dual authors Barton and Williams prove that when it comes to tight plotting and deep suspense, two heads are most definitely better than one. Here's dialogue that snaps like a hot fire, and a poker deck of memorable characters, not one of which is above suspicion. Maybe best of all, in Jefferson Davis King, these writers have a Western protagonist durable enough to carry a whole *Manhunt* series. I'm already waiting for the next one."

—Bruce H. Thorstad, author of *The Gents*

"*Manhunt* is a good-time suspenseful read. Get after it!"

—Max Evans,
author of the classic Western *The Rounders*

"Barton and Williams have merged the western and mystery into a . . . period whodunit that will satisfy, if not excite, readers of both genres."

—*Publishers Weekly*

Praise for Wayne Barton's
RIDE DOWN THE WIND

"A tight and historically accurate novel with suspense, interest and plenty of action, all of it plausible. A good job."

—*Roundup*

"Tight writing, solid plotting . . . a taut, well-told yarn. The battle scenes are done with authenticity. . . . Barton handles the violence necessary to the story with a touch a lot of old pros in the writing game could envy."

—*Sulphur Springs News Telegram* (TX)

"A most interesting tale. . . . A thrilling Western."

—*Booklist*

"Barton blends smoothly . . . the conflicting forces of the fugitives and their pursuers . . . an informative, perceptive story."

—*Bookmarks*

Both Available from Pocket Books

Books by Wayne Barton and Stan Williams

High Country
Manhunt
Live by the Gun
Warhorse

Books by Wayne Barton

Return to Phantom Hill
Ride Down the Wind

Published by POCKET BOOKS

HIGH COUNTRY

WAYNE BARTON & STAN WILLIAMS

POCKET BOOKS

New York   London   Toronto   Sydney   Tokyo   Singapore

This book is a work of fiction. Names, characters, places and incidents are either products of the author's imagination or are used fictitiously. Any resemblance to actual events or locales or persons, living or dead, is entirely coincidental.

Portions of the article "2 Midland Men Hitch Wagon to a Literary Star" by Elizabeth Edwin, copyright © 1990 by *The Midland Reporter-Telegram*, are reprinted by permission.

An *Original* Publication of POCKET BOOKS

POCKET BOOKS, a division of Simon & Schuster Inc.
1230 Avenue of the Americas, New York, NY 10020

First Pocket Books printing November 1993

10 9 8 7 6 5 4 3 2 1

POCKET and colophon are registered trademarks of Simon & Schuster Inc.

Cover art by Darryl Zudeck

Printed in the U.S.A.

For Kristin
There's a scene in here
that's just for you.

and

For Wendy
Whose time has come at last.

HIGH
COUNTRY

Chapter 1

The sound was muted by distance, no louder than the snap of a dry twig, but it was enough to bring Adam Hunter to his feet, tense and alert in the teeth of the sharp northerly wind. The first report was followed by another, then by a low rolling clatter in which Hunter thought he could pick out the sharp bark of a pistol and the deeper, more attenuated crack of rifles.

Hunter moved to catch the reins of his grazing sorrel. He was a tall, angular man, lean and bearded, his face a sculpture in leather tooled by sun and wind over months in the open. At first glance he looked older than his twenty-eight years, partly because of the fine lines that creased the skin around his eyes and mouth, partly because of the hard and humorless brown eyes that quartered the deep valley below him.

His backtrail was a tangle of brushy slopes and barren rocky ridges through which he had ridden steadily since sunup. He figured he'd made twelve miles north and most of two thousand feet in elevation from the edge of New Mexico's high plains. Near noon he'd stopped in a hollow just beyond the mountain crest to give his horse a breather and to eat a cold lunch. Now he stood motionless, listening to the fitful sounds of gunfire windborne from somewhere ahead.

"Trouble," he said aloud.

The valley was broad and shallow, its floor a lush,

vivid green broken by stands of pine, its gentle folds offering little protection from the wind that lashed across it. Deep, rippling grass marked it as ranchland as clearly as a fence. This at last was the rim of the San Antonio Valley, the place Hunter had come a thousand miles to see.

Hunter's sorrel shifted uneasily under his hand, blowing out a quick rush of breath through its nostrils. Hunter absentmindedly patted the animal's neck.

"Not our business, boy," he murmured, his attention still centered on the distance. The volume of gunfire had dwindled to an occasional shot. He judged both sides had found cover and were picking their shots. "Not our business. We've got no friends in Colorado."

Nor anywhere else, his mind added. Not anymore. His face showed no change at the familiar thought, but he bent to tighten the sorrel's double cinch and then stepped up into the saddle. A gentle pressure of his knees took the horse up out of the hollow and sent it angling down the long slope toward the valley floor.

"Still, we've come a good long way." Like many men who'd ridden alone, he'd fallen into the habit of speaking his thoughts on the trail. He reached forward and drew a heavy Winchester rifle from his saddle boot. "Might be there's somebody over there that we ought to meet."

Close up, the valley floor wasn't as flat as it had appeared from above. Rolling swells of ground limited Hunter's vision. Stirrup-high heads of grass rose and fell before the driving wind like ocean waves, and the sorrel cut a wake through them in the general direction of the unseen fight. Finally Hunter saw a break in the smooth green horizon and urged the horse off in that direction.

Within a hundred yards the ground fell away into a deep hollow surrounded by low hills. Sheltered from the wind, stunted pines clung to the sides like the painted rim of a green bowl. At the bottom of the bowl lay a dead horse with a man huddled in the lee of its body.

Reining up short, Hunter evaluated the scene with the eyes of a professional. The man on the ground laid his arm across the horse's back and fired a revolver twice toward a patch of boulders on the far side of the bowl. Almost at once a plume of smoke spurted from a gap between two of the boulders, whipping to tatters in the wind before the boom of a heavy rifle reached Hunter's ears. Studying the ground, Hunter located three more riflemen in the rocks and guessed at a fifth man somewhere back in the trees to tend the horses.

The man with the pistol fired again. All Hunter could see of him was a hat, the back of a shirt, and a set of the wide, hairy chaps that upland cowhands seemed to favor. The dead horse was lying on his rifle. His work with the pistol seemed more a gesture of defiance than anything else. Both the range and the odds were too long for effective shooting, and Hunter couldn't imagine why the men among the boulders weren't already spreading out to take him from the flanks.

"It's not our business," he told the horse. The words failed to convince either of them. Leaving a lone man to face four rifles went against his grain, but he didn't know anything about the situation. The lone man might be a rustler or a killer, the others a posse trying to bring him in. From the high ground he occupied Hunter was in a position to decide the fight either way. What he needed was an idea of which was the right party to join.

Hesitating, he had let the sorrel drift nearer to the rim of the bowl. A puff of smoke from the rocks and the heavy hornet-buzz of a bullet passing nearby showed him his mistake. He piled out of the saddle on the wrong side, giving the sorrel a sharp slap on the rump. Another bullet screamed by, closer than the first. Cursing his stupidity for being caught on the skyline, he threw himself flat on the dense carpet of pine needles and rolled for the cover of the nearest tree.

Behind him the sorrel screamed and reared, breaking back clumsily from the rim. Hunter twisted around to look, then ducked back as the trunk of his pine shuddered at the impact of a heavy lead bullet. In his brief glance he had seen that the sorrel was bleeding, hurt, maybe dying. His own position offered little enough cover and nowhere at all to retreat. Even the shelter of the pine's slender trunk wouldn't last much longer the way things were going.

His mouth a grim line, Hunter thrust the muzzle of his Winchester around the base of the tree and thumbed back the hammer. Whoever had started this little war, it was partly Hunter's now.

Four riflemen, he reminded himself. The black-powder man seemed to be the most dangerous. He'd been the first to open fire at Hunter, and with surprising accuracy, considering he was shooting uphill from a fair distance. Holding a little low, Hunter sighted on the gap between the rocks.

The barrel of a rifle eased into sight, and then something else—part of a man's arm, maybe, a dark sleeve. Hunter squeezed the trigger. The deep boom of the Winchester came at the same moment the man below fired. Powder smoke burst from the rocks. Another powerful blow shook the pine, and yellow splinters split through the bark above Hunter's head. He levered another shell into the chamber as echoes of the shots died away. In the gap nothing moved.

The trapped cowhand had twisted around to stare at Hunter, his mouth open in comic surprise. The other guns had fallen momentarily silent. Hunter lay motionless, waiting, the rifle steady on his aiming point, his eyes unblinking across the sights. A rifle cracked—not the black-powder man—and a bullet buried itself twenty yards below Hunter without breaking his concentration. Then the long barrel appeared again between the two rocks.

This time Hunter fired first. Almost on top of the Winchester's report he heard the whine of his bullet striking rock. The black-powder rifle jerked, steadied, fired. Its heavy slug cut through the branches six feet up, showering Hunter with twigs and pine needles. Then the rifle's muzzle wavered, cocked itself skyward, and fell backward out of sight.

The man behind the dead horse resumed pocking away with his revolver, but his opponents seemed to be caught in confusion. Disorganized firing slashed the slope around Hunter, none of it coming very close. Dust rose from among the boulders, and presently the drum of hooves sounded from below. Four riders burst from the pines on a dead run away from the clearing. A horse with an empty saddle trailed them, its reins dragging.

Rolling to his knees, Hunter tracked the leading rider in his sights for a dozen yards, then slowly lowered his rifle. No need, he decided. Whoever they were, they'd quit. He didn't know enough about them to shoot them down on the run.

The bark of a pistol startled Hunter. He looked down, half-raising the Winchester again. Evidently the ambushed cowhand didn't share his reluctance. He was on one knee, his heavy pistol braced in both hands, firing steadily. Just when Hunter decided the range was too long for any chance of a hit, one of the running horses stumbled and fell. Its rider kicked clear as it went down, rolled over twice, and came to his feet to snatch at the reins of the riderless horse. In a moment he was mounted and pounding north after the others.

"Shoot!" The shout drifted up to Hunter from the man in the bowl. "Why don't you shoot?"

Shaking his head, Hunter rose to see to his sorrel. The horse was hurt and skittish, bleeding into its mane from an ugly raw slash across its neck just ahead of the saddlehorn. Hide and muscles had been torn by the bullet, but bone and the deeper blood vessels were unharmed. Satisfied the wound wasn't immediately dangerous, Hunter went to his saddlebags and reloaded his Winchester. Then, leading the sorrel, he picked his way down the slope toward the bottom of the bowl.

The ambush victim was bending over his fallen mount, methodically stripping off what he could. He straightened, grinning, as Hunter approached.

"Edge Pardee," he proclaimed, holding out a big hand. "And damn proud to meet you, even if you're Satan hisself."

"Adam Hunter."

Hunter shifted the rifle to his left hand and shook, considering the other man with practiced care. Pardee was probably five years his junior, even though his round, freckled face made him look younger. A checked shirt, damp with sweat, strained across muscular shoulders, and the hairy whitish chaps partly hid faded denims. His pushed-back hat showed unkempt blond hair. His grin and the laughter in his innocent blue eyes seemed to invite Hunter to join in some sort of fun not yet revealed.

"Adam, huh. Don't suppose you're traveling with Eve."

"No."

"Hell," Pardee said, "just funning. You a lawman?"

"You see a badge?" Hunter said.

"No," Pardee answered. "Anyway, I'm downright pleased you happened along just when you did. That bunch of yahoos pretty near had me heeled and dehorned. I'm obliged to you, and I won't forget it."

"No need. That buffalo hunter took a shot at me, winged my horse. That's the only thing made it my business."

A hint of puzzlement wrinkled Pardee's forehead. "You'd've left me otherwise?" he asked. Then his grin returned and he shook his head. "Aw, hell, don't you never smile? You pretty near had me believing you. Come along, let's get a look at the one you shot."

Hunter followed him across the grassy floor of the bowl and up the slope on the other side, moving warily with the Winchester ready while Pardee cast ahead like a half-grown puppy. When he reached the boulders, though, the young cowhand stopped abruptly and straightened up. Hunter found him standing over the body of a lean, dark-skinned man.

The man lay on his back, pale eyes open to a pale sky. A black gun belt of tooled leather circled his waist, the pistol still in its holster. His clothing was fancy and well-kept, a dark coat with matching trousers and a fawn-colored vest over a white shirt. There was a dark bloody patch on the vest. Beneath and around the body blood stained the grass and pooled on the dark earth.

Pardee swallowed. His face had gone pale, the freckles standing out against white skin. "Lord God. Guess you got him pretty near right through the heart," he said. He stared at the blood, then at Hunter. "What was you shooting, anyways—a cannon?"

"Smaller than his," Hunter said.

He stepped across the body and bent to pick up the fallen black-powder rifle. It was a Sharps Creedmoor '77 with long-range sights. Hunter hefted it, frowning at the barrel-heavy balance, then leaned it against one of the boulders.

"Your lucky day," he told Pardee. "I expect he didn't miss too often. Do you know him?"

Pardee was still staring down at the welter of blood. He pulled his eyes away with an effort. "Never seen him before." For the first time his voice held a note of bitterness. "Still, I reckon I know where he worked. Looks like them Circle Eighters have gone to hiring their killing done."

"Circle Eight? What's that?"

The blond cowhand looked at him, surprised. "You're for sure a stranger around here, then! Circle Eight's the biggest spread in this county but for Pine Valley Ranch. Uncle Avery—he owns Pine Valley—and old Ellis Watkins from Circle Eight haven't passed a civil word in years."

"I guess not."

"But there ain't been no shooting to speak of, not until today. Those fellers seemed to take a right personal interest in me."

"So I noticed," Hunter agreed. "Are you certain—" Then he interrupted himself, turning to squint back toward the far edge of the bowl. A rider, coming hard, had just emerged from the screen of pines. "Company. Is this fellow a friend of yours?"

Pardee looked, then grinned again with a sidelong glance at Hunter.

"Yes. I know *that fellow* right enough." The grin vanished, replaced by a frown of sudden concern. "Riding out alone, too! Some people just ain't got no judgment a-tall!"

A moment later Hunter understood Pardee's little joke. The rider was a young woman. She rode astride as if she hadn't heard of ladylike behavior, but at close quarters she could never have been mistaken for a man. Like Pardee she wore jeans and wide, shaggy chaps. A man's shirt emphasized the shape of her slender tomboy's body. Long honey-colored hair was tied back at the nape of her neck. Her face, fine-boned and delicate, was set in a determined scowl, and her full lips compressed into a tight line as she reined up her horse in front of Pardee and Hunter. Her right hand held a stubby carbine, its hammer back, its muzzle centered on Hunter's chest.

"Edge, I heard shooting," she said without looking at Pardee. Greenish eyes, hard and unfriendly, studied Hunter. "What happened?"

"Just a little trouble, Linda. I'd like you to take your rifle off Hunter. He's all right."

The woman hesitated a moment, then rested the rifle across the pommel of her saddle and lowered the hammer to half cock.

"If you say so." Her face still showed suspicion and distrust. "What are you doing here?" she asked Hunter.

"Mostly he was saving my skin," Pardee put in before Hunter could answer. "No need to be so uppity about it. Name's Adam Hunter, he says. Hunter, let me present Miss Linda Pardee." He grinned. "My kid sister," he added for Hunter's benefit. "Happens I got the looks in the family, and she got the brains."

Hunter touched his hat. "Ma'am," he said.

"So. You're a Texan. And you wear that pistol where you can find it, too. What brings you here?"

"Just passing through," he said.

"I see." She looked at Hunter a moment longer, then jerked her head toward the body on the rocks. "Is that your work?"

"I shot him."

"A bunch of them bushwhacked me," Pardee explained. "The dead one there killed my horse with that flagpole." He pointed to the black-powder rifle. "Hadn't it been for Hunter, I'd be crow bait by now." His tone changed. "Listen, you know better than to ride out here alone. Uncle Morg will about skin you."

She laughed. "Who's going to tell him? You?" She swung down from her horse, leaving the animal ground reined, and started toward the rocks. "Remember, *I'm* not the one that got ambushed."

"Linda, don't go over there," Pardee said. "You don't want to see anything like that."

She ignored him, advancing until she had a clear view of the dead man. Hunter watched the blood drain from her face as she looked. She swallowed convulsively but held her face expressionless as she turned away.

"You did that?" she demanded. Her voice was steady, and Hunter found himself admiring her. "With what?"

Hunter took a cartridge from his pocket and held it out to her. It was as big around as her index finger and almost as long. She turned away, leaving him with his hand outstretched, but Pardee reached out to take the shell.

"Winchester .45-90. But hell. Somebody's cut the copper jacket back off the nose so's the lead shows."

"A gunsmith I know," Hunter said.

Pardee turned the heavy cartridge thoughtfully in his fingers, then tossed it back to Hunter. "Really loaded for bear, weren't you?" he said.

"No," Linda Pardee said. "Not bear." Her expression was closed and hostile. "Are you sure you haven't picked the wrong side? It's the Circle Eight that's hiring killers, not us."

"Linda! Quit it!" Pardee said. "I've told you, he saved my life."

"It's a gun, much like any other," Hunter said quietly. "I don't use this rifle often. But when I do I mean it to stop what I shoot at. I don't take pleasure in it." Even as he said the words he realized they weren't quite true.

Linda Pardee, though, didn't challenge him. "If you don't kill for fun, then you must do it for money. What's the going rate for killing a man?" She gestured toward the body of the horse lying out in the open meadow. "Or for that horse?" She pointed back in the direction she had come. "Is the pay less if you only get the horse?"

"I haven't asked for pay," Hunter said to the woman. "If he got all the looks, you deserved another scoop of the brains. But I think he got it backwards." He nodded to Pardee. "Good to meet you."

Pardee took off his hat and ran his hand through his tangled yellow hair, his round face unhappy. He cleared his throat and said, "Hell, Linda, fact is I'm the one that shot the horse." He brightened a little. "It was an accident, though. I was aiming at the yahoo riding him."

Leading his sorrel, Hunter went to have a look at the bushwhacker's horse. He knew he was unlikely to find anything useful, but it was always best to be sure. Barney had taught him that back when they rode together.

Back before I left Barney to die, he thought.

The thought came like an old friend, and Hunter faced it squarely. Looking down at the dead horse, he saw instead—as he'd seen a hundred times in the past two years—the narrow, muddy main street of the little Arkansas town called Rocky Comfort.

Chapter 2

Rocky Comfort was a single main street, barely more passable than the hillsides from which it had been scratched. Sagging log buildings, weathered gray by time and lack of care, straggled among the trees on either side of the road as if they'd been dropped there by accident. A couple of horses drowsed at the hitch rail before the largest structure. At a cabin higher up the hillside two men were loading a sturdy drummer's wagon while a small audience of dogs and children watched. The place looked as sleepy as a church toward the end of a long sermon.

"Not a lot to it, is there?" Barney Lemmon had asked, resting a heavy foot on the brake lever of the prison wagon. "Still, it's the best thing for miles in the way of a town."

Hunter took a pull from the bottle they'd been sharing. "No matter. We don't aim to stay long." He squirmed on the hard seat of the wagon. "I'll be right glad to get this done. Feels like we've been wallowing around these hills for a month. Let's get along."

Barney Lemmon snorted. "All you youngsters are too blamed impatient," he grumbled. "Ain't no need to be in such a rush." But he shook the reins. The two big Morgans leaned into their harness, and the wagon rattled down toward Rocky Comfort.

Lemmon drove the wagon into the shade of a spreading blackjack oak. He wrapped the lines around the brake lever and drew a big leather wallet from inside his coat. The wallet was crammed with official-looking documents. Fumbling his reading glasses onto his nose, he began to sort methodically through the papers.

"Who are we after here?" Hunter asked.

"Impatient, just like I said. You hold your horses, son, I'm finding it."

Hunter grinned and sipped from the neck of the bottle. Looking after the warrants was something Barney always insisted on doing personally. Hunter had been a deputy of Judge Parker's court for over a year, riding western Arkansas and the Indian Territory, but Barney still treated him like a greenhorn. Hunter had a hard time resenting it. A man couldn't ask for a better partner than Barney.

"Here we are," Lemmon said, holding up a creased warrant. "For the arrest of one Albert Converse, also known as 'Red' and 'Bull,' for the crime of"—he hesitated, then sounded the words out a syllable at a time—"for the crime of bi-ga-mous co-hab-i-tation."

Hunter laughed. Laughter had come easily to him in those days. "Well, this citizen doesn't sound like much of a desperado," he said. "You'd think they'd have us chasing after the gang that's been robbing banks in the Nations instead of counting people's wives."

"That's a bad bunch, right enough." Lemmon frowned, watching Hunter take another drink. "Heard they killed two men over at Claremore last week. Still, Judge Parker signed the warrant, so wiving up with too many women must be against the law as well as just plain stupid. And Albert's worth good money to us in Fort Smith, same as if he was a bank robber."

"Let's go and fetch him, then." Hunter offered the bottle. "One for the road?"

Barney stepped down from the wagon box, rubbing the thigh of his game leg. "Not me," he said. "And I wish you'd take it easy, too. We got an arrest to make."

"There's nothing wrong with me."

"Course there's not. But maybe you ought to take it easy."

Defiantly Hunter tilted the bottle back again. Then he corked it and shoved it under the wagon seat.

"You don't need to talk to me that way, Barney. I'll be there when you need me. Always have, haven't I? Hell. There's nothing here I can't handle."

Lemmon grinned, rubbing his chin with a big hand. "You've got me there, partner," he said. "Sure enough, you've always been there when I needed you, Hunter."

"Mr. Hunter?"

He started at the unexpected voice. Abruptly the picture of Barney Lemmon faded from his mind, and he stared down at the horse Edge Pardee had killed.

"Mr. Hunter."

"Yes, Miss Pardee?"

He turned to find her close behind him, the carbine held in the crook of her arm. Her brother was nowhere in sight.

"The saddle on that horse. That's a Texas rig."

"That's right."

"Like yours," she said.

"I got mine there."

"You come from there?"

Hunter turned away and began to unfasten the cinches on the fallen horse. "Not lately," he said.

"Meaning I should mind my own business?" she demanded. When he didn't answer she went on. "Just what brought you here, Mr. Hunter?"

"As I said. Passing through."

"Meaning I should mind my own business."

Hunter glanced up at her, then went on with the chore of stripping the gear from the dead animal. As he'd expected, the saddlebags contained nothing that might lead to their owner. The horse was wearing a Circle-Bar brand with a couple of older brands canceled. None of them meant anything to him.

"Do you recognize these markings, miss?"

Linda Pardee bit her lip, frowning at him, then stooped to look. "The Circle-Bar is a big spread in New Mexico, I think, down near Las Vegas. I don't know the others."

"Doesn't tell us much."

"Neither do you."

Hunter straightened from his task and turned to look at the young woman. "I'm sorry, Miss Pardee. I didn't mean to trouble you," he said. "I'll be on my way."

"You'll wait right here until Edge gets back," she snapped. "He took my horse to bring back some of the Pine Valley hands. Your sorrel is in no condition to be ridden."

"Oh?" For the first time in many months, Hunter found his mouth wrestling with a smile. "I'm surprised Edge would leave you on foot and alone. Especially with a doubtful character like me around."

Linda Pardee looked at him disdainfully and folded her arms over the carbine. "I told him there was nothing here I couldn't handle," she said.

Hunter turned away from her, his eyes seeking the crest of the distant mountains. "Yes, ma'am," he agreed. "I expect you're right." He heard himself telling Barney Lemmon there was nothing there he couldn't handle.

"We may as well split up," Barney had said. "I expect you're right that there's nothing here we can't handle. You ask along one side of the street, and I'll take the other. Chances are somebody can tell us all about Albert and his women. We'll meet down to the stable and decide what to do next."

The first building Hunter came to was a shake cabin, its broken door hanging by a single hinge and its yard overgrown with nettles. Next was a low, unpainted log structure. Straggling letters daubed on a weathered board over the door identified it as the Traveler's Rest Mercantile and Tavern.

Hunter glanced across toward Barney. The older deputy was talking with a portly, aproned storekeeper. Hunter hesitated, then shrugged and turned toward the Traveler's Rest. He figured the tavernkeeper would be the man to steer him straight to Albert Converse.

In the darkness of the building's interior one doorway led into the store, another to a low, dirty room smelling of smoke and sweat and the raw bite of cheap liquor. Behind a counter of green-sawed planks a heavyset bearded man regarded Hunter with bovine suspicion.

Can't just ask him straight off, Hunter told himself. These hill folks are clannish. Better have a drink and work into it.

"Whiskey."

After that first drink things had been going so well that he'd had another. And another.

"Converse, you say? Family by that name back up on Reedy Creek. Reckon Albert's one of their boys?"

"Big man. Red hair and beard. Call him Bull."

"Well, Ben here, he'll just go and ask around. Here, drink up. Looks like your glass must have a hole in the bottom."

Hunter's next clear memory was the distant sound of gunfire. The crack of the first shot cut through the fog in his mind like the headlight on a locomotive. He lurched to his feet and started for the door as the second report came. He felt sick and dizzy, but his hand sought the pistol on his hip with blind certainty.

"Here, mister." Bristly face white with fear, the barkeep caught at him. "Hold up. You don't want to go—"

A swipe of the revolver silenced him. Hunter stumbled over the unconscious body, slammed outside into blinding afternoon sunlight. He was still blinking dazzled eyes when the last shots crashed out, three together. Too late.

*　　*　　*

Pardee was back in little more than half an hour with extra horses and five grim-faced cowhands. Hunter picked out a stocky gray gelding while two of the men lashed the dead bushwhacker across the back of a nervous pack horse.

"All right," Pardee said at last. "Let's ride." He grinned at Hunter. "Mount up. The big boss wants to meet you."

"Thought I'd already met her," Hunter murmured, loudly enough to draw a suspicious look from Linda. Nodding gravely to her, he rode forward so that she was between him and Pardee.

The Pine Valley cowhands seemed to have about the same idea. They spread out in a loose circle, watching the green horizon, rifles ready. Pardee led them northwest across the bowl and up the long ridge beyond.

They paused on the western rim, and Hunter had his first clear view of the land into which he'd ridden. On all sides mountains rose into the clear sky. Around the rocky knees of the mountains wide valleys flowed like intertwined green rivers. A waterfall dropped white and roaring down the sheer wall of the nearest peak, disappeared into the trees at its foot, then emerged as a winding silver ribbon dividing the valley floor. Along its far bank, maybe two miles away, Hunter made out the white walls and red-tiled roofs of a cluster of buildings.

"Pine Valley Ranch," Linda Pardee said behind him. "Do you like it?"

For a moment Hunter didn't answer. Something tightened inside his chest, a feeling that had nothing to do with the beauty of the scene before him. He'd been on his way here for almost two years, much of the time without even knowing that the valley existed. He had followed a trail there, a trail marked by stolen banknotes. He'd seen his first one the day Barney was killed.

By the time Hunter's eyes adjusted to the blinding noonday light the drummer's wagon was tearing out of town, bouncing wildly on the rutted road. A big, red-bearded man lashed the horses, his massive shoulders hunched against the drag of the reins. The man beside him was smaller, his face half hidden by the turned-up collar of his coat. Seeing Hunter, he flung up a pistol and fired. The bullet slashed the earth a yard from Hunter's foot, and then the wagon was lost among the trees.

A boy was tugging at Hunter's coat sleeve. "Mister! Mister," the boy cried, "your friend fell down!"

Barney Lemmon lay just at the edge of the clearing before the cabin. His Winchester, fired once, lay near his right hand. He'd been shot three times, though any one of the bullets would have done the job. A dozen yards from his body Hunter found a wooden baking-powder box that had fallen from the wagon as it lurched into motion. It had split open, and rust-colored bank-notes from the Claremore National Bank drifted like dead leaves across the rocky ground.

"Pine Valley Ranch. Do you like it?"

"Nothing like it where I come from," Hunter said.

He was a little surprised at the new tone in Linda Pardee's voice. She hadn't spoken to him before the ride began, and their last conversation hadn't been especially cordial. Now the determined set of her mouth was softened by a childlike joy. She was looking past him, down to the valley and the ranch headquarters. Her green eyes shone with a light that he momentarily wished might be directed at him.

He caught Pardee's grin and shook off the thought. "Nice," he said roughly.

Linda frowned at him curiously. "You weren't even here," she said, so softly Hunter barely heard. "I wonder where you were."

"You can't miss liking it," Pardee put in. "Right up your alley, too. Just the country for a hunter."

Laughing at his own pun, Pardee urged his mount

down the steep trail to the valley floor. Linda held back a moment, looking at Hunter, then followed.

They caught up with Pardee at a wide gate and met the scrutiny of a few hands who'd stopped work to watch the little party ride in. Others drifted from the stables or from the long bunkhouse to stare at the body roped over the pack horse. No one spoke until a man came out onto the gallery fronting the main house. He leaned heavily on the railing, supporting himself with both hands while he took in the scene. Then he straightened and came slowly down the steps. Linda Pardee slipped from her horse and ran to meet him. She would have taken his arm, but he drew back and glared at her.

"Fine thing, missy!" he snapped. "How did you get tied into a thing like this?" His faded blue eyes sought Pardee. "Edge, I've told you a hundred times—"

"It wasn't his fault," Linda interrupted sharply. "I'll not sit home and knit while—"

"That's enough. We'll talk about it later. Edge, what happened?"

Hunter saw Linda's lips tighten at the reproof, but she didn't bite at the old man. Pardee launched into an account of the ambush. Ignored for the moment, Hunter used the time to study Morgan Avery. The rancher was slightly built, no taller than his niece, and he walked with a stoop that took more inches off his height. His sandy hair was thinning, his face weathered and tanned from years of mountain sun. A heavy mustache hid the set of his mouth as he listened to Pardee's story. When Pardee came to Hunter's part in the rescue the rancher lifted his head with the quick, proud motion of a hawk and stared into Hunter's face.

"You're Hunter? Sounds like I owe you thanks. Edge ain't much shucks as a nephew, but he's a damn good foreman, and they're hard to come by."

"No thanks needed," Hunter said easily. He swung down from the borrowed gray to face Avery on even terms. "Anybody would have done the same."

Avery stroked his chin, his eyes still evaluating Hunter. He made up his mind.

"Could be," he conceded, "but you were the one who was there." He put out a thin, strong hand. "Morgan Avery's the name. My house is yours. You looking for work, by chance?"

Hunter caught a look of surprise on Linda's face. Before he could decide whether she was pleased or angry she saw him watching and smoothed her expression to blank indifference. Accepting the rancher's handshake, Hunter allowed himself a smile.

"I'm a poor hand with cattle."

"I can see that. Offer's still open."

"Thanks, but I have business to look after. I'll ask you to board my sorrel for a time, though. And I'd appreciate the loan of your gray until I can report the shooting to whatever law's around here."

The rancher squinted at him, then nodded as though in answer to some internal question. After a moment Avery stepped across to the pack horse. Pulling back the slicker that covered the bushwhacker's body, he bent to peer at the lifeless face.

"Anybody know him?"

Silence ticked by for half a minute. Then one of the hands, a short, square bulldog of a man, spoke up.

"That's Horace Webb. I've seen him around with the Circle Eight riders, all right."

Hunter shifted so he could see the speaker. Judging from the dead man's rifle and fancy clothes, he'd no more been a cowhand than was Hunter. He'd had the look of a man-killer, probably new to the territory. If that was right, it was surprising he'd let himself be seen openly with his employers—unless the Circle Eight was ready for a full-blown war.

Morgan Avery might have felt some of the same doubts. He dropped the fold of slicker back in place and squinted at the cowhand. "Sure about that, Tag?" he asked.

"You bet. He was in town with Abel Carson and them, not over ten days ago."

"All right. That's gospel, then." Avery raised his voice. "New orders. From this minute no man rides alone. No man rides without his rifle nor goes into town without leave from me." Turning to Linda Pardee, he added, "Nor no woman, either. You understand me, missy?"

"Yes, Uncle Morgan."

Hunter decided her submissive tone was for the benefit of the hands. The argument would come later, when she and Avery were alone. He'd pegged her for too much of a hellcat to give in without a struggle—not that it mattered to him, he reminded himself. He was looking for banknotes and men, nothing more.

"What about Watkins and the Circle Eight?" the man called Tag demanded. "When do we pay them back?"

"When I say!" Avery swept an arm at the crowd of cowhands. "All right. Back to work. Still running a ranch."

Talking and grumbling among themselves, the hands moved away. An older man came to examine the cut on the sorrel's neck, clucked reproachfully at Hunter, and led the animal off. Within seconds only Pardee, Linda, and Hunter were left around Morgan Avery.

"Edge, best you take Hunter into town," Avery said. "Tell Tobreen the way of things. Any trouble, you send for me. Hunter, we'll look for you at supper."

He turned away, gathering in Linda and stumping toward the house. Linda paused for a backward glance at Hunter, found him watching, flushed, and hurried after Avery. Pardee laughed softly. Swinging up into his saddle, he tugged the skittish pack horse around and started for the gate. A step slower, Hunter mounted and fell in behind him.

Secure behind the porch railing, Linda Pardee watched the pair ride away. Edge moved easily with his

21

pony's gait, but Hunter held himself ramrod straight in the saddle, seemingly unwilling to accommodate himself even to the rhythm of the gray's stride. Linda found herself wishing he would look back her way again. Then she pushed the girlish thought aside and turned away abruptly to meet her uncle's speculative gaze. Her face burned suddenly, but Avery didn't seem to notice.

"That Hunter," he said. "Seems an independent sort, don't he?"

Linda tossed her head. "Independent is the word. I haven't noticed him wasting much energy being polite."

Morgan Avery's mouth tightened a trifle, but he didn't smile. "Strange. Edge made a point how polite you were when the two of you first met." He thought a moment, ignoring her wordless protest. "Tell you, there's a man with something gnawing his soul. Might be dangerous to get mixed up with."

Linda felt her face redden again. "Then you'd better reconsider about offering him a job, Uncle Morgan," she said as coldly as she could. Turning toward the door, she added, "Perry's coming to call tonight. Did I tell you?"

"Can't remember that you did."

"Well, he'll be here for supper." She decided she didn't sound pleased enough about that. "Maybe he can meet Mr. Hunter then," she said brightly. "But we won't get mixed up with him."

Hunter and Pardee rode in silence until they were well along toward the main road into town. Then Pardee fixed Hunter with a questioning eye.

"You drew into some high cards with Uncle Morg," he said. "Ain't often he takes to a man so fast." He paused, then grinned. "I ain't quite sure how you stand with baby sister, though."

Hunter shrugged. "It's not likely to matter. I don't expect to be here long."

Pardee's grin widened. "A man never knows," he said innocently.

Hunter decided it was time to change the subject. "Who's Tobreen?" he asked.

"Ed Tobreen. Constable in Sublette City, which is where we're bound. He's a good man."

"Meaning he sides with Pine Valley in your feud?"

Pardee didn't answer for a few seconds. When he did his voice was noticeably less friendly.

"Tobreen sides with the law, nothing else. And it ain't a feud—not the way you mean. Pine Valley and Circle Eight have the high valleys cut up between them, save for a stretch of government range and a little spread Jack Harvey runs back to the west. Uncle Morg and Ellis Watkins—he owns Circle Eight—they haven't ever gotten along, and lately it's been worse. We lose stock to the Circle Eighters, though we surer'n hell haven't caught them at it. They claim we're rustling their stock, which we ain't, so they've got no proof either. Today's the first time it's come to shooting."

Hunter nodded thoughtfully, watching the country change around them. They had climbed out of the cut where the Pine Valley headquarters lay. Now the road ran again across open grassland, with wooded hills swelling abruptly from the plain every little while. The tall grass whispered and rustled busily in the wind.

"Seems that Avery and Watkins both own enough so's they wouldn't need to fight over what's left," he said, half to himself. Then, seeing Pardee's puzzled frown, he asked, "You're sure it was Circle Eight riders that ambushed you today?"

"Don't know who else," Pardee answered with a trace of impatience. "I ain't got all that many enemies. Besides, Tag knew the yahoo you shot."

"Tag. He'd be the stocky dark-haired one?"

"Sure. Tag Kelly. Been with Uncle Morg for four, five years, off and on." Pardee frowned again, the expression seeming foreign to his open face. "Hunter, for a feller just drifting through you ask an almighty lot of questions.''

"Guess you're right," Hunter agreed. He thought of asking if Pardee had ever seen a Claremore banknote but put the idea aside. "It's kind of a hobby of mine," he said instead, "mixing into things that aren't my business."

Chapter 3

"Has anybody ever *warned* you about horning in on things that aren't your business?" Ed Tobreen demanded.

"Ever' now and then," Hunter said. He leaned back in the ladderback chair and crossed his arms. Nothing he said was likely to make Tobreen much angrier. "Never been able to shake the habit, though—especially when somebody starts shooting at me. I take that sort of personally."

"And danged lucky for me he came along!" Edge Pardee put in indignantly. "Else it'd be me hanging across that horse, and maybe you'd like that better."

Tobreen turned his gaze on Pardee. Gradually the anger left the constable's face. Tobreen was a broad, solid man who looked as if he'd ridden some hard miles in his time. His grizzled hair made him look nearer fifty than forty, but Hunter couldn't see an ounce of fat on him. Looking at Pardee, he stroked his drooping dun-colored mustache thoughtfully.

"Now Edge, I didn't mean that," he said. "But it's hard to credit your story when you come in with *him*." He gestured as though Hunter were a spavined mule offered for sale. "He's a shooter. I know the signs, and they ain't all in that fast-draw rig he wears."

"It's just a tool."

"Yeah?" Tobreen said. "If it's a tool, carry a hammer in it."

"You know what I mean, Marshal."

"Constable." Tobreen's eyes hardened as they came back to Hunter. "I know what you mean. You mean you've killed a man or two in your time."

"Not for fun. Nor for money."

"No?" Tobreen studied him a moment longer. "Well, it means reports to fill out." He opened a drawer of his desk, then straightened to look at Hunter again. "Just for openers, suppose you let me hold that pistol of yours."

"Are you saying I'm under arrest, Constable?"

" 'Fraid so. When a homicide's involved, it's the law."

Hunter thought about it. A stay in Tobreen's jail would be inconvenient, but not seriously so. The people he was looking for had no way of knowing who he was. If they were in the neighborhood, they weren't likely to run. And it wasn't as if he had much choice at the moment.

"Anything you say."

Calmly Hunter rose and began to unbuckle his gun belt. Then Edge Pardee exploded.

"Now wait a minute here! Are you going to arrest him because he saved my life? That's a damn poor reward for a feller that risked his skin to do a good turn!"

"It's all right, Edge," Hunter said.

"You stay out of this!" Pardee leaned across the desk to tower over Tobreen. "Listen here, Ed, the way I remember it, this all happened away off up the valley, plumb out of your jurisdiction! Why, I bet we were clear over the New Mexico line, and what do you say to that?"

He plopped back into his chair, arms folded in satisfaction. Tobreen looked from Hunter to him and back, then gave his mustache another tug.

"Edge, be your age," he said. "You and Abel Carson knocking each other around in public places, I can overlook that. But this is a killing. Just because it was out-side the town limits, I can't make believe it didn't happen."

Hunter rolled his shell belt around the holster and laid it on Tobreen's desk. "There's lawmen that would," he said.

"Well, I ain't one of them."

"Didn't think you were." Hunter almost smiled. He liked Tobreen; in some ways the constable was a lot like Barney Lemmon. "How long do you figure to hold me?"

Tobreen leaned back in his chair. "Well, I'll give my report to the county sheriff—that *is* his jurisdiction, Edge. The grand jury sits the first of every month. Likely Sheriff Vargas will put you in front of the next one, say three weeks from now." He reached for a cigar, considered, then drew back his hand. "With Par-dee's testimony you don't have anything to worry over. But like I say, it's the law."

"Hell of a law!" Pardee grumbled. He waved a hand angrily. "Get out your tools, then. What do you need for that fancy report of yours?"

Tobreen unfolded a pair of wire-framed spectacles and perched them on his nose. "Well, for openers suppose you tell me everything that happened this morning."

Forgotten for the moment, Hunter leaned back and surveyed the office. A stubby shotgun was in the corner within easy reach of Tobreen's desk. Two rifles, a Win-chester and a bolt-action Krag, were chained to a rack behind him. A small sheet-iron stove, now cold and idle, supported piles of letters and legal documents, each bun-dle neatly tied with green string. A raft of wanted post-ers hung on one wall, new ones tacked over layers of old.

Hunter noted details absently, out of old habit. With the conscious part of his mind he was considering how much truth to tell Tobreen. If a stay in jail wouldn't threaten his plans, the grand jury might. He couldn't afford to spook the game he was tracking.

Tobreen finished with Pardee, then took Hunter over the same ground. At last he screwed the cap on his fountain pen and nodded shortly to Hunter.

"That'll do. Only thing is, you never mentioned exactly how you happened to be there."

"Riding through."

"Yeah." Tobreen blew on the report to dry the ink, then folded it and put it in an envelope. "Edge, you can go. Mr. Hunter, if you'll pick out a cell you like—"

"Hold on, Ed," Pardee said.

Tobreen gave him an annoyed glance. "Edge, we've been all through that."

"All right. But suppose some solid citizen would kind of adopt Hunter, be responsible for him and guarantee his appearance and save the county having to feed him for those three weeks. Could you let him out then?"

Tobreen stroked his mustache and smiled. "You figure you're that solid a citizen, Edge?"

"Well, I just might be. But it was Mr. Morgan Avery I had in mind." Pardee grinned at Hunter. "Fact is, Uncle Morg has already offered Hunter a job. I expect he'll be taking it now."

"I expect," Hunter agreed promptly.

Tobreen frowned, clearly not liking the idea. Hunter didn't push. After a moment the constable slapped his hand down on the gun belt and shoved it across to Hunter.

"You be at that hearing, Hunter, or I swear by God Almighty I'll have a fugitive warrant on you and chase you plumb to the gates of hell. And don't you go bringing me any more corpses. You understand me?"

"Every word." Hunter rose, scooping up his pistol. "Much obliged, Constable. Come on, Edge."

He caught Pardee's arm, hustling the blond foreman along before something changed Tobreen's mind. Just as they reached the door it opened inward. A slender dark-haired man in gray suit and vest stared uncertainly at Hunter and Pardee.

"Ah—excuse me." He looked past Hunter and spoke to the constable. "Sorry, Ed. I didn't realize you were busy."

Tobreen said, "Come on in, Perry. We're finished." He waved a hand Hunter's way. "Fact is, we were just talking about your business. Hunter, meet Perry Bonham, our town undertaker. He's been working on the feller you dragged in."

Bonham nodded to Pardee and gave Hunter a cool, level appraisal. At first glance the undertaker seemed average in every way—height, weight, the expression on his pale, handsome, clean-shaven face, even the neutral gray of his suit.

"Ah—yes," he said. "I've laid out the deceased. His personal effects are right here, Ed—two new double eagles among them. If you'd care to see the body . . ."

Tobreen planted his palms on the desktop and levered himself up. "I expect I'd better. Hunter, you want to come along and admire your handiwork?"

"I saw it. I'm not that proud of it."

"Me, too," Pardee said. A shadow of his earlier sickness crossed his face. "Never seen a man shot up like that."

Bonham gave a quick, professional nod. "A very severe wound," he agreed. "Just a single bullet, too. Surprising." He remembered Tobreen and coughed apologetically. "I'm afraid it's pretty messy, Ed."

"Well, that's just fine." Tobreen herded them all out onto the plank sidewalk, turning to lock the office door with a key that must have weighed half a pound. "We'll pick up Doc Richards to do the death certificate, then get this feller planted right and proper." He turned a glare on Hunter. "I don't like this kind of work. Remember what I said about bringing me any more of it."

Motionless on the boardwalk, Hunter watched Bonham and the constable stride off toward the doctor's office. Not until Pardee shifted angrily at his elbow did he shake himself and turn away.

"That beats all!" Pardee growled. "Wasn't my place to speak, but why'd you let him talk to you that way and not even answer back? That ain't the man I took you for."

Drawing in a long breath, Hunter let his jaw muscles unclench themselves. "No point in answering, Edge," he said. "Tobreen still had half a mind to lock me up. This way I have three weeks before that hearing. That'll have to be enough."

"Enough for what?" Pardee asked quickly. Getting no answer, he shrugged. "Then again, maybe it's none of my business. What we'd best do is eat ourselves a steak, then go back and tell Uncle Morg what I've saddled him with. There's a place—"

He broke off suddenly. Hunter glanced at him, but Pardee was looking off across the street, staring intently at a horse tied to the rail in front of a saloon.

"No," Pardee said softly. "First thing, we better have us a drink."

"Here, drink up. Looks like your glass must have a hole in the bottom."

Hunter had returned to Fort Smith with Barney's body on the day Judge Parker sentenced a killer named John Thornton to hang. Hunter's own trial was less formal, and the jury was inside his head.

"I hate to hear that about Barney," Deputy Marshal Heck Thomas said when Hunter brought the news. "I've known him pretty near twenty years." He raised his eyes to Hunter's face, and Hunter felt the measured judgment of every deputy in the Territory.

"It wasn't like Barney to run off on his own like that. Where were you? Did you see the shooting?"

"No," Hunter said.

Pardee shot him a quizzical look. "Well. You're about

the last one I'd've took for a teetotaler." The foreman ran a hand through his tousled hair and grinned. "No matter, come ahead anyway. I got a word to say to Carson before we go."

"Carson? He's the one Tobreen—"

Pardee was already striding away. Uneasy, Hunter lagged behind. He hadn't taken much of a look at the town when they rode in. Now he saw that it was laid out in a curious mirror image of itself. Two saloons faced each other across the main street—not unusual in itself, but Hunter quickly picked out two mercantiles, two livery stables, two harness makers, even two barber-shops, as though the rutted street were the border between hostile nations. Only at the far end of the street did the strange confrontation end. There, not far from Bonham's funeral parlor, a single church steeple lifted against the sky.

"Hunter? You coming?"

The saloon across the way was called the Aces and Eights, with a smaller sign advertising pocket billiards. Hunter glanced at its twin on his side of the street: Paradise O' The Pines. The best he could tell, Pardee was leading him straight into trouble. Still, the blond cowhand had kept him out of Tobreen's jail. And he was Linda's brother.

Hunter sighed. "I'm coming," he called.

With Hunter a step behind, Pardee slammed through the batwing doors and strode to the bar. Hunter heard the low murmur of talk as he entered, but there was a dead silence by the time he moved up on Pardee's right. Pardee ignored both the silence and the glares of a dozen men gathered around the billiard table at the back of the room.

"Whiskey," he told the bartender. "And a bottle of Pluto Water for my friend here. He's feeling poorly."

"Well, now," the barkeep began. He twisted a towel in his hands as he looked at Pardee. "Well, now, the fact is I just ran out," he said hopefully. "Maybe if you'd try across the street—"

"That killer'll feel a damn sight worse if he don't get out of here, Pardee," a deep voice cut in. "Him and you both."

"That's *Mister* Pardee, Carson. I don't let just every polecat bandy my name around."

Hunter kept his eyes on the long mirror behind the bar. It gave him a tolerable view of the crowd of men—Circle Eight riders, he supposed—watching him and Pardee. The billiard game had broken up. Only one man was moving, walking slowly and deliberately across the room. He was big, even bigger than Pardee, but he moved with an easy grace that warned he'd be more agile than he looked. Black hair bristled below his rolled-up sleeves and curled as thickly as a furry scarf at his throat. His gaze rested for a moment on Hunter's back, then shifted its weight to Pardee. Abel Carson, Tobreen had said; Hunter knew this was the man who went with the name.

"Killer," he repeated. His voice sounded as if it came from a mine shaft. "Shot poor Horse Webb to pieces, so Mr. Bonham says." He planted himself in front of Pardee, loose-jointed and easy, melon-sized fists resting on his hips. "Is that your way now, using hired killers?"

"Webb was your man," Pardee said. "Seems like you're the ones hiring guns."

"Not mine. I fired him last month. Spent too much time cuddled up to that gun—like this scum here."

Before Pardee could answer, Hunter straightened away from the bar and turned toward Carson. "If you mean me, friend, I don't care for your line of talk. A man ought to have something in his head before he opens his mouth."

Carson swung his head slowly like a bull buffalo annoyed by a coyote. He stared at Hunter with small bright eyes, and his face relaxed into a smile. Hunter watched his gun hand, but Carson made no move toward the holster that hung high and awkwardly at his waist.

Not a shooter, Hunter thought. He'll use his hands.

"Well, now," Carson said. "He can talk. Suppose we all have a look at your rifle, mister."

Pardee turned, about to say something. The look on Hunter's face stopped him. Hunter didn't even notice.

"It's an old Winchester Model 1886. I imagine you've seen one before."

"Me and the boys, we'd like to see yours."

"I don't think you would. People I have cause to show it to are apt to be looking straight down the bore."

"Hunter—" Pardee began uneasily.

Carson's eyes narrowed. "Pillbox," he said without looking away from Hunter, "go out to this drifter's horse. Fetch me his rifle."

Behind Carson a straw-haired Circle Eight cowboy pushed himself away from the wall to follow the foreman's order. He hadn't taken his first step when a Colt single-action army revolver appeared in Hunter's hand.

"Hold your place, son."

Hunter had misjudged Carson. He'd thought the big man might be slow, but Carson's massive fist lashed out like a striking snake. Its backhand sweep caught Hunter across the temple and sent him spinning helplessly away along the bar. Before he could recover, Circle Eight men had pinned his arms and torn the Colt out of his grasp. Hunter fought desperately to get free, expecting Carson to come at him while he was still dazed, but again he had misjudged his man. He felt the rising excitement among his captors. Twisting to look, he realized suddenly that Carson's quarrel hadn't been with him at all.

In the open space before the bar Carson and Pardee had squared off. For a dozen long seconds neither man moved. Then Pardee feinted his left at Carson's head and drove a hard right under his guard. The blow landed with a solid smack, staggering Carson back a step. He grunted and bored back in, fists high, punching for Pardee's face. The Pine Valley foreman blocked two fast lefts, caught a right on his shoulder, then took the next punch squarely in the mouth. He fell back, shaking his head and spattering the bar with droplets of blood from his split lips.

The Circle Eighters jostled one another for a clear view, almost forgetting Hunter in their excitement. None of them moved to interfere, and Hunter sensed he was watching a single round in a long fight. When Carson slipped one of Pardee's punches and plowed inside, pounding the Pine Valley man back with powerful blows to the body, the cowhands whooped and whistled as if they were hazing cows into the loading chute. They groaned and catcalled when Pardee came over Carson's lowered guard and snapped the bigger man's head back with two quick jabs.

Of them all, only Hunter heard the angry voice demanding attention over the noise. Then the voice fell silent. Everyone heard the crack of a pistol, sharp and deafening in the confined space.

The gunshot froze everyone in place for an instant. Then the men around Hunter boiled into motion, some of them grabbing him, some reaching for their own holsters, some instinctively seeking cover. All finished by staring at the slim, dark-eyed young woman who stood just inside the swinging doors of the saloon.

"Abel Carson, you're a fool."

She spoke in a normal tone, but her voice seemed loud in the sudden silence. Perfectly black hair showed beneath her hat, falling in two neat braids across her squared shoulders. Her gloved right hand held a small but businesslike nickel-plated revolver, its barrel tilted toward the ceiling. Powder smoke drifted around her, and she waved it away impatiently. From behind the skirts of her buckskin riding dress a younger, slightly bucktoothed version of herself peered eagerly at the motionless crowd.

The younger girl widened dark brown eyes at Hunter.

"Look, Barb, that's the killer!" she said in a loud whisper. "Miz Cole over at the mercantile says constable's afraid to lock him up!"

She was about thirteen, Hunter decided, five years or so the junior of the young woman with the pistol. The strong, well-defined bone structure of her narrow face promised she'd have the same haughty beauty as her sister before long. Hunter winked at her.

"Annie Laurie Watkins, you be still!" her older sister snapped. "And don't call me that. Abel, you round up your strays and get them outside. It's time we were riding home."

Carson stood with his back to her, his ponderous fist cocked like the paw of a winter-lean bear. His whole body quivered with unspent fury, but he mastered it and dropped his hands. Pardee stepped away, lowering his guard as well, and Carson turned toward the door.

"Lord's sakes, Miss Barbara, this ain't proper! Your pa will about raise up the devil and tie a knot in his tail when he hears you stepped foot in a saloon—and Miss Annie, too!"

"I'll attend to my father. Get the men."

Hunter could almost hear Carson's teeth grind. The big man turned savagely on his riders. "All right, you heard the boss," he bellowed. "Get moving! Pillbox, give the slinger back his iron so's he'll have something to cuddle up to tonight. Move!"

The straw-haired cowhand methodically shucked the cartridges out of Hunter's Colt and dropped the empty gun at his feet. Following Carson's lead, the group stalked out into the gathering dusk. Annie Laurie was the last, lingering to study Hunter with a wide, excited gaze until her sister's hand reached back to snatch her along.

As the Circle Eight crew reached their horses and began to mount, Hunter looked at Pardee. The Pine Valley foreman was grinning. He dabbed absently with the back of his hand at the blood on his mouth, but his eyes and his mind were clearly on the young woman who had broken up the fight.

"Who is she?" Hunter asked.

Pardee started guiltily. "Barbara. Barbara Allen Watkins. Her pa owns Circle Eight." He was no longer grinning. "The young'un is her kid sister, Annie Laurie."

"I see," Hunter said. "Business aside, Carson seems to take you pretty seriously. Something personal, is it?"

"Could be." Pardee's glance was quick and hard. "Old Tobreen said it right. You're a fair hand at minding other people's business. Now we got some privacy, let's have that drink."

Hunter looked around. Aside from the bartender, still nervously twisting a towel as he stared at the new hole in his ceiling, only one man was left in the saloon. In the confusion, Hunter hadn't seen him earlier. Now his hand dropped to the butt of his empty Colt with an eagerness almost independent of his mind. With an effort he checked the movement and pulled his attention back to Pardee.

"Let's have the drink another time, if it's all the same. I'd like to learn if Mr. Avery's still interested in hiring me."

Pardee laughed and slapped his forehead. "Sure! Tell the truth, that had plumb slipped my mind, what with one thing and another. Let's ride, then."

Hunter followed him outside, careful not to glance toward the man in the corner. One look had been enough. Like a man checking over a reward poster, he reviewed the picture in his mind. Squat, square shape. Wide shoulders jammed into the corner so no one could get behind him. Watery blue eyes fixed on the glass in his hand. A pair of revolvers just visible below the skirts of a dirty plaid coat.

And the hair. Fierce red hair tangling like brambles into a fiery red beard. No mistake. Albert Converse, the Red Bull himself, in the flesh.

"What?" Hunter asked.

Pardee was already in the saddle, looking down as Hunter untied the gray's reins. "I said you made a good choice. You'll like it here."

"Yeah." Hunter swung aboard his mount and kneed the horse around. "I think you're right. This is just the place I've been looking for."

Chapter 4

The north wall of Morgan Avery's study was a mural painted in tones of green and brown, a map of the San Antonio Basin. Originally it had shown almost a dozen ranches, with Pine Valley among the smaller ones. The old boundaries showed faintly through successive coats of paint, with neat lettering to indicate which had been bought out by Pine Valley and which by Circle Eight. Although the map wasn't completely accurate in scale, it did suggest faithfully that the two giants were pretty much the same size. Only a swath of free government range and the Sublette City township separated the two. To the south, just above the polished wood of Avery's desk, Jack Harvey's little spread clung like a burr to Circle Eight's flank.

Seeing the mural reminded Hunter of Edge Pardee's observations on Harvey. "That red-bearded feller in the back corner of the Aces? Why, that was Jack Harvey, owns the third spread in the valley. Place so dirt-poor that not even old Ellis Watkins has tried very hard to buy it. Yeah, Harvey lives out there with his wife and three or four hands—tough bunch, they are, too—not that he runs enough cattle to keep them busy. I swear, Hunter, you're a regular nonesuch for asking questions."

Seated in a leather chair with a cup of hot coffee, Hunter studied the map, working to memorize the lay of the land while he listened to Pardee and Morgan Avery.

"I want to know what he said about Horace Webb."

"Carson said he fired him."

"You believe him?"

Pardee took a minute to think about that. "Sure do," he said. "Carson's straight. He may be all kinds of a bastard, but I never heard him lie."

"Hunter?" The rancher's glance was sharp, probing. "You don't look so sure. What do you think?"

Hunter shrugged. "No opinion. I'm sure of two things about Carson: He doesn't like guns, and he knows how to hit the way a mule knows how to kick."

"Careful man, are you?" Avery rubbed his chin and smiled. "I'd took you for one." He leaned forward, resting his elbows on the desk. "Edge says he's set you up to work for me. Is that agreeable with you?"

"I'd like to ask two conditions," Hunter said. "The first is I don't start until day after tomorrow. Second is that I have some time to myself now and again, after my work's done."

Avery considered. "I'll go you one better. Tomorrow's Saturday. We take Sundays off, 'cepting for a skeleton crew—and it's a holiday besides. You'll go on the payroll come daybreak Monday, if that's agreeable." He waited for Hunter's nod, then added, "I know you have your own reasons for being here. I won't ask what they are. But I've got a couple of conditions for you. I'll expect you to give Pine Valley your loyalty, take your orders from Edge or me, and drink on your own time. Pay's thirty a month and found."

"Are you thinking you're hiring yourself a gun?"

"No. I'm hiring help. Want to stop a range war, not start one."

Hunter stretched out his hand. "Done."

"That's good. Being as you're still on your own time, I'll offer you a drink in the bargain." Avery unlocked the bottom drawer of his desk and produced a bottle of bourbon. "No need to call Anna back for glasses. Here."

Hunter felt Pardee's glance but held his cup while Avery's bottle clinked against the rim. The rancher poured a generous slug into each of the three cups, then lifted his own.

"To your long life, gentlemen."

"Thanks," said Hunter. He tilted the hot mixture of coffee and Kentucky whiskey to his lips. The warm, enticing scent filled his nostrils, awakening his old thirst. He clenched his jaws and lowered the drink untasted. "And to yours."

"Now—" A tap at the door interrupted Avery. "It's open," he called.

Linda Pardee came in, excusing herself for the bother as the three men stood to greet her. She wore a long maroon velvet dress, pinched in tightly at the waist and open at the throat. A single strand of pearls was clasped around her neck. Her surprise at the sight of Hunter seemed genuine, and her shock at the sight of Pardee's battered face certainly was. Casually ignoring her uncle's hasty removal of the bottle from his desktop, she said, "I'm sorry, but I was expecting Perry—Mr. Bonham—and I thought perhaps—"

"No, not yet." Avery's forehead wrinkled, but he did not quite frown. "Hunter is coming to work for us," he said.

"Oh. Please excuse me. I'll wait in the parlor for Mr. Bonham. I'm glad you'll be with us, Mr. Hunter."

Hunter didn't find her declaration entirely convincing, but he nodded to acknowledge the courtesy and watched her until she closed the door.

"Have to excuse me, Hunter," Avery said. "Got a special job I wanted to talk to you about, but I'd forgotten that damned Bonham was coming courting."

Edge Pardee started a grin at Hunter, but his split and swollen lips wouldn't quite permit it. "Not the fondest words in the world for my future brother-in-law," he said.

The rancher colored slightly. Lowering himself gently

back into his chair, he said, "Bonham's all right. He *is*. It's just that I get the feeling he looks at me like he's measuring me for a shroud and casket. Like he expects to inherit—" He broke off short. "Enough of that. Edge, show Hunter the lay of the buildings and make him acquainted with the boys. We can talk later."

Pardee led Hunter through the hallways of the rambling house toward the front door. As they passed the open doorway of the parlor Linda called to them.

"Oh, wait! Mr. Hunter, I behaved rudely to you earlier today," she said quickly, as if she'd rehearsed it. "I was upset about Edge and—and the killing. I am sorry."

"Why, thanks, Sis," Pardee said gravely. "Nice to know you care."

"I do. And I thank you, Mr. Hunter, for taking his part—even if he has been fighting again!"

"No need to apologize, Miss Pardee," Hunter said.

"I—" she began, but then a low, pleasant voice called from the porch.

"Linda?"

"I'm here, Perry. In the parlor."

Perry Bonham came into the hall, then paused in the doorway of the parlor, thrown a bit off balance by the presence of Pardee and Hunter. Linda Pardee moved quickly to him, taking his arm and drawing him into the room.

"Perry, I'm so glad you're here. Edge and I were just talking to Mr. Hunter. Mr. Hunter will be working here for a while."

"Edge," Bonham said amiably, and he put out a hand. "Good to see you again. And Mr. Hunter." He smiled slightly, showing even teeth and a humor he kept under control. "I met Mr. Hunter earlier today, Linda. He's one of the reasons I'm late for supper."

"Oh."

"I looked for you two this afternoon," Bonham said. "I wanted to welcome you to the valley, Mr. Hunter, but you'd already left town—not for good, I'm pleased to see. Our little community here will profit from new people like yourself joining it."

"Good for business, he means," Pardee murmured, and he chuckled at his own joke.

Linda shot him a scandalized look. "Edge! You should be ashamed!"

Bonham's laugh was pleasant. "It's all right," he told Linda gently. "I'm accustomed to it. Actually, it is pretty funny, even though it's not really true." He grew serious, raising his eyes to include Hunter and Pardee as well as Linda. "I take little enjoyment from my work and not much more in my pay. Undertaking is a job someone has to do, a service—a profession, if I can say so without boasting."

"No boasting involved," Hunter agreed quickly. "Where does a man learn a trade like that?"

Bonham smiled. "Oh, many places," he said. "I studied in Missouri, mostly. Why do you ask?"

"Hunter's a great one for asking questions," Pardee interjected. "You'd think he was one of them dime novelist fellers fixing to write a story."

"I think you half believe in those foolish books, Edge Pardee," Linda said. "And half the time you act like you belong in one."

"Nope." Pardee shook his head virtuously. "Me, I got my mind on simpler things, like supper. You don't suppose we could still find us something to eat around here, do you?"

"Well . . ." Linda hesitated, then said reluctantly, "I told Anna to keep something warm for Perry and me. You and Mr. Hunter are certainly welcome to join us, Edge."

Her lack of enthusiasm was clear enough for even Pardee to see. "No thanks, Sis," he said. "You'd just lecture me about tangling with that big ox Carson. Me and Hunter will just *hunt* something up ourselves, and we're sorry to deprive you of our company."

He ushered Hunter out of the room and onto the porch. "You just follow me, pard," he whispered. "We'll see who has the inside track with the cook around here."

He followed the open gallery around the side of the house and tapped on a wide Dutch door. Hunter heard shuffling steps inside, and then a tall, heavyset woman opened the upper half and looked out, wiping her hands on a dish towel.

"*Ja?*"

"Evening, Anna," Pardee said. "You got anything for starving men? Me and Hunter here was a little late for supper, and we're hungry as bears."

"Hm!" The cook wrinkled her nose at Pardee. She was still a handsome woman, Hunter saw. She had wide blue eyes and fair skin, a little flushed from the heat of the kitchen. A thick braid of hair, now mostly gray but with a few strands of pale gold woven in, circled her head like a coronet. "To miss a meal won't kill you, I think. Next time you will maybe come home without drinking and fighting."

She turned away to go back to her dishes but left the door open. Pardee grinned and reached down to open the other half, beckoning Hunter into the large warm kitchen.

"Aw, Anna, don't be that way. What will our new hand think?"

She gave Hunter a searching appraisal, beginning and ending with the holster at his hip. "He will think to be on time for meals, maybe."

"Now, Anna. You know none of those fellers appreciated your pot roast and apple pie the way we will." Pardee looked at her unresponsive back. "Besides, I hear you saved up some for Linda and her feller. You getting partial to him now?"

"Hm!" she said with a different inflection. "You are a pest, Edge Pardee, a bully. All right, you eat. Food is on the stove, fresh bread in the oven." With a hand that dripped soapy water she gestured at the kitchen table. "But eat here. You will not bother your sister and her young man."

"Wouldn't dream of it. Come on, Hunter."

"Much obliged, ma'am," Hunter said.

"Hm! Manners. You listen to him, Edge Pardee. Maybe you will learn some."

Anna pointedly turned her back on the two while they worked over the remains of a meat loaf, a bowl of fresh-snapped black-eyed peas, and half an apple pie. To Hunter, his belly shrunken by weeks of his own cooking on the trail, it seemed a feast. He finished a last cup of coffee with Pardee, nodding his appreciation.

"Right enough, Edge. You have influence."

Pardee gave a whoop of laughter. "Told you!" He sprang up and darted across to Anna, sweeping her up in a bear hug. "Anna, you are the darlin' of my heart."

Laughing, she kicked free. "My apple pie, you mean, is the darling of your heart! Go. Out of my kitchen! Now!"

Hunter let himself be shooed along behind Pardee. On the porch again, Pardee patted his belt and said, "Well, that's better. Let's you meet the boys and then turn in." He inclined his head toward Hunter. "Listen, I thought you was going to question old Perry plumb to death. Won't matter much with him, but you might not want to come at these boys just that way. Some of them's liable to be a little sensitive about their past."

"Good enough."

They crossed the graveled wagon yard to the big shotgun structure of the bunkhouse. A single cowhand sat on the porch rail, watching the stars and smoking a hand-rolled cigarette.

"Hunter, this here's Tag Kelly. You saw him when we first rode in."

"Sure did. Good to meet you, Kelly."

"Hunter." The smaller man pressed his hand with a quick, hard grip, released it, said nothing more. The darkness obscured the expression on his face, but not the reserve of his greeting.

Inside the bunkhouse it was the same. When Pardee and Hunter entered, eight or ten men turned from playing cards or reading or talking about horses and women and the day's events to look at the newcomers. Hunter smiled, enjoying the feel of the place, the mingled odors of horses and leather and tobacco smoke and men at close quarters. He was going to like it here, he decided. Whatever the reason for the men's coolness, it would pass; or, if not, he could stand it for the three weeks he had to finish his job.

"Gentlemen," he said in blanket greeting.

A rangy, mustachioed man pushed himself up from his bunk and came to stand in front of Hunter beneath the central hanging lantern.

"Name's Banner," he said. "They call me Tom. Don't know much about you, where you come from or what you are. But we hear you stood by Edge today. That's good enough for us."

"Thanks," Hunter said.

"Now, this here's Dub Axtel—good man with a rope. And the young'un there is Billy Jackson. And . . ."

One by one they came up, spoke a word or two, offered a brief handshake. When they were done Hunter was one of them, though none had said so.

"I sleep over at the big house," Pardee said half apologetically. "You can pick one of the empty bunks in here. Washhouse is out back."

"Thanks," Hunter said. "I better see to that gray. Thanks."

Stepping out into the starlit dark, Hunter paused a minute, looking at the lights of the big house. Kelly had moved on, maybe to the barn or some other errand, and the yard was deserted. Through the lighted window of the parlor he could see Linda Pardee and Perry Bonham seated together on the big overstuffed sofa, deep in earnest conversation. Then Linda squeezed Bonham's hand

and laughed, happiness and freedom in her face and the proud toss of her head. Hunter, watching, set his teeth against the dull ache in his throat and strode toward the pen where he'd left the gray.

"Adam, please," Sarah Lemmon, Barney's widow, had said. "You don't have to do this."

They had stood in the tiny parlor of the Lemmons' frame house in Fort Smith, Hunter tall and awkward, his hat in his hands. Sarah Lemmon, small and birdlike and motherly, looked at him in distress.

"Barney wouldn't have wanted it this way, Adam. Your badge isn't any good outside the Territory. You won't be a lawman."

"No matter."

"Adam—son—no one blames you for what happened. It wasn't your fault."

But he felt guilty, and he had found no answer except to take to the trail. It had led him first to the two women who'd thought they were married to Red Bull Converse; to the grave of one bandit, killed by Cherokee police in the Nations; to the dugout cabin where another would not be taken alive and spoke bitter words about his partners before he died. Finally it had brought him up to the high valleys of southern Colorado.

And now I have them, he thought. One of them, anyway. Red Bull Converse, calling himself Jack Harvey. And Sid Tate, the one I don't know by sight. The one who killed Barney. If the Red Bull is around, Sid Tate won't be far away.

Chapter 5

At four o'clock the sky was still dark outside. Hunter was already awake. Damn poor habit, he told himself. The cowhands in the bunks around him were wrapped in their last half hour of hard snoring before the cook's clanging gong would wake them for a new day's work. Nearby someone murmured a name in his sleep. Silently as a shadow Hunter rose and dressed. Sitting on the edge of his bunk, he drew on his boots, then gathered his gear and slipped outside.

Although it was early summer in the basin the pre-dawn breeze held the cold bite of mountain snows. Hunter shivered as he strapped on his gun belt, settling the oiled leather holster against his thigh. Also from habit he drew out the heavy Colt, set the hammer to half cock, and turned the cylinder to check the loads. Satisfied, he snapped the loading gate shut and went to saddle the gray.

When presently Hunter emerged from the stable he led the horse a couple of hundred yards down the road before stepping into the saddle. Had he looked back he might have seen a lone figure silently observing him from the porch of the bunkhouse. Tag Kelly watched horse and rider disappear out of sight along the road that led up and out of Pine Valley. Then he made himself a cigarette and lit it, the flare of the match catching his face characteristically empty of all expression.

At the crest of the ridge overlooking the ranch buildings Hunter turned his horse east into the first hint of dawn. His study of Avery's wall map the evening before had shown him a high trail that led cross-country to the Circle Eight headquarters, shorter and probably less traveled than the road that ran through Sublette City. Before long he crossed it and turned that way, reaching forward to loosen his rifle in its scabbard.

The morning chill would burn away when the sun rose, but now it was cool enough that Hunter burrowed into his fleece-lined coat. Steam came in puffs from the gray's wide nostrils. As the trail climbed the sun rose to meet them, sunlight transforming vague grayish shapes into trees, flowers, and rocks painted in vivid shades of green and brown and yellow. The low-hanging mist was already disappearing, and he realized that by noon the air would be as dry as on the New Mexico high plains.

The scale of the map was apparently farther off than he'd thought, because he rode for two hard hours without sign of fence or dwelling. He crossed a wide, rugged stretch of poor grazing that he took for the government range, then went back into the green hills. Scattered bunches of cattle grazed the hills, first marked with the pointed chevrons of the Pine Valley brand, then with the Circle Eight.

As he pulled up a long slope, scattering the chunky steers with his progress, another rider angled down from a nearby hill to intercept him. Clear of the cattle, Hunter drew up and waited. As the cowhand came closer Hunter saw he had his rifle out, its butt resting on his thigh and its barrel pointing upward. He reined in a dozen yards away, frowning slightly as he studied Hunter.

"You're on Circle Eight land, friend," he said quietly. "Can I point you on your way someplace?"

"You can. My name's Adam Hunter."

"I figured," the other man said. He was about Hunter's age, with dark hair and thoughtful blue eyes, now wary. He rested his thumb on the hammer of his rifle. "I'm Bob Golightly. Heard a bit about your run-in with Abel in town. And about what you did to Horse Webb.'

"A friend of yours, was he?"

"Not so much. But no enemy, either."

"Nor mine, until he took a shot at me." Hunter folded his hands over the saddlehorn. "I want to talk to your boss—Mr. Watkins, is it? I'd count it a favor if you'd take me to him."

Golightly considered. "All right." He tipped his hat back with the hand that held the reins. "I don't suppose you'd want to give me that handgun."

Hunter shook his head slightly. "Nope," he said.

"Mind riding ahead of me?"

"Nope."

"Good enough." Golightly nodded toward the hill where he'd stood sentry. "Straight up that rise there."

From the top of the ridge Hunter saw the ranch buildings a mile away in a broad, shallow valley. He felt a sudden respect for the man who had claimed the site and planned the placement of the buildings. No book-trained army officer could have chosen a better-protected position, and no stockman could have wanted better grazing.

Unspeaking, Bob Golightly shepherded Hunter straight into the wagon yard and across toward the ranch house itself. Halfway there a voice hailed him from the corral.

"Here, Bob! You're supposed to be on watch. What've you got there?"

Golightly jerked his head and took Hunter that way. Obediently Hunter reined up the gray and dismounted. A spare, wiry, clean-shaven man, as tall as Hunter and ten years younger than he'd expected, strode over and planted himself in front of him. Without fuss six or seven hands fell in around him, watching Hunter with the same expression Golightly had worn. Hunter caught a glimpse of Pillbox grinning from the fringe of the group and of Barbara Watkins watching from the porch of the house. Some of the riders must have been family men, he figured, because a half dozen children gazed at him furtively from the edges of the yard. He wondered for a moment where Annie Laurie was, but then the elder Watkins claimed his attention.

"Ellis Watkins," he said in a round voice. He looked at Hunter with curiously colorless eyes but didn't offer his hand. "I've heard about you. Why are you on my land?"

Looking at him, Hunter could see where his daughters had gotten their firm jawlines and finely cut features, but the dark eyes and hair and the stunning beauty had come from another source. Their mother must be something, he thought inconsequentially. Aloud he said, "I want to talk."

"Go ahead."

Hunter tilted his head toward the audience of cowhands. "I don't need this much help."

Ellis Watkins only then seemed aware of the men backing him. "Jesus, take over Bob's watch, *por favor.*" His voice was soft but filled with authority. "The rest of you have made your welcome. Go on about your business. It's all right." To Pillbox's quick motion of protest he added, "I'll be a damn sight older before I need protection from a lone man who's facing me. Go along, son."

"Thanks," Hunter said.

Watkins showed no sign of unbending. "From the hang of your pistol I'd guess you wouldn't know how a ranch is run. The time for long talks is Sundays and evenings. Get on with it."

"I met some of your hands in town yesterday. Met some others on the trail earlier. I wonder were they yours, too."

"That bushwhacker you brought down, you mean?" Watkins rubbed his chin, his strange eyes cold and steady on Hunter's. "I've got no need to explain myself to you, Hunter, but mark this: I don't hide behind another man's gun. Anyone rides out shooting in my name, you'll find me right ahead of him."

Hunter nodded. "I'd thought some of your boys might be exceeding their orders," he said. "Now I've met you, I doubt that."

"Hm." The rancher frowned a little. "Sounds as though—"

The approach of a horse, ridden hard, interrupted him. Both men turned to watch Abel Carson wheel into the wagon yard on a bulky black gelding. Carson reined up a few yards short of them and dismounted, dropping the reins.

The hint of a smile might have touched Watkins's thin lips. "Abel," he said.

Carson nodded but said nothing. His small, bright eyes were intent on Hunter. As if the interruption had never happened, Watkins turned back to finish his sentence.

"Sounds as though you're taking a special interest in Pine Valley's affairs."

"I've signed on with Avery, if that's what you mean. And I don't much take to being shot at."

Carson started to speak but was checked by a movement of the rancher's hand.

"Then you've chose the wrong profession," Watkins said.

"So my mother always told me," Hunter answered. "You make it sound like you're expecting it to come to fighting between you and Avery."

Watkins snorted. "Hell, he hired *you,* didn't he?" This time the rancher did smile, though there wasn't much humor in it. "I don't figure it was to make peace between us."

"Been a real waste of money, was that his idea," Carson muttered. Hunter glanced at him, then looked back to Watkins.

"He didn't hire me to make war, nor to rustle Circle

Eight cattle," Hunter told him. "I guess that's what I came to say."

"All right, it's said. I'd think it best if you was to ride out. My word that nobody'll hinder you on your way."

Hunter touched his hat. "Much obliged for your hospitality."

He reached for the gray's reins, but Abel Carson put out a big hand. "If it's all the same to Mr. Watkins, I still want to see that rifle of yours," he said.

Hunter looked at the burly foreman, and then he knew what had really brought him to the Circle Eight that morning. "In the saddle boot," he said to Carson, almost gently.

"The barn suit you?"

"Just fine." Hunter took the reins and led the gray along while Carson swung back one of the wide doors.

"Abel?" Ellis Watkins frowned, looking at his foreman. "You sure?"

"Personal, Mr. Watkins," Carson said. "We got something to talk about, the shooter and me." He unbuckled his gun belt and slung it across the end of an empty feed box just outside the door. "Hunter?"

Hunter hesitated a moment, then did the same. He could have stopped there, because that one action had told him all he wanted to know. But a fury was rising in him, the same fury that had driven him across three states. Already he could feel the release that came from giving it free rein, as good, almost, as a drink of whiskey.

The cowhands around the yard had dropped all pretense of working now, staring openly at the two men. Carson nodded toward the open dimness of the barn, and Hunter led the gray inside, putting it into an empty stall while Carson swung the door closed behind them. As Carson shot the bolt Hunter turned, flexing his hands at his sides.

"Now then, shooter," Carson said, turning to face

him. "The scripture's been read and the hymns sung. Let's get on to the sermon."

Hunter met him between stall and doorway, shifted slightly to spread his feet, and swung with his left hand instead of his right.

If the offhand punch surprised Carson, he didn't show it. He took the blow on the side of his jaw, shook his head, and waded into Hunter with the same methodical, pounding attack he'd used earlier on Pardee. Hunter blocked, but one blow got through with Carson's twenty-pound weight advantage behind it. It staggered Hunter. He slipped, went to one knee, and scrambled to regain his feet just in time to catch Carson's blunt elbow across his temple.

Hunter landed hard on his back, odors of dust and straw and fresh horse manure around him, the ceiling beams of the barn blurring above him. Instinctively he twisted away from Carson's boots, but the big foreman wasn't that kind of fighter. Instead Carson stepped back and waited stolidly while Hunter rolled to his feet and brought up his guard.

Gasping for breath, Hunter realized for the first time how thin the air was at this altitude. His chest heaved with the effort of drawing breath, but he seemed to be drowning anyway. He knew he had to finish the fight quickly if he was going to finish it at all.

"Winchester. Model 1886," he panted, buying himself some time. "Big bore. The .45-90. Must have glanced off. The rock. Tumbled. Hit him that way."

Carson's face drew into a scowl. Disappointment, Hunter thought, rather than anger. The big man was breathing deeply but far less raggedly than Hunter.

"You throwing in your hand?" he demanded, his small eyes glinting with suspicion.

"Not today."

Hunter launched himself, driven by pain and anger and a deep-set determination not to lose. He landed a flurry of short, sharp blows and danced back, catching

most of Carson's return pounding on his upraised fore-
arms, driving a hard knee into the larger man's belly
when Carson tried a rush. That gave Hunter time to set
himself and drive upward, all the power of his legs and
back and shoulders going into a punch that snapped Carson's head back and sent him reeling into one of the
heavy beams that supported the loft. The foreman's
spine crashed into the post an instant before his head
hit it with a solid thud.

Hunter caught his breath, half fearing the foreman
was dead. Carson's knees buckled, but he didn't fall.
Shaking his head, he lunged. His huge arms clamped
around Hunter like the jaws of a trap snapping shut.
The two of them staggered along the barn runway in a
clumsy, exhausted dance while Hunter struggled to free
his arms and to breathe against the massive strength that
compressed his ribs.

They burst blindly through the slatted door of an
empty stall, Carson taking most of the impact. He
slipped off balance, and Hunter desperately drove a fist
against Carson's temple. The vise around his chest loos-
ened for an instant, long enough for Hunter to twist
free. Still in the same motion he pivoted, ripped a heavy
draft collar from its pegs on the wall, and swung it at
Carson in a whistling horizontal arc.

The edge of the collar caught Carson across the side
of the head, slamming him against a feed bin. He hung
for a moment, then folded forward at the waist as limply
as a wet leather hinge and slumped to the dirt floor.

Hunter dropped the collar in the dust and went to
kneel beside the fallen giant. Carson's eyes were peacefully closed, his breathing deep, his heartbeat strong and
steady. Except for being unconscious he looked much
better than Hunter felt.

Hunter rose, supporting himself on the slats of the
stall, kicked the broken door aside, and staggered out
into the runway. He found his hat and was about to
back the gray horse out when he heard someone else

breathing. He spun around, hand going automatically to his hip, where his holster should have been. Then he straightened, relaxing, as he saw who was there.

Barbara Watkins leaned against a side door watching him. Her weight held the door slightly ajar so that sunlight framed her black hair and the sculptured perfection of her face. Through the haze of floating dust particles Hunter saw her dark beauty wrapped in golden light, a vision of warm animal appeal. But she seemed to see him in another light. Her beautiful face was twisted with anger and disgust.

"I suppose," she said coldly, "you would call that a fair fight where you come from."

Hunter didn't feel like arguing the question, even if he'd had the breath for it. His head felt like a split melon.

"Seen lots of fights," he said. "Been in a few. No such thing as fair. One side wins. The other one loses."

"So the method doesn't matter, according to you?"

"Ask Abel." Backing the gray out of the stall, he wondered if he had the strength to mount. "No. Not so long as the right side wins."

Her full lips tightened into a line. "Well, you've picked the wrong one this time, mister. Circle Eight's never stooped to bushwhacking, nor to rustling, nor to hiring killers like you. Nor will it while my father or I live to run it." She stared at him, eyes full of challenge, but he didn't answer. "Go oil your guns, then, and get ready for a fight. But don't lie to yourself about being on the right side."

"I'm not a hired gun, Miss Watkins," Hunter said. "Or if I am, you'd be some surprised by my employer."

Barbara Watkins snorted. "Surprised at the Devil? No." She leveled a finger at Hunter. "But if you mix into this, he'll get you back sooner than you'd like."

She flung out the door, slamming it shut behind her. Hunter shook his head—a serious mistake, because it rang like a blacksmith's anvil—and dragged himself into the saddle.

"It's just a feeling I have," he muttered aloud. "But I don't think these folks like me."

"Barb doesn't," a cheerful voice said from above him. "I know who she does like. But I won't tell, 'cause they'd get in trouble."

Hunter stared upward. Annie Laurie Watkins gazed down at him with interest. She was propped on her elbows on the floor of the loft, her neck craned to watch what had gone on below. At the cost of considerable pain from his split and swollen lips, Hunter grinned at her.

"You keep turning up," he said. "Well-mannered young ladies don't spy on their elders. Aren't you scared, alone in here with a killer?"

She wrinkled her nose at him. "Barb's a young lady," she said. "But I'm not, and I won't be until I absolutely have to. But you're not really a killer, not really. You didn't kill Abel."

Hunter touched careful fingers to his mouth, then to the side of his face. "Abel would take a powerful lot of killing," he said. "Besides, I think we might get along, him and me." He tipped his hat to the girl. "So long, Annie Laurie. Don't be so quick to make up your mind about people. Being wrong could be dangerous."

"But I'm not wrong," she said with assurance, and Hunter swung back the broad door and rode out into daylight.

Three of the children he'd seen earlier had crowded against the barn wall, sharing the view through a crack between the boards. They stared with round eyes as Hunter leaned painfully down to recover his gun belt. When he straightened and looked at them they scrambled away around the corner of the building.

At the corral Ellis Watkins sat on the top rail smoking a stubby cigar. He paused with it halfway to his lips when he saw Hunter. Nearby several cowhands stood idle and unrebuked, staring almost as incredulously as the children had. Hunter nodded gravely to them, then swung the gray toward the gate.

"Damnation!" Ellis Watkins said. "Won't wonders never cease!"

Nearby Pillbox nudged Bob Golightly. "Pay me," he said. But none of them stirred until Hunter had ridden out; then they went to see what had happened to Abel Carson.

Chapter 6

Sublette City was in a quiet mood when Hunter arrived there shortly before noon. Now that he had visited with Abel Carson he intended to meet the others whom Pardee had identified as newcomers to the basin. He still figured that one of them would be Sid Tate. He just hoped he could learn about the rest in a less direct manner than the way he'd measured Carson.

He saw Adrian Hanover first, less by plan than from necessity. Hanover's Livery Barn stood at the north end of the town's only real street, near the church and the undertaking parlor. By a lucky coincidence it occupied the Pine Valley side of the street, so Hunter rode straight in without having to plan a more complicated approach.

Hanover himself was small and sleepily quiet, a thin, aging man with heavy, graying eyebrows and a big soup-strainer mustache that hid most of his face. He ambled out to meet Hunter, introduced himself, and led the gray back to a stall without spending more than a dozen words.

Hoping for a little more, Hunter waited, looking around the barn while the liveryman unsaddled the animal and baited it with oats. The place smelled of horses and hay and old leather. Hanover maintained a small feed store at one end of the livery and apparently had his living quarters there as well. A large yellowish dog of mixed ancestry rose from a nest of hay near the doorway to Hanover's rooms. It stretched itself, then loped over to Hunter, wagging its hairy tail with clumsily powerful sweeps.

"Hello, boy," Hunter said, standing still while the dog sniffed at his boots and trouser legs. Apparently satisfied, it sat back on its haunches and raised its right forepaw. Hunter glanced toward Hanover, now coming back along the barn's runway, then knelt to shake hands with the dog. Instead the dog licked his hand with a broad purple tongue.

"Hello," Hunter said again.

"Don't expect no hello from old Gen'ral Houston," Hanover murmured. "He don't talk much, least not to strangers. He does take to you, though, which he don't to most folks. Likes Texans, mostly."

It was the longest speech he'd made. Maybe, Hunter thought, General Houston's opinion means I'm all right.

"The General is a Texan, then?" he asked, scratching the floppy ears.

"Born and bred, same as me. Wonders why he ever left there, same as me. Whines and kicks in his sleep, dreaming about those woods back home."

"Same as you?"

Hanover smiled, opening his eyes a trifle wider to consider Hunter. "Been a long time gone," he said. "Years and years."

"What part of Texas do you hail from, Mr. Hanover?"

"Oh, here and there," Hanover said easily. "No place you'd likely recognize." He inclined his head toward Hunter. "Meant to ask you sooner. Did that gray horse trample you?"

"No. That wouldn't have hurt as much." Hunter rose and stretched himself to ease the tightness in his muscles. Dull aches answered from every part of his body. "I had a little disagreement with a friend."

"Oh." Hanover thought that over, thrusting out his lower lip through his brushy mustache. "Well, I'll make it a point never to downright *argue* with you, then. Don't want to tell you your business, but there's a barber down the street might have a bath for you and a dab of witch hazel for those cuts."

"I was just headed there," Hunter said truthfully. "Man named Sears, I understand, William Sears."

"Oh, now," Hanover said. "Not sure you'd want to do that. Will, he's over on the Circle Eight side of the street, and that horse says you're Pine Valley. Boyd Riley's your man."

Hunter nodded. "Thanks. Suppose you put that Pine Valley horse back there in a stall for me."

"You're the boss."

Hunter started to leave, then turned back. "Anybody else around that General Houston takes to?" he asked, feeling foolish because he was certain of neither man nor dog.

"Not so's you'd notice." The liveryman's eyelids drooped again, hiding his expression. "Excepting maybe that dad-blamed preacher, which is nothing he ever learnt from me."

At the mercantile Hunter paid what he thought a high price for a new shirt to replace the one he was wearing. With the package under his arm he paused on the high wooden porch of the store, looking across the street at the red-striped pole in front of the Eight Ball barbershop. It occurred to him that he'd made a mistake letting himself become involved with one side in a feud that wasn't his affair. Still, it beat sitting in Tobreen's jail.

Although the morning was well along, few people moved on the streets. Hunter judged that Watkins was right; on a weekday no cowhands from either party should be hanging around town. At least it was worth the chance. He strode quickly across the narrow street and went inside, then stopped in sudden confusion. The barber was a black man, tall and slender, with short gray muttonchop whiskers.

"Morning, sir," he said. "Can I help you today?"

"You're William Sears?"

"Surely am. But I don't recall having the pleasure."

"Name's Hunter." Hunter hesitated for a moment, uncertain what to do. He'd learned what he'd come to find out; William Sears wasn't his man. But leaving was more likely to attract notice than staying. And he did need to clean up after his encounter with Abel Carson.

"What do you get for a bath?" he asked.

The barber studied him for a moment, then smiled. "Seventy-five cents, most often. Shave and haircut is two bits each. You can have the whole works for a dollar."

Hunter raised his eyebrows. "That's a day's wages for some folks," he said.

"Worth every penny, too. Not meaning to be personal, you understand, but I'd recommend it to you. Got a wash boiler in back with all the hot water you want."

"You're quite a salesman," Hunter said. "Lead me to it."

The back room of the barbershop had a slatted plank floor, damp and a little slippery. The furnishings were a big claw-footed bathtub, a rickety wooden chair, and a copper wash boiler with coals glowing on an iron sheet beneath it. The air was warm and heavy with moisture.

"Here you go." Sears tripped the spigot of the boiler, and steaming water poured into the tub. "Hang your clothes on the chair—you can put the gun belt wherever you're minded. That spigot over there will give you cold water. Just stir it in until you're comfortable."

"Pretty fancy," Hunter commented.

"Only establishment in town with modern conveniences," Sears said proudly. "Got a tank set on the roof of the building. The fire department fills it every week with their steam pump." He stepped back through the doorway. "Towels and the like right here. I'll close the door. Just call if you need anything."

Hunter had intended his visit to town to be short and

businesslike. Stretched in water as hot as he could stand, he found his plans changing. He soaked long enough to ease the aches from Abel Carson's pounding, and he took a melancholy pleasure in the stinging smart that the alkaline water brought to his cuts. He had almost drifted into sleep when he heard the barber's voice raised in outraged protest.

"Now you wait just a minute. You can't go in there!"

A piercingly cold draft of air swept across Hunter's shoulders. The door of the room began to swing open. His drowsiness gone at once, he sat upright and reached for his holster, sliding the Colt halfway out. Then Annie Laurie stuck her head around the edge of the door and gave him her buck-toothed grin.

"Hello. You look silly."

Hunter felt silly. He let the pistol slide back into its oiled holster and sank back in the warm water, wishing for a few more soapsuds.

"Annie Laurie, what are you doing here? You have no business—"

"That's just what I was telling her," Sears said. "Miss Annie, you get right back here. It ain't decent, a young lady peeping in there."

"I'm *not* peeping," Annie Laurie said with dignity. She turned from one of them to the other. "I came into town on the supply wagon. And I'm here because I have important things to discuss with Mr. Hunter." She stepped all the way inside. "In private," she added, closing the door firmly in the outraged barber's face.

"Now, Annie, listen—" Hunter began.

Annie picked her way carefully across the damp floor and took a seat on the chair atop Hunter's clothes. "Papa sent three hands in with the wagon," she said. "Pillbox—you know him—and two others. You're lucky it's not haircut day. They wouldn't like you being here."

"Annie, do you know what they'd do if they came along while you were in here?"

The girl considered. "Something pretty awful, I expect—to you, not to me."

She squirmed into a more comfortable position and looked at him seriously. Beneath her tomboyish innocence Hunter caught a glimpse of the woman she would be in a few years—level dark eyes, impish humor, the firm line of jaw and cheekbone that would make her a real beauty.

"God help him," he murmured.

"Who?"

"The man you finally set your cap for." He started to stretch for the towel, then thought better of it and sat back. "What was it you wanted to see me about?"

"Well, I've listened to Papa and Mama and Barb and Abel and some of the hands all talking. They have different ideas about who you are and why you came here, but none of them sound right. So I thought I'd ask you."

"I'm just passing through."

She shook her head. "No. That's a story for the constable or Papa. You came *here*." For a moment she gazed at him with pursed lips. Then she said, "No matter what they think, I know you aren't bad. If you'll tell me, I'll help you—long as it's nothing against Circle Eight." She grinned again. "I won't tell. I keep lots of secrets."

For a moment Hunter was tempted. Child or woman, Annie Laurie clearly had her own ideas. Maybe she really could help—but not if it meant putting her in danger. If he knew nothing else about Sid Tate, he was sure the outlaw would kill to protect himself.

"I'll have to think on it, Annie Laurie. Maybe—"

He broke off because the door had opened again. Constable Ed Tobreen filled it, with Sears peering around him.

"Now, by thunder!" Tobreen growled. He took a long stride forward and loomed over Annie Laurie. "I thought Hunter was the biggest clod in my churn, but I guess it's still you, young lady."

Annie Laurie stood up. "I'm not," she said defiantly. "A young lady, I mean. And I had business—"

Tobreen shot out a big hand and caught her firmly by the right ear. Annie Laurie yelped as he marched her to the door.

"Not in here, you haven't," he said. "I've never yet had a female in my jail. But I swear to G—goodness you'll be the first if you pull another stunt like this. Now *git!*"

He turned his back on her protests and nodded to Hunter.

"Constable," Hunter said. "Good to see you. Sure you don't have a few friends you'd like to ask in?"

"Heard you were over in Circle Eight territory again." He almost smiled. "Trifling with their women, too. Can't say I think much of your judgment."

Hunter waved a hand at the wash boiler. "My own fault," he said. "If I'd wanted a little privacy, I should have taken my bath in the horse trough in front of the church. You want to close that door?"

Tobreen did, then he came up and squatted beside the tub. His dun mustache drooped like a wet sheepdog in the humid warmth.

"Thought you might have ridden on by now," he said.

"You warned me not to."

Tobreen grunted. "Just heard from the doc. He's been out to Circle Eight. They're saying somebody's put right smart of a dent in Abel Carson's skull."

"Oh?"

"Don't know as I would have done that. I own myself surprised that you did. Then there's Annie Laurie. She likes you, and that little imp is smarter than most men grown around here." Tobreen passed a hand over his mustache, shaking water droplets from it. "I mean to know more about you, Mr. Hunter. Could be I've judged you wrong, and that grates on me. I hate to get a man wrong."

"Sorry."

"Likely. Meantime, like I told you, don't bring me any more bodies like a puppy dragging in bones." Reaching out carefully, Tobreen lifted Hunter's Colt from its holster. "Nice piece," he said.

"Where I come from it's not polite to handle another man's iron."

"That's my point, son. You're where *I* come from." Tobreen rocked the hammer back to turn the cylinder, allowing the shells to fall one by one into his palm. When all six were out he cocked the gun and pulled the trigger, catching the hammer with his thumb just before it fell. "Smooth action. Hammer falls a little sudden for my taste, though. Could be dangerous."

"Maybe you'd better not play with it, then."

"Seems like it doesn't want to stay on half cock, either." Tobreen raised his eyebrows. "Now that's a real danger. Maybe you should see the gunsmith."

"That's what I thought, Constable. I'm headed there next."

With his hair cut and his beard trimmed short Hunter strode up the boardwalk toward the church. Across the way from Bonham's funeral parlor he found a small cabin with a sign burned into a wooden plank beside the door: Ammunition and Gunsmithing, Melvin Cox, Proprietor.

Hunter stepped inside, blinking in the relative darkness. The pleasant smells of gun oil and worked leather and fresh sawdust welcomed him, reminded him of happier days. He looked at shelves of neatly stacked boxes of ammunition and at cartridge belts and holsters hanging from metal racks, but no guns were in sight.

"Anything I can help you with?"

The voice came from the darkest corner of the room. Hunter turned that way to meet the blank gaze of a pair of tint-lensed eyeglasses. The man who wore them was seated at a wooden counter, his large head seeming balanced over his narrow chest and shoulders as precariously as a melon on a post. He wore a narrow-brimmed felt dress hat, but his shirtsleeves were rolled up and his hands stained with oil and varnish.

"Melvin Cox?"

"Yes."

"A box of shells for my Winchester."

"Caliber?" The man did not move. "Load?"

"It's a .45-90, smokeless powder. I want the heaviest loads you carry."

"The shelf to your lower left, in the bottom row. Not much call for that caliber. What else?"

"I'd like you to take a look at my pistol. I've been having trouble with—"

"No, wait," the man interrupted quietly. "I'd rather make my own diagnosis." He put out a slender white hand in Hunter's general direction. "May I see it?"

See it? Hunter thought. After a second's hesitation Hunter drew the Colt, shucked out the shells, and placed the gun in the blind man's hand.

"Good practice, unloading," the gunsmith observed absently. He kept his open stare on Hunter as his thin, sensitive fingers caressed the Colt. "Yes," he murmured. He cocked the pistol, dropped it to half cock, felt delicately for the safety position. "Yes," he said again. Then, as if he'd just remembered Hunter's presence, he said, "The hammer notches are worn. You must use it quite a lot."

"Over a long period of time."

"I can install a new hammer for five dollars, but that's a third the price of the weapon. For two dollars I can machine this one for you." He reached below the counter and took out another Colt, offering it butt-first to Hunter. "Try this. It had the same problem."

Automatically Hunter thumbed open the loading gate to be sure the gun was empty. His fingers touched a multitude of fine lines. He looked closely, squinting in the shadows of the room, and found a wealth of delicate engraving scored into the cold metal. Vines twined about the barrel, twisting and overlapping in complex patterns. Sprays of leaves covered the frame. Flowers, some just opening and some spreading petals wide to an unseen sun, seemed to grow up naturally to cover the cylinder.

"That's a moss rose," Cox said. He shrugged at Hunter's unspoken question. "Used to be I'd read a good deal. Can't anymore, and the engraving helps pass the time. That big Winchester of yours, now, that gives a man room to work. Look on those pegs above the door."

Hunter laid the revolver on the counter and turned to take down a rifle, the twin of his own. On the broad, flat plate around the loading gate a pair of elk grazed in belly-deep grass. Wooded mountains rose behind them, an eagle hanging tiny and stiff-winged near the tallest peak. On the other side of the receiver a mountain lion screamed defiance from a rocky crag backed by tall pines.

"I call that my high country pattern." The gunsmith chuckled deprecatingly. "Not something you'd be interested in. Try the action on that Colt."

Reluctantly Hunter put the rifle aside and picked up the revolver again. He eased the hammer back through its positions, delighting in the silky smoothness of its movement and the crisp, sharp snick of the half cock and cock. "That's something." He lowered the hammer carefully and offered the gun to Cox. "Feels more like a gold watch than a gun."

"Eases the trigger pull a mite, too. Helps you stay on target. Might even be a shade faster—if that's important to a man. Two dollars."

"You must polish the surface some way."

The gunsmith's bloodless lips twitched in a smile. "For two dollars more you can watch me work," he said. "Take the secret back to—well, to wherever you're going back to. I'll even tell you stories. It's nice to have somebody to talk to while I work."

"Where would you be going back to," Hunter asked, "if you went home?"

"We'll work that into the conversation, too, if you'll stay and visit."

Hunter hesitated. "I guess I'll have to put that pleasure off until I come back for the gun," he said finally. "But I don't think I'd better be unarmed right now. Do you think—"

"Oh, you can take this one until I'm finished. I don't believe it'll disappoint you. Yours will be ready Tuesday, unless you'd like a bit of engraving on the frame— a marshal's badge, maybe?"

Hunter stiffened, staring at the blank glasses. "Now why would you think that?" he asked.

Cox shrugged. "Oh, just an idea." He smiled a directionless smile. "I heard a voice like yours once, and its owner was a marshal. Was it you?"

Hunter hesitated, then managed a laugh. "No. I'd favor the high country scene for my rifle, though, if I had the time." He took two silver dollars from his pocket and laid them on the counter. "This ought to cover fixing my Colt."

Cox felt for the coins, then rolled them nimbly between his fingers. "Oh, I'd trust you, Mr. Hunter," he said. "Just as I do with the pistol. Don't forget to load it."

"I won't."

"It would be a challenge, but I think I could do the high country on a pistol. Think on it, Mr. Hunter. Call Tuesday."

An hour later, with a warm meal in his belly and a sense of having wasted his time, Hunter rode out toward Pine Valley. He'd had his look at the basin's newcomers, except for the preacher Pardee had mentioned and Perry Bonham, whom he'd already met. He put a mile of road behind him before he turned aside into a stand of pines. He waited there long enough to be certain no one was on his trail, then went on.

He was restless, impatient, dissatisfied with what he'd learned so far. Maybe it would have been better to go straight after Jack Harvey, to get him in a quiet place with a club and beat the truth out of him. At least, he thought ruefully, it would have been more fun than tackling Abel Carson.

"No," he said aloud. The borrowed horse, unused to his habits, cocked an eye at him but didn't break stride. "No," Hunter repeated. He'd thought it best to get a line on Harvey's partner first, and he'd made a little headway. He was pretty sure who wasn't Sid Tate. William Sears clearly wasn't the man he'd seen that day in Rocky Comfort, and the half-blind Melvin Cox couldn't have killed Barney. As for the others, he couldn't tell. Not yet.

Engrossed as Hunter was in his own thoughts, he still caught the movement near the road a half mile ahead. He reined up, uncertain what he'd seen. After a few seconds three horses showed briefly in the scattered timber above the road, climbing to the east. Hunter watched until they disappeared, then took his horse off the road, angling upward on a course he thought would bring him in sight of these riders who didn't care to use the road.

He moved slowly with a stalker's patience, finding cover in the pines just below the crest of the ridge. If his calculations were right, he was above and well behind the others. Here he had a wide view of the slope below, but he himself wasn't visible from any great distance. Urging the gray into an easy lope, he pushed along faster, though still carefully, toward the crest. He wasn't sure whom he was following, and it seemed best to get the first look.

The pines along the far slope thinned away gradually as if they'd been scattered by a careless planter long ago. The ground opened out into natural pasture, deep in lush grass and many-colored wildflowers. Nothing moved in Hunter's range of vision except a lone red-tailed hawk quartering the clearing for mice or rabbits. Apparently the hawk didn't see anything either, because it drifted gradually off to the east.

Hunter moved again, crossing the open space and reining up among the scattered trees. Drawing his field glasses from their case, he scanned the slope below. Down where the trees began to grow more thickly he saw three horses standing with weary patience. A man in a plaid shirt walked into sight for a moment, struck a match, cupped hands to his face. A puff of gray smoke drifted downwind. Hunter lowered the glasses. Five hundred yards. He would have to get closer.

Tag Kelly drew deeply on the cigarette he'd rolled and shook out the match, holding it until it was cool, then tucking it into his vest pocket. "How about my pay?" he asked without turning around.

"You'll get your damned money." The man called Jack Harvey showed his teeth in a snarl. "Soon's you've done something to earn it. You're supposed to be bringing news from Pine Valley."

"Just go easy, Jack. He'll get to it," Bob Golightly said. Hunkered comfortably against a fallen log, he looked up at Harvey. "If things at Pine Valley is going as smooth as at Circle Eight, there ain't much to report."

"Shut up. Let him tell it."

Kelly turned, squinting at the big man with the scowl. "Bob's spoke true; it's all going just how you said." He paused and rubbed his nose thoughtfully. "One thing, though. That new man—Hunter—he rode out before first light on Mr. Avery's gray horse. I expect he's gone for good, so we don't have to worry about him."

"I ain't worried about him," Harvey said. "He's already done enough. Horning in when we had Pardee dead to rights was one thing, but when he killed old

Horse, that's too many. I'll settle him when the time comes."

Golightly had looked up sharply at Hunter's name. Now he grinned. "Didn't know you were sentimental, Jack," he murmured.

The heavyset man shifted his glare toward Golightly. "That ain't your affair. I want to know is Avery ready to fight. And what about Watkins?"

"Avery hates Circle Eight enough to fight," Kelly answered. "But he ain't ready yet."

Jack Harvey nodded. "All right." He pulled a thick hand from his pocket and counted out a few bills into Kelly's hand. "You keep watch and don't make no mistakes in judgment. I'll tell you when it's time." He turned to Golightly. "Well? What's your story?"

"Well," Bob Golightly said, "we did have us a little entertainment this morning. That man Hunter, he rode in first thing after breakfast and had a long talk with Mr. Watkins. Then—"

"What the hell!" Harvey interrupted. "What do you mean, talk? What did they say to each other?"

Golightly eyed him with mild amusement. "Fact is, they didn't invite me to listen in. And Mr. Watkins ain't got around to telling me yet. Then," he went on quickly as Harvey started to speak again, "Hunter politely invited Abel Carson into the barn and whaled the tar out of him."

"Aw, hell," Tag Kelly said, grinning. "You're drawing the long bow, Bob."

"I'm sure as hell not. Made a noise like a cyclone, they did. Then after a while Hunter came out looking like the nigh end of a train wreck—but he came out. Abel was asleep in the barn. Cost me ten dollars of my own money."

"Huh!" Harvey combed his red whiskers thoughtfully. "Strange business. What's the chances Carson will shoot Hunter down for us?"

"None," Golightly said firmly. "Ain't his way, shooting people. Doubt they'll fight again, even."

"Huh!" Harvey said again. He frowned; struggling with an idea too complicated for him. "You know where Hunter went from there?"

"I do," Tag Kelly put in softly. He was rolling another cigarette, looking casually off toward the crest. "Don't nobody turn to look. There's a gent up the hill a piece watching us like we was ladies bathing in a stream. I can't see his horse anyplace, but I'd bet it's Avery's gray."

"I don't see anything," Harvey growled.

"Don't know how you've lived this long, then. He's there, but I figure he's too far off to make out who we are."

Without haste Bob Golightly unfolded himself and stood up. "About time I was riding, I expect. Just count out my share of the money, Jack."

"Hold it. We could rush him. Or two keep him busy while the third slipped around his flank."

"Nope," Golightly said.

Kelly bent his head to light his cigarette. Jack Harvey scowled.

"Why's that? You yellow?"

"I ain't a killer nor ain't planning to be. Told you that up front." Golightly smiled. "Besides, I got the idea Hunter ain't a good man to go sneaking up on. Didn't work out too well for your high-paid shooter."

"I said I'd kill him for that," Harvey growled.

"Go right ahead." Golightly swung aboard his horse and turned its head downhill. "See you next week, if nothing happens."

"Tag?" Harvey said.

"No nevermind to me," Kelly said without turning. "Let Bob get on away. Likely Hunter will follow one of us two. If it's me, I'll do my part. Killing ain't agin my religion."

*　　*　　*

Hunter lowered the glasses as the men dispersed, each riding out a different way. With the binoculars he'd recognized all three men. There was no mistaking Jack Harvey—Al "Red" Converse—and he'd met both the others. There was no way to be sure, but it seemed a good bet Harvey had spies on both ranches. That could be just a prudent precaution with a range war brewing, but more likely Harvey was helping bring the brew to a boil.

He waited what seemed a safe interval, then went back to his horse and found the road again. No reason to try catching up to Kelly, and he certainly didn't want to follow Harvey. He was riding slowly back toward Pine Valley, turning over what he'd learned in his mind, when the shot came out of the trees to the west.

The bullet screamed past within a yard, and Hunter reacted as quickly and instinctively as a tarantula disturbed by an insect. He swung the gray viciously, spurring straight up the hill into the eye of the sun, straight for the hidden gunman. Bending low in the saddle, he jerked his rifle from its boot. Another bullet snapped past, and then he was in the trees, a poor target and a deadly danger for whoever was above him with a short-range rifle.

Once among the pines he dismounted and swung wide, working uphill until he judged he was level with the spot where the rifleman had been. He cut across the slope until he found the fallen tree that had served as a blind and two empty .44-40 shells. The ground was marked with hoofprints where a rider had come and gone. Kelly or Jack Harvey, he guessed, and even odds either way.

It was too bad. He'd taken a hand in a feud that was none of his business, and now his job would be that much harder. Shaking his head, Hunter found the gray and rode out, still headed for Pine Valley. But now he carried his rifle across the saddlebow, and his eyes, scanning the trees to right and left, were never still.

Chapter 7

Jack Harvey waited in a pile of boulders more than an hour for Hunter to follow him. Finally he put up his rifle and headed for Sublette City. By the time he got there Harvey's mind was on whiskey and the death of Adam Hunter, and both thoughts were pleasant to him.

What didn't please him was the sight of three of his men loading a wagon in front of the general store on Pine Valley's side of the street. That meant a bill to settle. Besides, payday was coming up for all his men. He would have to get money before nightfall, and getting money was always more of a problem than he figured it ought to be, given that he was a wealthy man.

Riding past the store, Harvey dismounted and tied his horse in front of the harness shop. He went inside like a man with urgent business and talked to the bored clerk about the weather and the state of the grass on his north range until he was sure the wagon had pulled out. Then he broke off the conversation and strode swiftly back to the general store.

"Well, Mr. Harvey," the proprietor greeted him. "I was hoping you'd come in today. Hate to bring it up, but your account—"

"Sure, Titus, sure," Harvey broke in with heavy joviality. "Just stopped in at the bank yesterday, and on my way in to pay. What's the damage?"

The storekeeper wiped his hands on his white apron

and reached up for a notebook bound in limp leather covers. "Now let's see," he muttered. "According to my ledger book, it totes up at ninety-six dollars." He raised his head and peered at Harvey through gold-rimmed spectacles. "That's counting what them boys of yours just bought, of course."

"Ninety-six dollars!" Harvey clamped his jaws shut and glared at the grocer. "That's a hell of a sum! Why, I've known men who could run a ranch for a year on that, back in—" He stopped abruptly, cleared his throat, and said, "Why, I got a good mind to take my business across the street!"

"Well, I hope you'll see fit not to do that," the storekeeper said. "Overhead's high, and nothing I can do about it. Costs money to freight my goods up from the railroad. Seems like Morgan Avery understands about—"

"Avery, hell! Avery's got money enough to burn a wet mule! It's always the little man—like me—gets squeezed out."

"I hope not, Mr. Harvey, I surely do. And you can take your business wherever you think best. But I've got to make my living, same as you. Same as Jim Cole across the way. Don't believe you'll find his prices a bit better than mine, no, sir."

"Hmmp! Likely not!" Harvey glared around him, finally waved an impatient hand. "Give me a dozen of them cigars—no, not those, the good ones."

Still grumbling, he pocketed the cigars, paid his bill, and stomped out. It damn well wasn't fair, he thought. He'd worked hard and risked his life for what little he could lay his hands on. It wasn't fair for some smart-mouthed storekeeper to steal his money with talk about overhead and shipping costs.

"Bet that old skinflint's got two, three thousand hid out somewheres in that store," he muttered half aloud. "Good stake for a man, did he need one."

Slowly and with enjoyment Harvey caressed the butt

of his left-hand pistol. He had to keep up a front here. Sid said so, and Sid was the smart one—or so he thought. But one day things would be different. One day.

Harvey bit off the end of a cigar and lit up, puffing out a great cloud of gray smoke. Feeling better, he strode down to the Aces and Eights. It was still early, and the place was deserted except for Bill Epps, the proprietor.

"Jack," Epps said. "Pick yourself a seat. It's a slow day."

Harvey started for the bar, then pulled out a chair instead, deciding to make Epps work for his money. "You got any more of that tequila, Epps?"

Without looking Epps reached back to the shelf behind the bar, took down a bottle, and tilted it back and forth. "About a pint left. I guess I'd best order some more." He reached under the bar for a shot glass and carried bottle and glass and a shaker of salt around to Harvey's table. "You're about my best customer for this south-of-the-border stuff. About my onliest one, in fact."

"That's because these ridge-runners around here don't know what's good," Harvey said with satisfaction. "Learned to drink this in Sonora, back when I was just a pup." He dug into his coat pocket for a coin, scowled, then tried each of his other pockets in turn. "Hell," he said finally. "I got some urgent business back in your outhouse, Epps. Hold that bottle for me, and I'll be back directly."

"That's fine," Epps said. "Come back when you're easy in your mind." He set the bottle on the bar and picked up a towel. "I ain't expecting any big run of business on this stuff."

Silently cursing himself, Harvey walked out the back, headed toward the bank, then turned down the narrow alley that ran beside it. That bloodsucking grocer had taken almost the last cent he had on him. He shouldn't have let that happen. He had plenty of money, and more's the pity he had to sneak around like an egg-sucking dog to get it. Tate's idea again, damn him.

Harvey cut behind the bank between the building and the steep rise of hill that sheltered that side of town. Tufts of grass and flowers grew everywhere in the cool shade, but Harvey paid no attention. He walked rapidly along the narrow path, halting abruptly from time to time to be certain no one was watching. Reaching the back door of a familiar building, he tried the knob, then thrust himself quickly inside when it opened. With surprising grace for his build he moved silently along the hallway until he could look into a larger room where a man sat writing in a gray notebook.

"Sid."

The man whirled like a cat, spilling notebook and pen. When he brought up his hand it held a small shiny pistol.

"Sid, easy now. It's just me."

The man Harvey knew as Sid Tate rose quickly, but he did slip the pistol back into his pocket.

"Damn you, Red, you'll do that once too often," he said. Then his brows drew together in anger. "What do you mean coming here in daylight? I've told you before—"

"Now don't be flaring up at me, Sid. We go back too far. I'd not need to be here if we'd split the haul like I asked you."

"No. You'd be in some jail, or in a lonesome grave." Tate drew the curtains on window and door panes alike. "Latch that back door. Then we'll see."

By the time Harvey returned, Tate had taken up a candlestick and lighted the tall candles. He led the way to a narrow storeroom hidden behind a curtained doorway. Shelves were piled with boxes and dark glass bottles, but neither Harvey nor Tate glanced at them.

"You know where," Tate said. "Go on."

Grunting as he bent down, Harvey found an iron ring on the floor and lifted it. A square trapdoor creaked open, admitting a cool, musty smell to the stuffy room.

"You first," Harvey said.

"Like hell. You're the one that wants the money."

For a moment the red-bearded man glared at him. Then Harvey seized the candle and made his way down a flight of creaking wooden stairs. Tate followed, pausing to swing the trapdoor closed behind them. The candles burned blue and dim in the moist air, barely illuminating the slabs of moss-grown rock that lined the passageway on either side. The passage ended at another door. Tate opened it with an iron key, and the two entered an even smaller room.

Walls and roof were of the same square-cut rock as the walls of the passage. In places seeping water had stained the mortar, dripping down to form small puddles on the rough rock floor. Harvey's foot skidded in one of the puddles, and he cursed.

"Hell of a place to keep our money! Hell of a place, anyway!"

Tate laughed shortly. "Where would you suggest? You know how safe banks are."

Harvey turned to stare at him, and after a moment he also laughed. "Now that's the truth," he said. "We know about banks, Sid, you and me. Damned if we don't. Got your key?"

The room was bare except for a long wooden box set upon a pair of sawhorses. The lid of the box was secured by two heavy brass padlocks. Harvey reached inside his shirt and drew out a key attached to a long leather thong. Holding the candles high, he bent to peer at the locks.

"Harvard six-lever, that's me." He thrust the double-bitted key into the lock and opened it. Tate opened the other, and Harvey swung up the lid of the box.

Candlelight fell on a sparkling heap of gold and silver

coins mixed with currency and other papers. Here and there a stone set in a piece of jewelry returned white or green or red reflections. A crude boxwood divider cut the box into two compartments, one noticeably better stocked than the other. Harvey frowned at the one nearest him.

"This don't seem right. I ought to have more than that. You been sneaking into it when I wasn't looking."

"Don't start that again. Neither of us can open it without the other's key—at least not without leaving traces, and you're welcome to look for any. We started out fifty-fifty. If your side's lower, it's because you've drunk and whored it away."

"You got no call to talk to me like that," Harvey growled. "You're running a good business here while I'm stuck on that hardscrabble ranch."

"Not for much longer."

"Now's long enough. I got a payroll to meet—twenty hands at forty a month. And I got expenses. I'm a married man."

Tate sighed. "All right, all right. Here's four hundred from my side to help meet your payroll. But this is the last month I'll go for it. Once we get Avery and Watkins settled for, you'll have to tend to your own bills."

"Tend to my own bills? Like hell! Don't you go making up no new rules in the middle of the game." Harvey turned, his hunched shoulders seeming to fill the narrow room. "Listen, I don't cipher as good as you, but I still remember how we set this deal up—an even split, and partners until we got the lock on things in this valley. There's coming a day to count it all out even, Sid, and don't think I'll forget it."

"All right," Tate said smoothly. "Take it easy, Red. We'll settle our accounts when the time comes, right down to the penny. You have my word on that."

Harvey blinked at him uncertainly, then shrugged. "What it is, Sid, is I don't see my way clear," he said in a softer tone. "I ain't sure what you're waiting on. I ain't sure we're big enough to handle something this size. And it's taking a hell of a time."

"We'd be a lot farther along if you'd handled Pardee the way you bragged you would."

"That ain't my fault, nor the boys I sent after him. Old Horse was as good a man-killer as money could buy. It was that damned meddler Hunter. And I mean to put him through for it, too."

"I've been thinking about Mr. Hunter," Tate said. "Let him be for now. It may be he'll work into our plans just right." He slapped the larger man on the shoulder. "Come on, Red, keep a tight rein. You've never lost money by letting me do the thinking. Just you be ready to move when I say."

Jack Harvey tugged his red beard uneasily at Tate's mention of Hunter. "Well," he muttered. "Well, you might give a wink when you're about to change trumps. But I'll let it ride for a while. Things better work out soon, though, or I'll take my half out and try my luck somewheres else."

Without answering, Tate half turned away and lowered the lid on the long wooden box. He snapped the big brass lock in place and waited while Harvey did the same.

"Why, sure, Jack," he said then, smiling easily. "If things don't work out, you can do just that."

"Don't get that look in your eye with me, Sid, else I'll think you and me is finally about to have it out."

"Thinking's never been your longest suit, Red. But don't get that stupid."

"I ain't. You're flat out the best man with a handgun I've ever seen, Sid—so good you never left anybody behind can tell what you look like. But you think you're about ten times smarter than anybody as ever lived, so maybe you don't know I'm good enough to bring you down."

"Red, Red—"

"Oh, I don't figure I'd live over it. I know suicide

when I see it. Just you remember it'll be your funeral the same day as mine."

Tate smiled again. He took up the candlestick and motioned Harvey out of the room. "Let's get out of this hole, Red," he said. "It's making us both talk foolish. We're partners. Once this is done with you'll have Pine Valley for next to nothing, and I'll take Circle Eight. All it'll take is just a little more patience."

"All right. But it's me taking the risks and spending the money whilst you sit in town like a hen on her nest."

"I'll be there when the time comes, Red. Meantime don't go talking about us shooting each other. We need each other."

"I said all right—for a while."

Checking carefully to be sure the alley was empty, Harvey slipped out the back door and lumbered toward the saloon. Need each other, he thought. That's right enough. We need each other—for now. And smart as you are, Sid Tate, never think I don't know your killing look when I see it.

A couple of Circle Eight hands had come into the Aces and Eights during Harvey's absence. Worse, the tequila bottle was gone from his table. He stalked to the bar, interrupting Epps's conversation with one of the cowhands.

"I'll have that bottle now," he growled, and he slapped his dollar down under a thick hand.

"Sure thing, Jack," Epps said. "Would have left it for you, but you were gone so long I figured you forgot. Big crowd at the outhouse?"

Jack Harvey took the bottle by the neck and walked out without answering. He got his horse and wheeled away at a trot, hardly sparing a look at Adrian Hanover, who stood watching from the wide doorway of the livery barn. Beside Hanover a big yellowish dog sat upright and growled as Harvey passed.

Damn hypocrites, Harvey thought. Him and that worthless mutt both. But my time's coming, and then we'll see who's the smartest after all. And I'm starting with Hunter, no matter what Sid and his big ideas say.

At the edge of town he kicked the tender flanks of his horse. The animal gathered itself into a gallop, and Harvey rode out leaving a cloud of fine, thin dust hanging in the air behind him.

Chapter 8

Linda Pardee absently brushed back a loose strand of hair without raising her eyes from the big green ledger that lay open before her. Almost lost in her uncle's massive leather chair, she leaned forward to make an entry in the book, then sorted through the stack of bills that lay on the desk. When she was satisfied she'd entered them all she set them aside and began totaling the column. She was rechecking her figures, unconsciously worrying the tip of her tongue between her teeth, when the door to the study opened. Morgan Avery came in, stopping short in surprise at the sight of her.

"Linda! I thought you were off somewhere doing chores."

Linda smiled quickly up at him, returned to the book long enough to put a neat check beside the total, then blotted the entry and closed the ledger.

"I am," she said.

"I meant helping Anna with supper for the hands, or prettying yourself up for that Bonham feller. I've told you time and again all this ciphering ain't no job for a woman."

She made a face. "It ain't no job for a cowhand, either," she mocked gently. "I spent the whole morning finishing this dress for Perry's sake. But that didn't get the bookkeeping done."

"Now just you keep a civil tongue, missy. I don't see

why you want to worry about things that aren't your concern anyhow."

"Uncle Morg, you know expenses are down twenty percent since I started handling the purchasing. We might even make a profit this year. Why are you so stubborn about it?"

"No such, missy," Avery growled. "There's not a stubborn bone in my body. Now you just get along. I want to use that chair."

"Yes, sir." Linda rose meekly and made way for Avery, hiding her quick concern at the way he leaned for support on the edge of the desk.

No use to mention the doctor again, she thought. Not a stubborn bone anywhere in this family! Aloud she said, "Oh, there's an invoice from somebody called Jacob Haish and Company, almost fifteen hundred dollars. Did you place an order with them?"

Morgan Avery had sunk into his chair. He looked up almost guiltily. "Yes. Yes, I did. It's just a little something I been studying on. I'll have to send somebody down to the depot in Antonito to pick it up."

"Oh, good," Linda said. "I'll go along to do some shopping." She smiled at him. "Something to pretty myself up for that Bonham feller."

"That'll be fine."

Linda waited a moment to see if he would explain further, then shrugged. "All right. I'll see if Anna needs any chores done."

Avery nodded, already preoccupied with something else, and she let herself out.

She walked briskly along the hall, annoyed half at Avery and half at herself. Uncle Morg wasn't willing to see her as anything except a china doll, and she was ridiculously reluctant to stand up to him. Maybe it was because he'd been father and mother to her and Edge since the death of their parents in the fire, or maybe it was because she was frightened by his steadily failing health.

"Maybe it's because I'm not half as brave as I'd like to think," she murmured aloud. But what did Perry think about woman's work? What would he say after they were married—if they were to be married at all?

Emerging from the side door of the ranch house onto the covered porch, she paused. A rider was just entering the wagon yard, mounted on a gray horse she recognized. Hunter, she thought. Adam Hunter. Without effort she transferred much of her annoyance to him. She'd already entered his name on the payroll in spite of her own misgivings, and here he was slacking half a day's work. On impulse she called to him.

"Mr. Hunter."

He stopped abruptly, turning toward her in a quick, smooth motion that startled her.

"Maybe you're not used to our ways," she said. "Around here the workday runs until sundown."

Hunter had dismounted to lead the gray to the barn. Now he turned and came to the porch, looping the reins around the top of the railing. He took off his hat.

"That's my fault." He inclined his head gravely, not even a trace of humor in his voice. "Maybe your uncle failed to tell you. I don't start work until Monday."

For some reason his distant courtesy annoyed Linda even more. She started to answer sharply, but then she saw his bruised and swollen face.

"You've been fighting," she said. "Just like Edge."

"A lot like Edge," he said. He chuckled, but then his voice was serious again. "I'm afraid you're right. I got into a little disagreement."

"And you didn't settle this one with your gun?" The words were out before she really thought about them, and she saw that he didn't like them. His face seemed to close.

"There was no need." He reached to untie the gray's reins. "I'd best get this horse tended to—if there's nothing else, Miss Pardee."

"No. Nothing."

He nodded to her again and turned away. After a step or two he stopped and looked back. "You look especially nice today, Miss Pardee, if you don't mind my saying it. That dress suits you."

Her uncle's criticism still fresh in her mind, Linda frowned. "Better than what you saw me in yesterday, you mean?" she demanded. "More ladylike?"

Hunter looked surprised. "Why, no," he said. "That's not what I meant at all. Good day, Miss Pardee."

Linda stared after him for a moment as he led the tall gray horse toward the barn. Then she turned away to see if Anna needed help with supper. Her anger was still as strong as ever, but now she was angry mostly with herself.

Adam Hunter was tired and sore, out of sorts with the world, and angry at himself. No matter where he met Linda Pardee or what he said to her, it seemed to put her on her guard. She'd already seen him as a gunman and hired killer. Now he'd added brawler to the list and had somehow angered her besides with his clumsy attempt at a compliment.

No matter, he thought as he unsaddled the gray and turned it into the corral to roll. This country's too much of a good thing for me anyway. Best I do my business and be on my way.

He felt the old familiar thirst for a drink, and that brought back the memory of Barney Lemmon. Thinking back, he could not remember Barney in any pose except that of death. He knew there had been good times—jobs well done together, quiet nights around the campfire— but none of them would come to mind. Barney, he thought, I'd rather have killed any man I ever met before I let you die.

"Hunter?" Edge Pardee came from the direction of the kitchen, looking back over his shoulder. He rested a foot on the lower rail of the corral and grinned at

Hunter. "Been chewed out by the boss again, huh? Women's hard to figure."

"Maybe not so much," Hunter said morosely. "She's got nothing invested in me, nor any reason to start."

Pardee glanced at him quickly, then away. "I've always felt like baby sister thinks too much for her own good. But maybe she ain't the only one." Before Hunter could sort that out, Pardee went on. "Heard you had a little talk with Carson."

"Word gets around."

"Sure does." Pardee rested his arms on the top rail of the fence, watching the gray shake itself and trot around the enclosure. "I kind of figure he's pretty much my problem."

Hunter laughed sharply. "You're welcome to him from here on out," he said. "We had something to settle, that's all. Now it's settled."

Pardee nodded shortly, still not looking at Hunter. After a moment he chuckled. Then, quietly, he began to laugh.

"Well, hell. I'd've paid a month's salary just to see that—and won it back on the betting." He straightened and grinned at Hunter. "You must have had yourself a pretty busy day."

"Not so much. I just met some of the people you'd told me about."

"And asked them a hundred questions a minute, if I know you. Miss anybody?"

"Well—I didn't manage to call on the preacher— Walker, you said his name was?"

"That's right, the Reverend Wendell Walker. You'll get your chance at him tomorrow if you come in for church and the doings afterward."

"Wouldn't miss it."

Laughing, Pardee clapped Hunter on the shoulder. "Best you get washed up for supper. Anna's already rung the bell. You can tell us the rest of your adventures then."

"I'd better tell you one of them now," Hunter said. "Somebody shot at me this afternoon, about two miles down the road."

"The hell!" Pardee's round face turned serious at once. "You should've said something sooner. Come on."

He hustled Hunter along into the dining hall. The cowhands were just taking their places at the long wooden table, laughing and talking among themselves. Pardee found a vacant space and hammered on the tabletop for attention.

"Listen up, now. Just so's you'll remember Mr. Avery's orders about going armed and working in pairs, somebody tried to bushwhack Hunter out on the main road today."

Startled faces—young Billy Jackson's, Tom Banner's, Tag Kelly's—turned toward Pardee and Hunter. Tom Banner spoke up for all of them.

"How's that? What happened, Hunter? You all right?"

Hunter shrugged. "It wasn't all that serious," he said. "I'd seen a couple of riders up ahead but didn't think much of it. Then somebody took a couple of shots at me just after I started that big curve coming up the hill. When I went to make his acquaintance he'd already gone."

"How many were there?" Banner asked.

"Did you recognize them?" asked Tag Kelly at the same instant.

"Just one man, I think. If there'd been more of them, they probably wouldn't have let me off so easy. No, Kelly, I never saw him." He reached in his shirt pocket. "Got a couple of his cartridge cases, though."

Pardee grabbed them eagerly, then passed them to Tom Banner. "Forty-fours," he said disgustedly. "Could be anybody. You're about the only one around whose rifle signs its name, Hunter."

"That's so," Banner said. "Likely I wouldn't have

stayed to face that field piece myself." He gestured. "Light and eat, gents. Anna's just about to bring in the steaks."

Pardee hesitated. "Go ahead, Hunter," he said. "Best I have a word with the boss first." He lowered his voice. "I expect he'll want to see you after supper."

"That's good," Hunter said. He'd lost a partner once through his own carelessness. He couldn't bring trouble down on these folks the same way. "Tell him I'd like to talk with him this evening."

"Let's take a walk, Linda," Perry Bonham said. "There are some things I'd like to talk over with you."

"I really should help Anna with the supper dishes," Linda said. Then, disgusted with herself for the coquetry—the kitchen swamper could handle the cleaning up, and Perry knew it as well as she—she shook her head. "No, you're right. I'll get my shawl."

The moon was just showing its edge over the shoulder of the mountains. Above, stars shone like dewdrops on summer grass. Linda held tightly to Bonham's arm, feeling the lean muscles beneath the smooth gray suit as he led her across the yard and toward the north meadow. She'd noticed that among men Perry always seemed quiet and diffident, but with her he was different— stronger, more confident. When they reached the corner of the split-rail fence beside the old wagon shed he stopped, as she'd known he would, and kissed her.

She gave herself up to the kiss and to the tight, urgent pressure of his hands against her back, letting herself be drawn into him. Is this how it feels? she wondered. Should there be more? She pressed her face against the cool fabric of his coat while he held her, then relaxed his hold.

"Let's go inside," he whispered, nodding toward the dark doorway of the shed.

She looked up at him, the starlight reflecting in her eyes. "What would Uncle Morg say?" she teased.

"You don't ride the horse until it's yours to saddle."

Linda tried to smother her laugh, but it came out anyway. Bonham's voice was a perfect imitation of her uncle's irascible growl, his words very much what Uncle Morg probably *would* have said. "All right," she agreed.

She followed him inside among the wagons parked there in the dark. She felt a moment's relief when he passed by the buggy with its deep leather cushions and boosted her onto the seat of a light runabout instead. The wagon's springs squeaked as he climbed up beside her.

This time she turned to him. They kissed again, and Bonham drew her to him until she was half lying in his arms. His hand stroked her hair, brushed against her cheek, moved down to rest lightly on the bodice of the new dress she'd made for him.

"Perry," Linda said. She reached up to capture the hand. "Remember," she whispered with a smile. "You don't own the horse yet."

"That's not what I want." Bonham's voice was quiet, deeply serious. "I don't want to own you, Linda."

"What, then?"

"If you marry me—you know how much I want that— it has to be your decision, what you want, too. I haven't pressed you for an answer—"

"I know," she put in quickly. "That's good of you, Perry."

"—but now I have to know. I'll go down on my knees if you like, for the form of it, but you must decide."

"Why?" It sounded like a little girl's question, and Linda was ashamed of her hesitation. "I told you I wasn't sure, and you agreed to wait. What's changed, Perry?"

"There's trouble coming to this valley. Oh, don't look surprised, everyone can feel it. A range war—Pine Valley and Circle Eight." His voice dropped for a moment. "I've seen the first of what that means already, and there'll be more. I want to be where I can help, Linda, where I can look out for you."

"But—" She looked up into his face, wondering. She hadn't seen this side of Bonham before. "What about your business? I wouldn't want to leave Pine Valley— not while there's trouble."

"Then you wouldn't have to. I have some savings. If your uncle's willing, we could build a little house right here, out in the meadow. If it comes to a fight, I can pull my weight, no matter what Edge and the others may think—I haven't always been a businessman. Then, when things are settled, we'll see."

"I—" Linda swallowed, trying to get her thoughts in order. "Perry, what do you think is woman's work? I— I do things here, on the ranch. Uncle Morg doesn't like it, but I'm good at it. Where would that fit—with us?"

Bonham laughed happily. "Afraid I'm going to tie you down to dishpans and babies, Linda?" he asked. "Well, maybe I would, with the babies, anyway." He smiled again at her sudden confusion. "But it's not my intention to tie you down. I've told you, I want you to be free." When she didn't answer he looked at her more sharply. "What is it? Do I have competition now, since Hunter came?"

"Hunter?" She hadn't even thought of Hunter that way. "No!" She stared up at him in surprise. She stopped, suddenly aware she wasn't telling herself exactly the truth. "No," she said again, more softly. "No competition, Perry."

"Then you must decide," Bonham said. Standing almost behind her, he put his arms around her and drew her against him. "I know you don't want me the way I want you." His hand tightened against her chest with such confident power that she caught her breath. "But in time you will. And you know I'm patient."

"Yes," she murmured. I know you're patient, she thought. And I've tried to want you—the way you want me. How much time is it supposed to take?

"Yes, Perry," she said. "I'll marry you."

Almost fearfully she drew his face down to hers, sealing her lips before she could take the words back. For a time she lost herself in the touch of his hands and mouth and strong wiry arms, and then he moved away from her.

"I should speak to your uncle now," he said.

"Not alone." She sat upright, straightening the rumpled dress. "We'll both go."

Bonham and Linda Pardee had been gone perhaps five minutes when Adam Hunter straightened himself from the darkness along the back wall of the shed and stepped out into the open moonlight. The shed had seemed a good place for some quiet thought before his talk with Avery, but it hadn't turned out that way.

You never were much on judgment, he told himself wryly. Damn well serves you right. Startled into silence by their entry, he had sat like a snake in the henhouse while Perry Bonham and Linda had pledged their love for each other. No, come to think of it, there wasn't that much said about love. But it was none of his business. He'd said it right to Pardee: Linda had nothing invested in him, and no reason to care—even less if she'd known the truth about who and what he was. He had nothing in his past to be proud of, and his future might prove to be violent and short. His face grim, he walked back to the bunkhouse and sat on the porch, wrapped in his own thoughts until Pardee called him to talk to Morgan Avery.

Avery still sat behind the big desk as if he hadn't moved since the last time they'd spoken. To Hunter, the lines in the rancher's face seemed etched a bit deeper, either from pain or worry, but that might have been a trick of the lamplight. Avery's growl was cordial enough.

"Got a riddle for you, Hunter," he said. "Ever see an undertaker happy with nobody dead?"

Hunter answered politely and said appropriately pleasant things when Avery explained. Then the rancher folded his hands and looked at Hunter from under heavy eyebrows.

"I hear you visited with Ellis Watkins today—and with his top hand."

"That's right."

"Well, today was your doing. That took sand, and I like you for it. But whiles you're working here you'll stay clear of Circle Eight unless I order different."

"That's fine. I said what I wanted to say."

Avery chuckled. "I suppose you did," he said. "I'm sending down to Antonito for some things I ordered. It'll be a two-day trip, maybe with some trouble along the way. I'd like you to take the wagon down Monday and take care of it."

"Maybe you'd better hear what I have to say first."

"All right." Avery sat back and cleared his throat. "I said up front your business is yours. You needn't say anything you don't want to."

Hunter nodded. "Thanks, but things have changed a little," he said. He paused a minute, deciding where to start. "Fact is, I'm a deputy marshal from Indian Territory. I can show you some credentials if you want."

"No need."

Briefly Hunter sketched in the situation for Avery, telling him about the robberies, about Red Converse–Jack Harvey, about Harvey's unknown partner. He didn't mention Barney or the personal reasons for his quest.

"Well, Harvey's a hardcase for sure," Avery said when he'd finished. "Not surprised he has something in his past. But he's been a good enough neighbor, and nothing says he's tied up in the troubles here."

"That's true," Hunter admitted. "I'm pretty sure he has a spy on your ranch, though, and one on Circle Eight."

"A spy!" Avery half rose, his face darkening. "Who is it? And how do you know?"

Hunter described the meeting he'd witnessed. "There's no doubt it was Kelly," he finished. "And it's a reasonable bet he's the one who shot at me."

"But you didn't see him."

"No."

"Huh!" Avery rubbed his chin. "I'd hate to think it of Tag. He's been with me quite a time." He looked up at Hunter. "Best I call him in and give him his chance to explain."

"I'd rather you kept it dark for now. I still don't know the second man I'm after. And if Kelly's a traitor, it'll be better if he doesn't know you're on to him."

"There's something in that," Avery agreed reluctantly. "All right. But that doesn't change things about Antonito. I'd like to send Edge, but I need him here. Pick yourself a good man to take along."

"Tom Banner. He looks like the best you have."

"I'd thought of him, too. You're a good judge." The rancher looked at him thoughtfully. "What would you say about Bonham?"

Hunter hesitated. "Seems a little cold to me," he said at last. "But I think he means the best for Miss Pardee."

"Good enough. By the way, she wants to go along to Antonito—one reason I wanted you there's to watch after her."

"Oh." Hunter was silent for a moment. "Listen, maybe I ought to stay around here. We don't know when trouble might break out."

Morgan Avery laughed and shook his head. "That's a fact," he said. "But from what I've seen so far, I figure the trouble's more likely to follow you than to stay around here."

Chapter 9

The Reverend Mister Wendell Walker dwarfed the rough pine pulpit as he stood watching his flock file to the seats. He was a tall man, broad in proportion, with iron-gray hair and a rugged, pockmarked face that fit well with the rustic furnishings of his church.

Compared to the rest of Sublette City, the church building was new and raw, its pine planks sawn locally and still uncured. Before it had been built the congregation had met in Baker's saddle shop, and before that in the Paradise O' The Pines Saloon. Now Walker took quiet pleasure in the newly painted steeple, the pump organ on which Barbara Allen Watkins was playing a halting prelude, the dozen rows of uncomfortably small pews that flanked the narrow center aisle.

As always, the pews were filling by a strictly predictable formula. Ellis Watkins bulked grimly in the front pew on Walker's right. Beside him sat his wife—still handsome enough to show where her daughters had gotten their beauty—and Annie Laurie, fidgeting in a frilly blue dress. His cowhands ranked themselves in the rows behind him, most of them looking almost as uncomfortable as Annie Laurie over the forthcoming ordeal.

Across the aisle the story was the same, except that Morgan Avery and his niece and nephew held the front pew. But today something was different. Perry Bonham sat with them, holding Linda Pardee's hand in a proprietary way.

Frowning slightly, Walker let his gaze drift farther back among the crowd. The new man, Hunter, was in the next row, looking attentively back at him. Toward the rear of the church sat a scattering of townspeople, most of them ignoring the division between the two ranches. Bill Epps was there with his wife and twin sons, and the Coles from the mercantile, and a dozen or so more. Far back in one corner, as usual without her husband, Myra Harvey sat on the edge of a pew as though uncertain of her welcome.

The organ wheezed to a stop. With a last glance at Bonham Walker said, "Let us pray."

He led a short prayer, then called for the first hymn, one of his favorites. A few members of the congregation began leafing through their own hymnals, but most had to rely on memory. The church had no hymnals yet, no parsonage, no true organization. Someday, Walker thought. Unless— He broke off the thought resolutely and joined in the hymn:

> Must Jesus bear the cross alone,
> And all the world go free?
> No, there's a cross for every one,
> And there's a cross for me.

Walker led them through it, at times hearing little more than his own droning baritone and the voice of Edith Cole, who aimed at the soprano part and missed it by almost half a tone. He nearly smiled, but then the jagged point of his conscience pricked him. For a moment his voice faltered. Unconsciously he gripped his thigh, to find no comforting revolver holstered there. He held on to the pulpit, looking from face to face in the congregation. If they knew, he thought.

He thought of telling them everything—all about his past, his true nature, his reasons for being where he was. He almost decided to do it. He pictured the warm, cleansing wash of it, the relief that a public confession held out to him. But he kept on with the hymn, and the sweet danger of self-exposure had passed by the time the organ pumped on to the final verse:

> The consecrated cross I'll bear
> Till death shall set me free;
> And then go home my crown to wear,
> For there's a crown for me.

After that he preached them a sermon about peace through forgiveness. He spoke that gospel so compellingly that he came close to accepting it himself.

At the benediction Linda Pardee lifted her head, feeling the touch of Adam Hunter's gaze. For the briefest of moments she met his eyes fully before turning to take Perry Bonham's arm. She spoke to Barbara Watkins, remembering the days they'd been friends before her parents had died and she'd gone to live at Pine Valley. Maybe the trouble Perry sees won't come, she thought. Maybe Barbara and I will be friends again. But she didn't really believe it.

"Founder's Day," Edge Pardee had told Hunter. "Story is, old Ben Sublette built himself a trading post right where the mercantile is today—pretty near fifty years ago, that must have been." Pardee grinned and shrugged. "I misdoubt it's true, but it's a pretty good excuse for a town picnic every June."

As Hunter watched from the sidelines a dozen eager cowhands transformed the church. The pews were moved back to make room for a larger crowd, and four men moved in a long table along one wall. Before long the table was piled high with box lunches, with Walker standing by to act as auctioneer.

"Now, gents," he said, his deep voice only a trace

less solemn than when he'd been in the pulpit, "the rules are these: The baskets sell to the highest bidder. All the money goes for upkeep on the church and cemetery. The lucky man that buys a basket gets to eat with the lady who prepared it." He stopped for a wink at his audience. "And of course, nobody knows which basket is whose."

"Not much, Mary Ann," Pardee murmured Hunter's way. "If a lady wants you to know, she'll sure enough see that you do."

They were standing with the knot of Pine Valley hands who had come in from the ranch that morning. Automatically, it seemed, the Circle Eight riders had moved to the opposite side of the room. Hunter caught a quizzical look that Ellis Watkins sent his way, but then the rancher turned away to speak to his wife.

"Do you have a basket picked out?" Hunter asked Pardee, but the blond cowman waved him to silence as Walker began to speak again.

"Now we'll be eating outside on the grounds, so I'm going to act like a minister just once more today. Before we get started I'd like to ask Mr. Bonham to say a blessing for us."

Bonham looked up in surprise, breaking off his conversation with Linda and Morgan Avery. Then he smiled.

"All right, Wendell. If you'll bow your heads, please."

Hunter dutifully did so while Bonham spoke a short prayer. Then the minister turned to the table and held up the first box that came to hand.

"All right, here's number one—and a fine-looking package it is. What am I bid?"

The crowd was larger than the congregation had been, Hunter noticed, with new people slipping into the back of the hall all along. Most of the others he'd met in town were there, and many he didn't know. He caught a momentary glimpse of Jack Harvey, his face set in an uncomfortable smile, standing beside a gaunt, blondish woman, but then Pardee nudged him, and he brought his attention back to the minister.

The first two lunches had sold quickly, one to a boy still in his teens who grinned shyly as he claimed the basket and its pigtailed owner, and one to Bill Epps of the saloon. Now Walker was holding up a cloth-covered basket that Hunter recognized, the one Linda Pardee had brought in that morning.

"You oughta give old Perry a run for his money," Pardee whispered. He looked at Hunter with guileless blue eyes. "Just so's baby sister will make a good showing."

"Now this one looks something special," Walker said. "In fact, I'll start the bidding at four bits."

There was a ripple of polite applause. It was a handsome gesture on the minister's part, the price of a good steak at the local restaurant. Bonham joined in the clapping, but Hunter saw the swift, almost angry look he shot at Walker. Walker met his gaze firmly, his pockmarked face stern. For a moment almost too brief to notice their eyes locked in a silent duel, and then Bonham's face relaxed.

"One dollar," he said.

"Well, that tops me." Walker made a show of looking around for other bids, then started to hand the basket over.

"Two," Hunter said.

The minister raised his eyebrows. "New horse race—if you'll pardon the expression." He paused for his listeners to laugh. "I have two dollars from this gentleman. Do I hear—"

Bonham shrugged good-naturedly. "Three," he said.

"Five."

It was a challenge. Necks craned as the watchers sought a glimpse of Hunter, then of Linda Pardee. Linda flushed, her cheeks going red under a dozen inquiring gazes—including her uncle's.

Perry Bonham turned to look at Hunter. He was still

99

smiling, but his inspection was no less deep and searching.

"Ten," he said with quiet finality.

Hunter backed off. He'd drawn more than enough attention to himself, and for no good reason he could see. He nodded to Bonham but got no response beyond a level stare.

"Thank you, gentlemen, thank you," Wendell Walker said, seeming unconscious of the sudden tension in the room. His voice was full and hearty, but from under his heavy brows he was studying Hunter as intently as Bonham had. "With help like that we'll soon have those new hymnals. Then you can all sing along with us on Sunday. Let's show our appreciation for Mr. Bonham's generosity."

Hunter joined in the polite applause, then drifted slowly to the back of the room as the minister held up a basket adorned with pink ribbons and asked for bids. Out of the focus of attention, Hunter leaned against the wall and wondered at the impulse that had led him to bid against Bonham. Probably nothing but a pretty face, he told himself in disgust, though deep down he thought it was more than that.

Walker sold two more baskets without incident. Hunter watched as Jack Harvey, scowling, bought one of them for fifty cents and left with the blond woman. Then the minister held up a box decorated with a bright yellow neckerchief.

"Of course, I've no idea who prepared the meal," he said, "but earlier I saw Miss Barbara Watkins wearing something that looked a lot like this. Do I have a bid?"

"Two dollars," Abel Carson said promptly.

Hunter saw Edge Pardee straighten, his easy grin disappearing. "Three," Pardee said.

In a way it reminded Hunter of the fight in the saloon. Carson bid stolidly, expressionless as a gambler with a pat hand. Pardee showed more style, pausing to count on his fingers, delaying until the last call to raise the bid. Cowhands from both sides cheered them on. For the first few minutes some of the town's young men stayed in the race, but they dropped out as the bids rose. In a few minutes the two foremen had the better part of a month's salary on the table.

"Stay with him, Edge," Billy Jackson urged. "Come on, boys, pass the hat. Edge is going to rustle Circle Eight's prize filly."

"That's forty-two dollars. Do I hear any advance?"

"Forty-five."

The Circle Eight hands gathered behind Carson, offering their own money and encouragement. But gradually Carson's raises became smaller, the intervals between bids longer.

"Sixty-eight. Sixty-eight dollars."

The Circle Eight hands looked at one another. Pillbox spread his hands helplessly. With a final fierce scowl at Pardee Abel Carson turned and walked quickly out of the building. The Pine Valley hands cheered and slapped Pardee on the back, urging him forward.

Almost forgotten in the competition between the two men, Barbara Watkins stood erect and tight-lipped, pointedly ignoring the stares of the crowd and the Pine Valley celebration. When Carson gave up she started toward the front of the church and the basket waiting there.

"Stop!" Ellis Watkins pushed to the front of his group, his face as red as a turkey's comb. "I won't have this."

"It's all right, Papa," Barbara said.

"Ellis!" her mother said at the same moment.

Watkins ignored them both. "I won't have it," he repeated. "No Pine Valley saddle bum can insult my daughter this way."

"I'm not any saddle bum, nor ever have been," Edge Pardee said. "And I don't mean Miss Watkins any disrespect. You've no call to say that."

Watkins started to speak, but Wendell Walker's deep

voice cut him off. "You're in the wrong here, Mr. Watkins," the minister said. "Whatever celebration we're holding here, this is a church. Leave your fights outside. Edge's bid is a handsome gesture in a good cause, no more."

For a moment Watkins stared at him. Then the rancher visibly gained control of himself. "Sorry, Parson," he said. "You're right. It's a good cause. And I'll bid a hundred dollars for my daughter's basket."

The crowd gasped. Pardee took a short, angry step forward, but Morgan Avery caught his arm. The two spoke softly for a moment, and then Pardee in his turn wheeled and stalked out of the room.

"Damned fool," Hunter heard him mutter as he passed. "I should've known."

Chapter 10

The confrontation between the foremen chastened the crowd but didn't end the auction. Hunter saw Barbara Watkins exchange a few quiet, angry words with her parents, then leave the church. Perry Bonham and Linda had already gone. A few of the other cowhands bid on baskets, and gradually those who failed to buy drifted away to pay a dime for a share of the food prepared by the church ladies. Hunter stayed on, partly to gain a bit of privacy from the other Pine Valley hands, partly to take a closer look at the Reverend Mr. Walker. The auction was nearing its end when he noticed Annie Laurie standing anxiously near the table that held the lunch baskets.

Hunter hadn't seen her parents leave, but she was alone now. She looked toward one of the few remaining baskets, then toward a group of three boys who were whispering and nudging one another near the doorway. When the minister turned away from the table for a moment Hunter thought she would reach for the basket, but she didn't.

Walker sold two more lunches rapidly, then reached for the one Annie was watching.

"Not many left," he observed. "Better move fast if you're looking to eat with a lovely lady. Now who'll open the bidding?"

He looked around expectantly. At first nobody answered. Then one of the boys by the door called out, "Two cents."

"Well, that's a start." Walker shot a quick glance at Annie. Her cheeks had reddened a little, but she stood as straight as Joan of Arc at the stake. Walker's gaze roved over the remaining bidders until his eyes met Hunter's. "Still, it's not much of a bid for the privilege of a lady's company. Perhaps some gentleman in the crowd will improve on it."

Hunter hesitated, then nodded. "A dollar."

Walker's long face creased in the hint of a smile. "Much better. Any more bids?" He waited, then said, "Sold to Mr. Hunter. Congratulations, sir."

"We missed the filly, but Hunter's got the yearling," Billy Jackson snickered. Both Hunter and Annie Laurie ignored him. Hunter walked to the front to claim his basket, then offered Annie his arm.

She took it gravely but didn't say anything. Hunter led her outside and picked a spot for them near a tall pine, a little distance from the other picnickers. Spreading the cloth from the basket on the ground, he looked up at her.

"That's a mighty pretty dress, Annie Laurie. Have you changed your mind about becoming a young lady?"

Annie shook her head vigorously, her braids flying. "Ma made me wear it," she said quickly. "Else I wouldn't have." She looked at the ground. "I should thank you—even if I wasn't your first choice. If you hadn't bid, I would've had to eat with that Lee and Charley Epps."

"Mmm. Fried chicken." Hunter offered her a drumstick and, when she refused, bit into it himself. "Then I was your first choice, Annie Laurie?"

"Well"—she studied the toes of her white shoes— "well, not exactly." She sat down on an edge of the cloth, folding her hands daintily in her lap. "I'll break that Jerry Haskell's nose for choosing Sarah's basket instead of mine."

"I wish you wouldn't. I'm grateful his bad judgment gave me the chance to have lunch with you."

Annie Laurie giggled. "That's the way Barb's beaux talk," she said. She selected a piece of chicken and nibbled at it. "I'll bet you just want to ask me questions, the way you do with everybody else."

Hunter rubbed a hand across his mouth. "You keep up with what's going on, don't you?"

"Somebody has to." She sighed and shook her head. "Mama isn't interested, and Barb's *so* calf-eyed over"—she stopped and looked sideways at Hunter—"over *things* that she wouldn't notice a cow in the woodshed. Someone needs to watch over her."

"Seems like that's your pa's job."

"Oh, Papa has lots of worries—and now you're one of them. Besides, I think a woman should look out for herself, don't you?"

"I think that's a wise policy." Hunter put aside his plate of chicken bones and peered into the basket again. "A whole cobbler seems kind of ambitious. What kind is it?"

"Blackberry. And I didn't forget the sugar this time."

"That's good. Tell me, is Jack Harvey one of the people you keep up with?"

The girl put down her spoon, the cobbler untasted. "He scares me. I don't like the way he looks at Barb. Nor at me." She shivered. "I still don't think you look like a killer. But he does."

"Don't be fooled, Annie Laurie. You can't always tell a killer by his looks."

"Really?" She looked at him eagerly. "Do you know lots of killers?"

"Enough. We were talking about Harvey. Does he have any special friends around town?"

Annie frowned in thought. "Well, mostly he's in the Aces and Eights when he's in town. He trades at Mr. Haskell's store and stables his horses with Mr. Hanover." She shrugged. "That's all I know, 'cepting when

105

the reverend's tending his flock he rides out to visit with Mrs. Harvey." Her voice dropped a little. "I heard Pa say once they likely wasn't married legal at all!"

"Likely," Hunter said. "You've been a big help, Annie—and the cobbler was first-rate. Reckon you can keep quiet about our talk?"

"Oh, I'd better!" With a swift glance around Annie began stowing the leftover items in the basket. "Papa will just about raise the devil and tie a knot in his tail if'n he finds out I was with *you*." She stood and made a little curtsy. "I enjoyed it very much, Mr. Hunter. Thank you."

"The pleasure was mine, Annie."

She dashed away like a young colt, her blue dress flying. Hunter tidied up, then strolled around the grounds watching the other events of the day. The saloons were closed for the Sabbath, but a few enterprising celebrants had brought their own liquor. Constable Tobreen gently herded them away from the main party, and most of the town settled into the various contests: a horse race, games of quoits and horseshoes, booths for apple bobbing, pie eating, and the like.

Over against the hillside Titus Haskell and Jim Cole, the two storekeepers, had set up a shooting range. Hunter was standing in the background watching Adrian Hanover plunk shots at a target when a deep voice called his name.

"Mr. Hunter, is it? Do you like our town?"

Hunter turned to look into the minister's pockmarked face. "Surely do, Parson," he said. He'd seen enough of Hanover's shooting. If the liveryman was Sid Tate, he wasn't showing it in public. "I've not seen the high country before."

"I noted you were listening during my sermon. Not everyone does. May I ask what you thought of it?"

Hunter hesitated a moment. "Well, I'm afraid I'm no judge of sermons. I was listening to what you said about making this a peaceful community."

"I had not taken you for a man of peace," Walker said. "Neither for the valley nor within yourself."

Hunter looked at him sharply, but there was no judgment in the way he said it. Walker's deep-set eyes were sad and thoughtful.

"Maybe I'm not," he said. "But this is a hard country full of hard men. I don't think you know what you're asking when you tell these folks they should settle their differences without violence, the way they do back east."

The minister's long face creased in a rueful smile. "I don't know what they do back east," he said. "But I've seen what violence can do, one place and another. I know there has to be a better way." He looked past Hunter. His face changed, relaxing into a welcoming smile. "Hello, Tom. And Billy. Are you looking for us?"

"For Hunter, really, Parson," Tom Banner said. He took off his hat. "Hunter, me and Billy here and the other boys, we'd take it favorable if you'd do some shooting."

"Well, I don't know," Hunter said.

"We'd be right glad to pay your fee and all," Banner said. He shifted uneasily, then added, "Fact is, we've made sort of a little wager on the outcome."

"There are times when a man wants to lay his gun aside," Walker said. "You should be able to see that, Tom, and to respect it."

Standing in Banner's shadow, Billy Jackson grinned. "Fine one you are to say so, Reverend," he said. "Talk is you keep a Colt right under the pulpit." He grinned again and ducked his head from Walker's gaze.

"That's no way of talking to a man of the cloth," Tom Banner told him sternly. "You'll have to forgive the young'un, Parson. He ain't but about half civilized." To Hunter he said, "If you're not willing, that's one thing. But we'd take it favorable if you could see your way clear."

107

Hunter considered a moment. "Tell you what," he said slowly. "I'll shoot if Brother Walker here will—providing you're not opposed, sir."

"Well—" Surprised, Walker stared at him for a moment. Then the minister laughed softly. "Very well, Mr. Hunter, if it will oblige you. And with the understanding there'll be no wagers, Billy."

"Yes, sir," Billy Jackson muttered, but Walker had already turned away. He walked with long strides back to the church. In less than a minute he returned, cinching a wide black gun belt around his waist under his long coat.

"I'll swan! I bet he does keep it in the pulpit," Jackson said under his breath.

On the firing line Walker removed his coat, revealing an ivory-handled Smith and Wesson American holstered on his right hip. He handed the coat to Titus Haskell and took up a stance beside Hunter.

"When you're ready, sir."

"Ha! We got just the thing for the two of you," Jim Cole said. He gestured toward a bullet-splintered wooden board standing against the hillside twenty yards away. On it was a crude painting of a masked outlaw poised to draw an enormous pistol. "Old Black Bart is pretty shot up, but he can still give the two of you a tussle."

"No," Hunter and the minister said together. "Mr. Hunter and I are peaceable men," Walker added when the storekeeper seemed disposed to argue. "Tin cans are more our speed, if you please."

Frowning in disappointment, Cole set up a dozen cans. "Ready," he said, stepping aside. "But I still think—"

Walker moved, drawing and cocking the long American with a fluid motion that seemed unhurried until Hunter realized how quickly the first shot came. It smashed the can on the left, and the minister worked to his right, cocking the gun as it kicked up on recoil and firing as it came level again. Hunter heard a long whistle from someone in the crowd as Walker reversed the pistol back into its holster.

"Your turn," Walker said.

Hunter nodded and turned. He drew the engraved Colt more slowly than Walker and fired with a touch more deliberation, but he did manage to knock down all six targets. "Again?" he asked, raising an eyebrow toward Walker.

"I think not. Good shooting, Brother Hunter."

"Good shooting, Brother Walker."

With a nod the minister turned and walked away toward the church, seeming unconscious of the sensation he'd created. Hunter reloaded the Colt, watching Walker's back. "It's never simple," he murmured aloud.

Jim Cole heard the words but didn't understand. "Guess not," he said. "That's about the second-best shooting we've saw today."

"Oh? Whose was the best?"

"That gunsmith, Melvin Cox." Seeing Hunter's surprise, Cole laughed. "Couldn't even see the cans sitting on the shelf there, so he said. Had Titus throw them in the air, and he'd shoot when he saw the sun glint on them. Never missed a shot. Ain't that something?"

"Surely is," Hunter agreed. He moved away, frowning, thinking about sunlight glinting on a marshal's badge back in Rocky Comfort, Arkansas. "It's never simple at all."

Abel Carson forced the bit between his horse's teeth, looped the bridle up over its proud ears, and fastened the strap. "Hell, no, Blue Eye," he said. "It's because you're a horse that you'd even ask such a question. If you was a man, you'd know that God must have made woman as a afterthought, and likely that when he was tired or in a bad mood."

A young woman's voice interrupted him. "Abel? I thought I heard you talking to someone."

"Steadying my horse." He looked up at Barbara Watkins. Then he drew the girth up tight and cinched it.

"Are you leaving?" she asked.

"Aim to."

"But I thought you were going to drive me home after lunch."

"I'm not hungry anymore."

"Oh Abel, I'm sorry about the auction."

"Sure enough? It looked to me like you really wanted to eat with Pardee. Anyway, I'd just rather ride on back by myself and eat some hardtack." He stepped up into the saddle.

"Abel, please don't be angry." Barbara Watkins stood by Carson's horse and tilted her head back to look up at the big man. She put her small hand on his big beefy paw. "I really wish you'd drive the buggy and take me home. Is that such a bad job?"

" 'Don't be angry'? Why, hell. Everybody in the basin saw my shame when I couldn't come up with enough cash money to buy your basket."

"Shame? There wasn't any shame in that."

"I've got more money."

"I'm sure you do."

"I just didn't have it with me."

"A man shouldn't need to carry a lot of money."

"I try to keep up with every dollar I can so that one day I can ask you a special favor. And now I'm shamed because I didn't bring enough of that money to pay for your lunch so I *could* ask you today."

"Abel—"

"I hate it."

"It doesn't matter."

He stopped his horse from stirring and rested his eyes on Barbara Watkins. " 'Doesn't matter'?" he asked. "What don't?" He stepped down so that he could see into her eyes. He took her by the shoulders and pulled her toward him. "Do you mean I can ask you without that lunch together?"

"Abel . . ."

"Or do you mean it don't matter because your answer was going to be 'no' anyhow?"

"Abel."

A thought came to him. "Wait a minute," he said. "What did you mean asking if it'd be a bad job to drive you? Did you mean that job's as close as I'll ever get to you? Did you mean I'm working for your pa when I drive you?"

"No."

"By God, today is Sunday."

"Yes."

"I don't owe a Sunday to no man."

"I know."

"No woman either."

"I know you don't. You're right. It's your day off."

"All right, then, I'll drive you home. But it's not part of my *job*. It's a thing I *want to do*."

"All right."

Nothing was going the way Abel Carson had intended it. If this was a fight, he thought, I'd be whipping myself. "Well then. I'll just tie Mr. Blue Eye onto the back of your buggy."

He helped Barbara Watkins up to the buggy seat. Then he tied his horse to the tailboard without loosening the saddle girth. "Let it be a lesson to you while it's squeezing your insides," he told the horse, "so's you'll maybe learn about women."

He took his place on the buggy seat, left the whip in its stand, and spanked the draft horse with the reins. They moved sharply out of the churchyard and onto the Circle Eight road. "Only thing is," he told Barbara Watkins, "I thought you was supposed to be eating with somebody else." The idea painted a smile on Carson's wooden face.

Barbara Watkins had been looking across the yard

toward a little knot of men from Pine Valley. In the middle of the knot was Edge Pardee. She turned back to Carson and smiled brightly. "I got confused about who I was supposed to eat with," she said, "so I brought the lunch along in hopes that you would consent to eat with me after all."

Abel Carson laughed out loud. "Well now, I know just the place," he said. Several minutes later he swung the buggy off the main road and through a set of stone gateposts into the Mount Hope Cemetery. "Plenty of chaperons," he said, laughing again. "None of them noisy."

They drove slowly around the loop between fine stands of green grass on both sides. At the rear of the cemetery the road ran beneath a small grove of tall old cottonwoods. Abel stopped the buggy, set the brake, and stood down to ease the animals. Then he lifted a heavy blanket out of the boot and spread it out on the grass in the deep shade. He took a warm pleasure in watching Barbara Watkins carry her flowered picnic basket to his crude table on the ground. He had never seen any forest animal as graceful.

"What are you staring at?" she asked him. "Here. Take this jar down to the spring and get us some fresh water. By the time you get back I'll have things ready."

Abel Carson got the water and sat down across from the girl. "I was staring at you," he said. In his entire life he had never spoken so boldly to a woman. "I aim to make a practice of it."

"Abel." She spooned potato salad and beans onto his plate. "Would you care for some chicken?"

"Yes. I'm always partial to your chicken. I aim to stare at your chicken while I ask you my question."

"Truth is Annie Laurie fries chicken better than I do."

Carson saw tears well at the rim of her eyelids like the water in the spring behind him. He stripped the meat off half his wishbone, chewed it a moment, and nodded with great satisfaction. "Annie Laurie fix this chicken?"

Barbara Watkins nodded without looking up.

"Is *she* spoke for?"

The girl shook her head. "Abel," she said again. It seemed to be the only word she could speak.

Carson swallowed hard, washed the dry chicken down his throat with a draft of spring water, and did his best to grin. "Hell, let me help you get the rest of it said, girl. What you mean is you really like me. You about love me, the way a sister loves her brother. And what you want is for me to be a big brother to you and stand between you and your father when he's on a tear. And—"

"Oh, Abel."

"—you wish I could be happy being your big brother and not never wanting to put my arms around you and hold you close and say those things I've been saving up my whole life just for you."

"Abel!" She tried to get to her feet, turned over the water jar, and slipped back to her knees. Then she leaned toward him until her hair brushed his chin, tried to suck in one great sob, failed, and fell against him, crying as if they had come to Mount Hope for a burial.

Abel Carson hesitated, touched her shoulders, finally drew her against his breast, and held her while she cried. He hoped she would cry for a long time because he knew he would never have her in his arms again. He would have cried himself if he'd remembered how.

He heard the pistols begin to bark over by the church where the men were shooting at targets to raise money for hymnals. Damn fools, he thought. Practicing for the war that's coming in this basin.

After a long time she was still. Her voice was hoarse from the crying when she told him that he was the kindest and best and most understanding man in the world. He damned himself roundly for each of those virtues.

113

"Would you always be here to watch over me?" she wanted to know.

He thought about it. In the distance the guns continued to speak. "Only the worst kind of fool would stay here under them conditions and without no hope." He felt a new sob rising in her chest and spoke quickly. "But of course, the worst kind of fool is surely what I am. So I expect I'll be right here, loyal to you and your father till the day I die."

Chapter 11

At four-thirty on Monday morning Hunter and Tom Banner ate scrambled eggs and hotcakes and sausage in the kitchen while Anna packed a lunch of biscuits and cold fried chicken.

"Ain't going to be much to tide three hungry people over on a two-day trip," Banner observed with a wink at Hunter. "Even though Miss Linda does eat like a bird."

Anna turned away from the counter to look at him. "About Miss Linda you will keep a civil tongue, Tom Banner," she snapped. "Plenty of food I have packed for you on the wagon."

"Better come along and cook it for us, Anna."

"Hm! For yourself you will have to cook. But that will not kill you in two days, I guess."

Banner chuckled and uncoiled himself from the chair. "Don't hurry yourself, Hunter," he said. "I'll go on out and see to the team."

"I'll be right along." Hunter finished the last of his eggs, tarried a moment over the last of his coffee, then rose and reached for his hat and his rifle.

"You, Hunter," Anna said. "You will look after Miss Linda, yes?"

Hunter paused to look at her in surprise. "I'll do my best, Anna. We both will, Tom and I."

"No." She shook her head firmly. "Tom Banner I

know. He will do all he can. But you are a different sort of man. It is for you to keep her safe.''

"Is there some danger to her, then?"

The cook snorted. "You are not a fool, Hunter," she told him. "Don't treat me as one. It is for you to keep her safe.''

Hunter straightened slowly. "I'm afraid you mistake me, Anna. I'm just another man, like Tom," he said. "But as you say, I'll do all I can."

He went outside to find that Banner, with a little help from a sleepy-looking Edge Pardee, had a team harnessed to the big platform market wagon and a saddle horse ready at the hitch rail. Linda Pardee and Morgan Avery stood on the porch talking quietly.

"Glad you could come, Hunter," Pardee greeted him. "Reckon you figured this was an afternoon tea we was having."

"Morning to you, too, Edge," Hunter said. "Mr. Avery." He touched his hat. "Miss Linda."

"Hunter," Avery said gruffly. He turned to Linda. "You're sure you want to do this?"

Linda laughed. "You know I do," she said. "Where else will I find a wedding dress?"

Avery's face clouded. "Your mama always hoped you'd wear hers one day," he said. "If she'd lived—" He stopped, shrugged. "You're a lot like her, girl," he said.

"Oh, Uncle Morg." Linda smiled and turned to give him a quick hug. "Not a girl any longer, I'm afraid. But—thank you.''

She turned away quickly, accepting Hunter's arm to help her onto the wagon seat. As she swung up he saw the shine of tears in her eyes, but she kept her voice light.

"It's just for a few days," she said brightly. "And I'm sure Tom and Mr. Hunter will take good care of me.''

"Yes, sir. We'll surely do that," Tom Banner said.

He climbed stiffly up to the wagon seat and took the reins. "Hunter, suppose you take the first turn outriding."

"And suppose you get on along." Edge Pardee's voice seemed a little rough, but his grin was sunny as ever. "There's some of us got work to do, and it's blamed near daylight already. Tom, you see you keep Hunter out of trouble. He's apt to run plumb wild in the big city."

"All right," Avery said. "We'll see you toward the week's end. You men take care now."

It seemed to Hunter that the rancher wanted to say something more, but instead he turned away abruptly and stumped into the house. With practiced care Banner took a last look at the wagon, then snapped the reins and guided the team out onto the open road, Hunter trailing behind.

Sunrise found the travelers near the sunken pasture where Hunter had intervened in Pardee's fight with the bushwhackers. Cattle stirred along the edge of the pines, drifting slowly away from the moving wagon. A rider— one of Avery's hands from the southeastern line shack— paused on the skyline to wave his hat in greeting, then drifted along behind the herd.

Hunter rode a little apart from the others, glad of the morning silence. Seeing the ambush site again reminded him how few days had passed since he'd first set eyes on the valley. Somehow it seemed he'd been in the high country much longer, that he'd come to know the valley and its people well. But he knew he was only fooling himself. He was still the outsider, maybe more than ever. If he'd doubted it, the moment's talk on the porch—memories shared by Avery and Edge and Linda of which Hunter knew nothing—had proved it again.

Just as well, Hunter thought. He still had his job to do. Whatever else he remembered or forgot, there was still Barney Lemmon dead because of Hunter's failure.

Until that was settled he had no business thinking of anything else.

Instead of retracing the path Hunter had ridden that first day, Banner turned due east across the bowl. On the far side he found a narrow road that presently led down into the brushy foothills in a series of switchbacks. Chipmunks scurried to the top of the jutting boulders to watch with tense curiosity as the wagon passed, and an eagle circled high overhead. Hunter smiled to think how much easier his hard climb through those hills would have been if he'd only known the road was there. Banner turned left at a fork into what seemed the head of a new canyon. Before long its walls rose steep and rocky to cut off the sun.

"The right fork goes down into New Mexico," Hunter said, bringing his mount up level with the wagon. "I came up that way, more or less. Where does this one take us?"

Banner squinted up at him. "Dead Horse Canyon," he said. "We'll pick up the crick in about an hour, and that's a good place to stop for beans. Come nightfall we ought to be in the valley where Antonito lies." He twisted uncomfortably on the padded seat. "About time, too. I tell you, this is worse duty than riding nighthawk in a thunderstorm."

"Oh?" Linda pulled her smile into an exaggerated pout. "Is it so bad, then, nursemaiding a woman to town to do her shopping?"

Banner looked around, his deeply tanned face taking on a shade more color. "Oh, no, Miss Linda. I didn't mean it like that a-tall," he said in haste. "It's—well, it's a pure honor to escort you. I just meant—"

"—that you wish somebody else had drawn the short straw for the honor?" Her laugh was low and clear. "How about you, Mr. Hunter? Are you as uncomfortable with the job as Tom?"

"I don't believe that was Tom's meaning," Hunter said gravely.

"That's a fact," Banner said. "All's I meant was I'm built more for a saddle than a wagon seat. God made me for a cowhand, not a farmer."

"Well, then, it's only right the two of you should share the hard work. Maybe Mr. Hunter will spell you on the wagon." She gave Hunter a cool, level stare. "Would you agree to that, Mr. Hunter?"

"Of course, Miss Linda."

Tom Banner glanced at Hunter, then back at Linda. Raising one gloved hand from the reins, he rubbed it across his mouth. "Well, bad as it is, I believe I'll last it out a spell," he said. "At least until we stop. After that we'll see."

Within a couple of miles the canyon walls began to open out. For a space the road ran steeply down along one wall, with a sharp drop at its edge and pine trees below. The horses, instead of pulling, were holding back now, fighting the heavy wagon that threatened to run them into the ground. Banner took them down slowly, using the brake often until the road leveled out on the canyon floor. To the left the walls fell away where another canyon joined the first. A cold swift stream, its banks cut sharp and deep, seemed to come from nowhere to parallel the road. Banner took the horses splashing across a ford to a broad bench shaded by the high red rock walls, and then he reined in.

"Dead Horse Canyon," he said again. "Best place we'll find to stop for a bit. Hunter, if you'll tend the animals, I'll see what vittles Anna packed us."

Hunter released the team from the wagon but left collars and harness in place. He led them and the saddle horse a little way downstream to drink, then hobbled them to graze on the scattered tufts of grass. When he got back Linda had withdrawn into the brush along the canyon wall. Banner knelt bareheaded by the stream, splashing cold water over his head and neck. Hunter joined him.

"Food's over by the dead tree there soon's you're

done washing up," Banner said. His dark eyes, studying Hunter, were friendly but thoughtful. He rose stiffly and stretched, hands on his hips, arching his body backward. "Can't say I'm sorry for the halt. Getting old, I expect."

Hunter smiled. Smiling had become easier for him the last few days, he realized. "Not likely, Tom," he said. He straightened as Linda came to sit on the trunk of the fallen tree. "Maybe a little of Anna's cooking will make you feel better."

They ate slowly, then sat for a while longer to chat, Linda laughing at the hummingbirds that dived and darted at the wildflowers along the stream. No one seemed eager to set out again, but finally Tom Banner rose and stretched.

"Best we move along if we're to get to the river by sundown," he said almost apologetically. "Hunter, I'd welcome a turn in the saddle. Maybe you'll fight the wagon for a while?"

"Glad to."

Linda looked up, a hint of the teasing smile back on her lips. "I think that's very noble of you, Mr. Hunter. Shall we go?"

Hunter led the team back down, and Banner fastened them into their traces. Mounting the sorrel, he passed Hunter's rifle across to him and took his own in return.

"Best I ride ahead, since I know the way. If the ruts give out, just keep to eastward of the crick."

They traveled for a time in silence, Banner a hundred yards ahead, often out of sight in the trees. Linda seemed lost in her own reverie, and Hunter didn't interrupt. The canyon continued to open out, the slope of the walls softening until it was more of a valley, narrower but no less green than the one where Avery's ranch lay. Far ahead Hunter saw the land stairstepping down to a band of trees along a broad river. He started to point it out to Linda, then hesitated.

Though he'd really wanted to talk with her, he now felt awkward beside her on the wagon seat. A moment later she leaned gently toward him, her head resting for a moment on his shoulder, her body swaying to the steady roll of the wagon. He realized her silence had been due to drowsiness and wondered whether to wake her. Before he made up his mind she jerked suddenly erect on the seat.

"Oh! I'm sorry, Mr. Hunter," she said. Her cheeks reddened as she realized where she'd been. "I didn't mean—I must have fallen asleep."

Hunter grinned and watched the color in her face deepen. "My pleasure, Miss Linda."

"I—I ought to be better company. Riding in anything with wheels puts me to sleep faster than a toddy. You should see me on a train."

I'd like to, Hunter thought. Aloud he said, "You must have been up late last night."

She looked at him sharply. "Why do you say that?"

"Woke up once myself. The lamp was lit in your room."

"I didn't know you could see my room from the bunkhouse."

Hunter cursed himself. "Can't," he said. "That is, I don't imagine you can. I'd stepped outside for a minute."

"I see." Linda's gaze searched his face a moment longer, and then she looked away. "I was—reading," she said. "I had some things to think out." She changed the subject abruptly. "I'd taken you for a Texan. Now I think I was wrong."

"Well, I've been there, but never for very long. I hail from Missouri."

"Are you a traveler, then?"

"After a fashion."

Linda waited. Hunter knew that she wouldn't ask another question, wouldn't pry into a man's past, but he felt the silent pressure of her interest.

"I used to see the trail drives come past my folks'

farm. Thought that was the best thing in the world. When I was fifteen I went with one of them."

"And liked it?"

"Enough. I came back for a while, then went out again when I turned eighteen. Worked in Texas, Montana, the Medicine Bow country, places like that."

"But you came to us from the south, so Edge said."

The wagon lurched into a narrow gully, righted itself sluggishly. For a minute Hunter was busy with the reins. "That's right," he said then. "Lately I've been in Arkansas and the Nations."

"The Indian Territory." Linda's eyes seemed to darken a bit. "I've heard that's a lawless place," she said carefully.

"Like anywhere else," Hunter said. "Some good people and some bad ones."

She nodded thoughtfully. "I see," she said again. "Still, I guess there are many ways a man can get crosswise with the law."

For one instant Hunter was tempted to tell her the truth, to explain himself and his reason for being there. Then he choked off the impulse. There was too much danger in it. Besides, she was promised to another man. Her interest in him could only be casual at best. Before long, one way or another, he would be out of her life.

"Yes, Miss Linda," he said evenly. "I expect that's true."

Throughout the long afternoon they wound steadily downhill through a mixture of wooded and open country. By the time the rim of the sun touched the western mountains they were among the cottonwoods along the river. Banner waved to them, then rode farther ahead until he was lost to sight. A few minutes later Hunter saw a wisp of gray smoke ahead. By the time the wagon reached the spot, Banner had already unsaddled his mount and turned it free to roam the area. A campfire burned in a rock firepit atop the ashes of many others.

"Surprised there ain't nobody else here," Banner greeted them. "Way it is, we can spread ourselves large."

Again Hunter tended the horses while Linda and Banner looked to supper. When he came back to what was now their camp stew bubbled in a skillet on the coals. Banner poured coffee from a blackened coffeepot and held the cup out to him. In half an hour they were enjoying a hot meal as the first stars began to show overhead. With full darkness a coyote somewhere along the rimrock began a series of high-pitched yips ending in a long, heartbroken wail.

"This must have been a wonderful country back in the old days," Linda said suddenly. "Before all the people came in and made it so crowded, I mean."

Hunter smiled into his tin cup as he drained his coffee. "Yes," he said, "but where would you be if they hadn't?"

She answered without hesitation. "Oh, I'd be here somehow. I'd have come here from any place, because this is where I belong."

Tom Banner chuckled. "Too many for me," he said. He hitched himself to his feet and carried his plate and cup over to the wash pan to wait for morning. "I plumb enjoyed the meal, but I'm going to pull my bedroll over a piece and leave you young folks to talk about belonging to places."

"Wait, Tom," Linda said. "Wouldn't you like some peaches?"

Banner shook his head, looking from her to Hunter. "Thank you, no, missy. Bedtime for an old bobcat like me. But I'm betting Hunter will split a can with you."

"Oh. Good night, then, Tom." She turned hopefully. "Is that right, Mr. Hunter?"

"All right." He picked up the can, snapped open his jackknife, and cut into the top. "Here you go." As she poured a helping onto her plate he said, "Must be a nice feeling, belonging."

"It is."

She raised her head, a question in her eyes. Hunter didn't want to answer it. Before she could speak he said, "You were born at Pine Valley?"

She nodded. "It was two ranches then, Uncle Morg's and ours. My mother was his sister. But one night—" She stopped and bent her head over the plate. Firelight caught in the flow of her hair and broke into tiny sparkles. It reflected for a moment in her eyes as she looked up at Hunter again. "One night there was a fire."

"I'm sorry."

"You know what it's like, I guess." Her voice was soft and uncertain. "Losing someone."

Mister. Mister, your friend fell down.

"Yes."

"I don't remember much—just what Edge has told me. I was three, and he was seven. Since then Uncle Morg has been our folks." She smiled suddenly and looked up. "He's not nearly so fierce as he seems. I don't think he ever raised a hand to either of us. That's why I'm such a spoiled brat."

"I hadn't noticed," Hunter said, and he was surprised when she laughed.

They shared the last of the coffee with their peaches, listening to the murmur of the stream and watching an ebbing campfire. Then Hunter took his bedroll from the wagon so that Linda could sleep there. Casting an eye toward Banner's blanket-wrapped figure, he made his own bed the same distance from the wagon. It was odd. Banner was a veteran at Pine Valley, deeply trusted and aware of Linda's engagement. Yet he'd intentionally withdrawn to throw the two of them together for a time. Hunter wondered why.

An hour later, running over his talk with Linda in his head as he watched the moon clear the sharply cut canyon rim, he was still wondering.

Chapter 12

Adam Hunter stopped the wagon and set the brake at the crest of the last long hill. Below them the town of Antonito lay cradled like a jewel in the green velvet cushion of a settled valley.

Linda Pardee smiled like a little girl. "As many times as I've seen it before, I'm still surprised all over again at how beautiful it is!"

North and east the land sloped gently downward into plains already cut up into the neat checkerboards of irrigated farms. South and west the foothills rose until they gave way to the pine-clad slopes of the mountains. Compared to Sublette City Antonito looked large and prosperous, prosperity brought by the railroad that followed the river in from the plains, then parted from it to begin the hard climb toward Cumbres Pass.

From their position above the town Hunter had agreed with Linda about its beauty, but close up he found Antonito less beautiful. Many of the buildings had a raw, impermanent look caused by too much unseasoned pine planking and too little paint. Back from the main street, the residential section was a mixture of substantial homes and hastily thrown up cabins, with a few tents pegged out in bare lots. Around the town square, though, the courthouse and the stone structures of the business quarter showed the town was there to stay.

"There." Linda pointed to a storefront in a block of joined buildings. "Madame Sophie, Dressmaker."

"Good enough," Tom Banner said. He reined his horse a little closer to the wagon. "The hotel's just down the way. What say we get settled in? Then we'll walk you back here, and Hunter and me can see what's in our shipment before suppertime."

Following Banner's directions, Hunter brought the wagon to a stop in front of a two-story frame building. He and Banner carried the luggage and their rifles inside. At the desk a woman awaited them with a painted smile and a massive register book.

"I'm Bonnie Miles, your hostess, Mr.—Hunter," she said, squinting to read his name upside down. "Will you and your wife be wanting a room with a view of the street?"

Hunter ignored Tom Banner's quiet chuckle. "No," he answered without looking up. "Miss Pardee will have her own room."

"Oh!" The woman looked hard at Linda. "Well, of course, Miss Pardee," she said sweetly. "From Pine Valley, isn't it? My lands, I should have known you right away."

"Thank you," Linda said with equal sweetness. "I'm surprised you didn't."

Leaving their gear in their rooms and the wagon to the hotel's hostler, they returned to the dressmaker's. With Linda happily busy there, Hunter and Banner walked on down toward the railroad station. While Banner was inside Hunter leaned against a post on the platform, idly watching the flow of the town's business.

Before long a boy of ten or eleven rode up on a sun-faded red bicycle. He shot a quick glance at Hunter, his face showing equal helpings of suspicion and freckles, then looked longer at the empty ticket window. Satisfied the stationmaster wasn't watching, he leaned the bicycle against the platform and bent to search the ballast beside the railroad tracks.

Hunter watched with increasing interest, but before the boy found whatever he was seeking the door from the depot swung open. Banner and a man in a blue uniform came out, Banner frowning as he listened to the other. The boy shot them a startled look and vanished like a rabbit under the platform.

". . . Right down here," the stationmaster was saying. He pulled off his cap and mopped his forehead with a bandanna. "I thought it best to put it out of sight, but the word's got around. I swear, I don't know what Avery can be thinking about!"

"His own business, I expect," Banner replied. Worry showed in his face and voice. He jerked his head at Hunter, motioning him along.

The stationmaster stopped in front of a big double door and opened its railroad padlock from a ring of keys. In hurt silence he slid one door back and gestured inside.

Banner peered inside, then shook his head. "Sure enough, though I'd never have believed it," he murmured. He started to add something but glanced at the agent and changed his mind.

Hunter looked, then stepped back, almost as surprised as Banner had been. Stacked inside the storeroom were rolls and rolls of barbed wire, kegs of staples, and a crate of tools for stretching and cutting wire.

"You see what I mean," the stationmaster said. "Nobody's ever thought of fencing the high country before. People ain't going to like the idea, either."

"It's not people's business," Banner said absently. "How much to leave it here until we pull out?"

"In the storeroom, you mean?" The agent thought a moment. "Well, it ain't in the way, but the railroad ought to get something. Dollar a week be all right?"

Banner fished in his pocket and drew out a silver cartwheel. "Won't take us that long," he said, "but I'll pay for a week. Don't talk about this any more than you can help."

"Never fear. I'll have a receipt for you when you're ready."

He relocked the door and hurried back inside the station as though unwilling to be seen with the Pine Valley hands. Banner waited until the door had closed, then gave Hunter a worried look.

"I hate to say it, but that feller's right. That wire's apt to bring trouble."

"Maybe," Hunter said.

The boy had emerged from beneath the platform. He gave Hunter a quick, toothy grin, then resumed his search along the tracks.

"Could be Mr. Avery figures the wire to stop the trouble," Hunter said. "Maybe what Pine Valley and Circle Eight need is a boundary between them. It's easier to patrol wire than open range."

Banner snorted. "Easy to say. Now all's you have to do is convince Ellis Watkins of that."

"Well—"

Hunter broke off. The boy delved beside a railroad tie and straightened with a grin on his face. He ran back toward his bicycle.

"Find what you were looking for, son?" Hunter asked.

"A dime." He held out his hand to display a thin, moon-shaped silver piece about the size of a half dollar.

"A dime?"

"I left it on the tracks." The boy cast another swift glance at the station window. "Thanks for not telling old Higgins I was here. He sure don't like us kids doing that."

"A dime," Hunter said again. "What'll you take for it?"

The boy frowned at him, suspecting a trick. "I told you," he said. "It's a dime."

Hunter searched a pocket. "Would you take a quarter for it?" He held the coin up, then placed it on the platform by his boot.

Cautiously the boy approached. Hunter took a step back while Banner looked on with a smile twitching his mustache. When he was a yard from the platform's edge the boy made a sudden dash, snatched up the quarter, and dropped the silver disk in its place. Then he leapt for his bicycle and pedaled swiftly away.

"A fool and his money." Banner chuckled as Hunter stooped to pick up the dime. "Why'd you do that, anyway?"

Hunter shrugged. "Don't know. He seemed like a nice kid, that's all."

Banner shook his head. "Hunter, you beat all." He hesitated, rubbing his chin. "Say, could you see Miss Linda to supper and all? I got me a little personal business here in town."

"Sure—if you'll trust me with the job."

Banner chuckled again. "Oh, I'll trust you right enough," he said. "Fact is, I'll buy you a beer down at the Pall Mall later this evening. They got a right fancy place there; you ought to have one drink with them while you're in the city."

Hunter felt his mouth go dry, felt the tightness in his throat. He'd been a long time dry, and there was no danger here. One drink wouldn't—

Dimness and rough voices and the smell of sweat. "Here, drink up. Looks like your glass must have a hole in the bottom." And nothing else clear, nothing until the shots came.

"Maybe," he heard himself say.

A momentary puzzlement came and went in Banner's eyes. "I'll give you a shout when I get back, then," he said. "And I hope you're right about that wire—though I wouldn't bet your dime on it."

An hour later, washed and shaved and wearing his newly brushed coat, Hunter presented himself at the door of Linda Pardee's room. Thinking of decorum, he made no move to enter when she answered his knock.

"I was hoping you'd have supper with me," he said. "The hotel dining room is open, or—"

"Oh, no," Linda said quickly. Then, seeing his face, she laughed. "No, I don't mean I won't have supper with you. But there's a much better place down near the depot—the Suarez family runs it. May we go there?" She peered down the hallway. "Is Tom coming?"

"Tom says he has other business."

"Oh? Oh, of course. I'll need just a minute. Would you mind waiting in the parlor for me?"

It took longer than a minute. Downstairs Hunter scanned the headlines in a week-old Denver newspaper. Finding nothing of interest, he turned to the window. The street lamps had been lighted, although the sun was barely behind the western mountains. Evening traffic was light—a loaded wagon starting back for a homestead somewhere in the hills, two couples on the boardwalk, a knot of men talking in front of the mercantile. Three men dressed in trail clothes came out through the wide doors of the livery stable across the way, paused to look around, then turned toward the depot.

Something in their movements attracted Hunter's attention. Idly he watched them until they were out of sight. Their faces were unknown to him, but still he felt a touch of uneasiness. He'd left his Colt in the room, figuring it was neither necessary nor appropriate for taking a lady to dinner. Now he felt a nagging urge to go up and get it. He turned from the window, tempted, but then Linda Pardee stepped into the doorway.

"Mr. Hunter? I'm ready."

She had changed from her traveling suit into a green dress Hunter hadn't seen before. Her dark blond hair shone from brushing. For a moment Hunter stared like a schoolboy, but he caught himself and smiled.

"I didn't know I'd be walking out with a lady of fashion," he said. "I'm afraid I show up pretty shabby by comparison."

"You haven't had the advantage of a visit to the dress-maker," she said, falling in with his gentle banter. "So-phie had made this up from my pattern and had it all ready for me when I arrived. You're the first to see it."

"I'm honored."

"Still, you look quite presentable for someone just down from the high country." She crossed to take his arm. "A lady—or even a ranch-bred tomboy—could do worse. Shall we go?"

The restaurant was far cleaner and a little less crowded than Hunter had expected. A plump, smiling woman of middle age took them in tow at once and led them to a table.

"So nice to see you again, Miss Linda," she said. "Will you take wine with your dinner? Our grapes do very well here."

"Of course," Linda answered. "Will you join me, Mr. Hunter?"

Hunter pressed his lips together. "I'm afraid I'm not much for drinking wine," he said. "But please go ahead."

"A drink then, perhaps, for the gentleman?" the woman asked. "We have—"

"Just coffee, please. Black."

When she had gone Linda looked at Hunter. "I hope you don't think I'd mind if you took a drink. After all, I grew up in my uncle's house." She laughed softly. "He still thinks no one knows about the bottle he keeps in his desk."

Hunter didn't answer. Neither the truth nor a lie appealed to him as something he wanted to tell this woman right at the moment. Instead he said, "You seemed to know where Tom got off to. I was surprised he didn't come with us."

"I'm not," Linda said. "I thought you knew. Tom's been keeping company with a widow woman here. I'm sure he's gone to visit her." She smiled. "And so you're stuck with the job of chaperoning me. I'm sorry. You might have found a friend of your own."

"It's Tom's loss," Hunter said gravely. "Linda, I was outbid for the privilege of eating with you Sunday. Tonight I'm the luckiest man in town."

She colored and looked down at the table. "Thank you," she said softly after a moment. "That was a nice thing to say."

During the meal they chatted easily about the valley and the ranch and her visit to the dressmaker. Hunter gradually relaxed his guard. Linda asked no personal questions, nor did she inquire about the shipment at the depot. Hunter didn't bring it up. Soon enough she would know about the wire and her uncle's plans for it. For this one night he preferred to let the matter rest.

They were finishing their dessert when Hunter saw Tom Banner passing along the boardwalk outside. In the pool of lamplight that spread from the restaurant's doorway Banner's face showed a deep dejection. Hunter turned, starting to rise, but then sank back as Banner passed into the evening without even a glance their way.

"Now what could be the matter with Tom?" Linda Pardee murmured. She had followed Hunter's glance and was watching him with anxious eyes. "Tom seems unhappy about something. Had you better see what's the trouble?"

For a moment Hunter didn't answer. Banner had been a picture, he realized, of the man he himself would be when the evening was past and he returned Linda to her room. "I'll talk to him when we get back," he said finally. "More coffee, Miss Linda?"

"Now you've turned sad on me," she said. She touched his arm lightly across the table. "And you dropped the 'miss' a while ago. Wouldn't you like to keep it that way?"

Hunter shook his head. "It helps me remember your engagement," he said.

132

She looked away. "Maybe we both need to be reminded."

They left the restaurant in silence, walking back toward the hotel in the cool evening. A passenger train was just leaving the station after a brief stop. The night wind carried the black coal smoke their way. Hunter was just beginning to tell Linda how good the smoke smelled when she made a face and drew her shawl across her nose. Neither seemed inclined to speak until they reached the hotel lobby. Then Hunter stopped and turned to face her.

"Linda," he began, "I—"

"Mister! Hey, mister!"

A boy burst through the front door and skidded to a stop just inside. Hunter recognized the youngster from the depot.

"Why, hello, son," he said. "You're out late, aren't you?"

"Got another dime on the tracks," the boy panted. "But then I saw your friend." He pointed toward the door.

"What's the matter?" Hunter said. But in his mind he heard another boy saying *Mister. Your friend fell down.*

"Your friend!" The boy pointed again, stabbing his finger frantically toward the door. "Seen him through the window. Your friend from the depot. Down at the saloon. Those men, three of them. You gotta hurry, he's in terrible trouble."

Chapter 13

Hunter didn't wait to hear more. Cursing himself for going about unarmed, he sprinted up the stairs. His rifle was leaning in the corner behind the door of his room. He snatched it up and stripped off its leather scabbard, then turned for the stairs again. In his mind he heard again the refrain that had followed him from Fort Smith:

It wasn't like Barney to run off on his own that way. Where were you?

"Mister—Adam, wait!" Linda called, but he hardly heard her. Nor did he see the astonished faces of the desk clerk and a couple of guests who'd stepped out of the parlor to see what the commotion was. All his awareness was concentrated on the saloon and the need to get there in time.

He ran, hardly aware of other people on the street, or of the boy who raced along at his heels. Just short of the lighted doorway he slowed to a stop. The Pall Mall faced onto a corner, with tall double glass doors set at an angle to the boardwalk. That was good. No one could be behind him or on his flank. He levered a shell into the Winchester's chamber and stepped onto the boardwalk.

"Thanks, son. You run on home now," he said to the boy without looking his way. Carrying the rifle ready in one hand, he opened the left-hand door and stepped into the saloon.

His first reaction was one of overwhelming relief. Tom Banner stood with his back to the bar, one boot heel hooked over the brass footrail, his hands dangling loosely at his sides. A bottle stood on the bar beside him, untouched. His pose seemed relaxed and natural, but Hunter saw the tightness around his mouth and the quick hard look of relief in his eyes.

A burly man with a handlebar mustache and a young woman in the gauzy trappings of a saloon hostess huddled at the far end of the bar, obviously trying to stay out of the way.

A yard away from Banner on either side stood two grinning men with their hats tilted back. One had collar-length blond hair and the start of a beard. The other wore a broad, Mexican-style sombrero that hid most of his face, at least from Hunter's vantage point. When the blond-haired one saw Hunter his grin broadened. A third man sat at a round table, and it was toward him that Banner was looking. Hunter recognized the three riders he'd seen earlier in the evening.

At some signal from the blond man the other two shifted position to look at Hunter. The one at the table stood up and pushed his chair away from him with his foot.

"You'd be Hunter," he said. Standing, he was taller than Hunter and almost skeleton-thin. His face was pale, but a hectic reddish flush—not from drink—burned in his hollow cheeks. He wore a long pistol in a curious cut-down holster that rode low on his hip. "Come a little farther inside and close the door. We were just about to have us a little party here."

Slowly Hunter moved out of the doorway, letting the door swing shut behind him. "I don't know you," he said to the standing man.

"Too damn bad."

"Gunfighter?"

"Some say so."

The bartender and the young woman edged a little

135

deeper into the shelter of the bar, leaving the five men facing one another at odd angles. The only other person in the room was an elderly man at a table in the far corner. He dozed with his head on the table, peacefully unaware of the others. Tuesday night, Hunter thought mechanically. Light crowd. Wish there were two less. Aloud, he said, "Tom, you come up this way."

"I don't think so," the man with the sombrero said. "You just stand right still, cowboy. Might be you'll live to see your lady friend again."

"Tom."

Banner didn't move. "They were laying for me, Hunter," he said. "But it's you they want. Back out of here the best way you can."

"Shut up," the lean man told him. He nodded toward the Winchester in Hunter's hand. "That the rifle you used on old Ace Webb?"

Hunter said, "You a friend of his?"

"Damn straight."

As the gunfighter spoke he was moving slowly to his left, putting distance between himself and the others at the bar. You're first, Hunter thought, although the way the deck was stacked, it didn't figure to make much difference. The tall gunman was obviously the most dangerous, but the other two wouldn't be any slower than snakes—and they were close enough to Tom Banner to make shooting tricky at best.

"Is that what this is about?" he asked, trying to buy a little time. He began edging to his right, away from the doorway, away from the men at the bar. "Shooting Webb?"

The gunfighter saw what he was doing. Bloodless lips drew back in a contemptuous grin. "Maybe," he said. "Or maybe it's about fencing the range. Or maybe we just don't like you."

"Deke?" the one with the sombrero said. "Somebody might come. Let's get it done."

136

"Shut up," Deke said again. He didn't look away from Hunter. "I'll say when."

"Who's paying you?" Hunter asked.

"The Devil."

Hunter nodded slowly. "That's lucky," he said. "I'm the Devil's paymaster." There was no point in more talk. He and Tom weren't going to draw any better hand than they already had. He took a deep breath, ready to move as he let it out.

"Paymaster?" The tall man grinned again. "That's good. I'll take your money for damn sure, just as soon as we're through with—"

He stopped in midsentence, his hand streaking for the butt of his Colt. By the bar Tom Banner was already moving. Ignoring the men flanking him, he snatched up the whiskey bottle and heaved it with a desperate side-arm throw. Deke's gun was coming up swiftly, its muzzle tracing a perfect arc to center on Hunter's chest, when the bottle caught him on the point of the shoulder. Instinctively he flinched away. His first shot went wild, but in less than a heartbeat he was ready for the second, steady once more on his target.

Hunter saw from the tail of his eye the flurry of movement from Banner, but he couldn't afford to look. An instant after the gunman's first shot the big Winchester roared. Without waiting to see the result Hunter worked the lever and fired again at the smoke-shrouded figure.

The first bullet took Deke at the beltline and lifted him up on his toes like a mule's kick. He doubled over, his face twisted in pain and shock, but he didn't drop the Colt. He slammed one bullet into the floor a yard in front of Hunter's boot. He'd managed to cock the pistol for another shot when the rifle's second heavy slug shattered his collarbone and drove shards of it downward to find his heart.

Hunter pivoted to his left, dropping to one knee as he searched for another target. He'd heard at least three shots from that direction. Now a fourth came, the bullet driving into the wall just above him. He saw that Tom Banner was down.

Hunter snapped a shot at a figure looming through the smoke, missed, slammed another round into the Winchester's chamber. As he fired again he saw Tom Banner move.

His eyes burning with anger, Banner had followed through on his throw by grappling with the blond gunman. A swipe from a gun butt had sent him staggering. Before he could recover, the man in the sombrero shot him low in the back. The impact spun Banner around so that he fell heavily on his left side, staring back at the one who had shot him. He knew vaguely that he was hurt, that Hunter's rifle was filling the room with noise, that all motion had slowed to a crawl. There seemed to be plenty of time to take out his own revolver. Now, even as Hunter found the blond man with the muzzle of his rifle, Banner fired his only shot of the fight. It struck his man just beneath the point of his chin, shaking trail dust from the sombrero that tumbled away behind him. The man arched backward across the bar, then slid nervelessly off and fell to the floor beside Banner.

Hunter was just starting to rise when the saloon's glass door crashed open. Not sure who was behind him, Hunter threw himself to the floor and rolled, swinging around to train his rifle on the doorway. Over the sights he looked into the face of Linda Pardee. She stood white and rigid as a marble statue, clutching the handle of Hunter's engraved revolver with both hands. She was staring toward the bar, her eyes very wide. Hunter followed her stricken gaze to the body of Tom Banner.

Mister! Your friend fell down!

Just like Barney, his mind told him. Too late again. Forgetting the other fallen men, he went to kneel by Banner's side.

* * *

At first Linda couldn't move, not even to lower the heavy pistol. Hunter moved past her like a figure in a dream, and she was unable even to feel relief that he was still alive.

She hadn't immediately understood when he rushed from the hotel. When she realized what was happening she went to find a weapon. The door to Hunter's room was open, and she'd taken the revolver from his holster and dashed after him. She was twenty yards from the saloon when the night had exploded into flares of powder and an almost continuous roar like the firing of a battery of great cannon. Brushing past a young boy who was peering eagerly inside, she entered, cold fear in her heart and the Colt ready in her hands.

Behind the bar the mirror was spiderwebbed with cracks radiating from a large hole with blood spattered around it. On the bar itself a black sombrero rested upright at the end of a long bloody streak. More blood spattered the floor around the body of a man in the center of the room, glistened like wet paint on the front of the bar, pooled beneath Tom Banner's motionless body. Through Linda's mind ran a blinding succession of images she hadn't thought of since she was a child.

The first snow lay white in the barnyard, covering the muddy ground. A hog ran squealing from the shelter of its pen into bright sunlight. Waiting his moment, a ranch hand swung up a freshly sharpened axe. Sunlight glistened on the blade as it fell to strike the running hog at the base of its skull. Blood sprayed; bright arterial blood shot ten feet into the cold air. And she—a little girl too young to understand—understood, heard herself scream again and again and again.

"Linda!" It was Hunter's voice, coming to her from a long way off. "Linda! He's still alive. Get a doctor!"

She dropped the pistol, hearing it clatter on the floor. One faltering step, then another took her to Hunter's side. Banner lay on the floor, his face deathly pale under its tan. His eyes were half open, unseeing.

"She wouldn't have me." His lips barely moved. "Said she'd found another."

Adam Hunter reached up and caught her arm, his face as white as Banner's. "Linda! A doctor!"

"Yes. Yes, of course."

She didn't realize she'd spoken, but she moved. The saloon hostess had come slowly out of her hiding place. Linda went to her.

"Please! Get Dr. Miles. His office—"

"I know where it is," the woman said. She looked at Linda for a moment, then nodded. "I'll go."

She hurried out, meeting in the doorway a lean, dark, gray-haired man with a silver badge on his vest. Linda heard the sound of heels clacking rapidly along the boardwalk, and then the dark man stepped inside and pointed a pistol at Hunter's back.

"Stand away from him, mister. And from that rifle."

"We need a doctor here."

"Mindy's gone for him. You stand away. Put your hands on the bar, hear me?"

"Sheriff!" Linda Pardee said. She came swiftly across the room toward him. "Sheriff Vargas, wait."

Hunter had done as he was told, leaving the rifle on the floor beside Banner. Still watching him, the sheriff quickly bent over each of the fallen men, then knelt to retrieve the Winchester. He looked up in surprise when he heard Linda's cry.

"Why—Miss Pardee, isn't it?"

"That's right. The wounded man is Tom Banner, and this is Mr. Hunter. They're employees of my uncle Morgan Avery at Pine Valley Ranch."

"Right now they're in a lot of trouble," Vargas said. His voice was grim, but his tone had changed when he saw Linda. In spite of himself, he'd been impressed by the Avery name. She caught the change and pressed her advantage.

"These men attacked them. I'm sure your investigation will show that."

140

"Maybe," Vargas said. He straightened, leaned the rifle against the wall well out of Hunter's reach. Finally he holstered the pistol. "Hunter," he said. "I know that name."

"Of course. I told you, he works for—"

"Your uncle," Vargas finished. "But that's not where I heard the name." He glared at Hunter's back. "Hunter. You're the one Ed Tobreen named in his telegram."

Hunter didn't answer. Linda wasn't sure he'd heard. He leaned heavily on the bar, bowed head hanging down. She thought his hands would be trembling if his palms didn't press so hard against the polished wood.

"Leave him alone!" she snapped as she knelt beside Banner. "Can't you see he's sick?"

"He should be sick," Vargas muttered. "To shoot down four men—"

"Two," Hunter said hoarsely.

"What's that?"

"Two." Hunter didn't look up. "Tom's been back-shot. I killed two of them, and they were damn well shooting at me when I did! Tom must've got the other."

"After he'd been shot, I suppose."

"Listen, Tom needs—"

A frail young man entered the saloon, satchel in hand. He stopped just inside the door. His eyes went wide at the bodies on the floor, and he snorted like a startled deer.

"Over here, Doc," Vargas said. "There's only one needs your help."

Briskly, motioning Linda out of the way, the doctor took her place beside Banner's body. In a moment he'd checked pulse and respiration, then ripped away most of the cowhand's shirt.

"No bullet," he said, half aloud. "Passed through. Below the ribs. Looks like it played hell with his intestinal tract. Primary bleeding internal." He pressed squares of clean white gauze over the wounds, then turned to Vargas as if just noticing him. "If he lives till I get him on my table, I might be able to help. We'll have to carry him."

"I'll carry him," Hunter said.

"Stand where you are, hear me?" Vargas waved a hand.

"Sheriff—" Linda began.

Hunter turned to Vargas. "I'm taking Tom," he said. "You can help or you can stand back. But you'd better not—by God—get in the way."

"Not a lot of time to talk about it," the doctor cut in. "Want him alive or not?"

Vargas sighed. "All right." He jerked a thumb at Hunter. "Let's get him."

Together they carried the moaning Banner to the doctor's quarters and laid him on the high, narrow, padded table. The doctor impatiently motioned Hunter and the sheriff out of the room. "Wait," he said when Linda started to follow. "You can help."

She stopped, looking from the door to the place where Tom Banner lay. "But—" she said, then stopped. She was worried about Hunter, more worried than she would have believed she could be. But Tom Banner needed her more. At least she hoped that was true.

The doctor was taking instruments from a metal cabinet and laying them out on a tray. "Scrub your hands," he said impatiently. "Use the soap. I'll tell you what to do after that." He glanced up, looking at her face for the first time. "You aren't going to faint on me, are you?"

"No." She turned away from the door. "No, I'm not going to faint," she said.

Hunter walked silently ahead of Vargas to the sheriff's office. Vargas waved him to a chair while he instructed a deputy on tending the bodies and taking statements from the witnesses at the Pall Mall. Then the sheriff turned on Hunter.

"All right, mister. Time for you to give an account of yourself."

"I was too late," Hunter said dully. "Again."

Vargas looked at him closely. "For the kind of hard-case you look to be, you're taking this pretty hard." He opened a drawer of the desk. "What you need is a drink."

"No. I thank you, but I'm afraid that's not what I need."

For a moment Vargas looked at him. "So. That's the way it is," the sheriff said slowly.

"Yes."

"And you're working something off on account of it."

Hunter raised his head. "You seem to know a lot about me," he said.

"I know the signs." Vargas closed the drawer softly and settled back in his chair. "Seen it before, close up. You'd better tell me the whole thing."

Hunter told him. He began with Barney and took it all the way through. As he talked he felt his strength starting to return. When he had seen Banner lying wounded Hunter had felt that old black hopelessness start to close in on him. Now it let go his throat and drew away, although he didn't think it had gone far.

"Tom said they were laying for us, and that it was me they wanted," he concluded. "Might be. I didn't know them, though the tall one called me by name."

"Umm." Vargas had listened without interruption. Now he frowned. "Why didn't you tell all this to Tobreen?" he asked. "It might have saved a power of trouble."

"I didn't know if I could trust him." Hunter shrugged. "Hell, I don't know that I can trust *you*, but I had to tell it."

"Umm. Morgan Avery know the grief you've brought him?"

"He knows who I am. He's got his own grief with

143

the Circle Eight, and my guess is barbed wire will make it worse.''

"Miss Pardee isn't going to like that. Edge, either." Vargas considered. "I'd better get up there. There's a trial starting here that I can't miss. Soon as it's done I'll ride through Pine Valley." He looked at Hunter again. "If I let you go back, you tell your tale to To-breen, hear me?"

He rose as the deputy came back. For a moment the two of them talked in tones too low for Hunter to hear. Then Vargas motioned to him.

"All right, Hunter, you can go. Bill here brought back your rifle." Vargas shook his head angrily. "Way things stand, you're most likely going to need it again."

"How's Tom?"

"Alive. Miss Pardee's sitting with him. You go back to the hotel and stay there, hear? Bill will walk along to see you get there—and to see you stay."

Closed inside the narrow room, Hunter drew off his boots and lay back on the bed, staring at the ceiling in the dim glow of the turned-down gas. He knew he should be thinking ahead, making plans, but the only picture his mind would hold to was that of Tom Banner groaning on the dirty floor of the saloon.

You're a hell of a man to have around, he told himself. Barney Lemmon lies in Fort Smith's cemetery because of you, and Tom Banner's an inch away from being buried in Antonito, long before his time. Be better for everybody if you'd just ride out and keep riding.

He swung his legs over the side of the bed and sat up. He knew he wouldn't sleep, and he didn't want to think. The Winchester leaned beside the door where he always kept it. Hunter rose, turning up the gas as he went, and picked up the rifle. He shook the gun free of its long leather scabbard, jacked the cartridges out onto the bed, and spent a careful half hour giving it a thorough cleaning and oiling.

Thoughtfully, then, he removed the flattened dime from his coat pocket and turned it in his fingers, reflecting on it with eyes whose pupils were unusually large. Finally he laid the silver disk on the flat of the Winchester's stock and slid it around until it seemed about right.

Then he did something he normally would never have considered. With the point of his knife he traced neatly around the disk until he had outlined it on the wood. For an hour or more he made sharp, delicate cuts, carving with great care, forming a shallow circular indentation in the hard wood. At last the silver disk fit when he tried it. He tapped it carefully into place with the butt of the knife, then examined the inlay with a critical eye. Glinting in the yellowish light, the silver piece lay flush with the oiled walnut surface of the stock.

Hunter reloaded the rifle, laid it beside him like a wife, and closed his eyes, ready at last for sleep.

Chapter 14

Hunter woke at six o'clock, still tired but feeling he had overslept shamefully. He dressed quickly and knocked at Linda's door, without result. Taking his rifle, he went downstairs, intending to check on Tom Banner. To his surprise, the deputy who'd escorted him to the hotel the night before was asleep in an overstuffed chair in the lobby. He woke as Hunter neared.

"Morning, Mr. Hunter." He rubbed his eyes and blinked owlishly. He was a tall, heavyset young man with close-cropped black hair. A Remington revolver was thrust with apparent carelessness through his belt. He touched it lightly, checking as he stood and stretched. "Looks like another warm day."

"Good morning. Bill, isn't it?"

"Yessir, Bill Stoner. Heading for breakfast?"

"To the doctor's first."

"I'll need to walk along. Sheriff's orders."

"Come ahead."

They found Banner pale and weak but awake, talking with Linda and another woman. Banner smiled and tried to hold out a hand to him. Hunter went quickly across and put a hand on the wounded man's shoulder.

"You're looking good, Tom," he said. "Sorry to drag you into my scrape."

Banner frowned. "Ain't how I remember," he whispered. "Figured as I got us in an' you got us out." He nodded toward the woman Hunter didn't know. "Lucille, this here's Hunter. Good man with a gun."

"Pleased to meet you, Mr. Hunter," she said. She was about forty and plumply handsome, although her face was haggard from worry. Her eyes showed she'd been crying, but she smiled at Hunter. "I'm so thankful you were there to help, and after what I'd done to poor Tom, too." She went to the bed and gripped Banner's hand. "You just rest now, sweetie. I'll be around."

The young doctor appeared in the doorway, lifted his nose, and barked at them. "Out!" he said. He waved an impatient hand at them. "I need time with my patient. He needs rest. Lucille, you can come back in an hour. Good day to the rest of you. Miss Pardee, thank you. No, he's doing just fine, sir. Out, out, out."

"You'll take the wagon back alone," Linda told Hunter as soon as they were outside. "I'm staying until Tom's better."

"I can't leave you—" Hunter began, but Lucille interrupted.

"It's a Christian thought, dear, but I can look after Tom. We'll move him to my place soon's he's able."

Linda looked at her coolly. "We understood you had another gentleman friend," she said.

"That never was true." Lucille sniffled and dabbed at her eyes with a lace handkerchief. "I was put out with Tom because he'd been away so long, and I made up that story to make him jealous. It was a lie, and I know the Lord'll remember it against me." She looked at them in real distress. "To think how close he came to getting killed, believing I'd put him by! I swear to you, Miss Pardee, I'll make it up to him."

Impulsively, Linda gave her a hug. "I'm so glad, Lucille," she said. "But I'll want to see how Tom is before I make any decision. We can talk later."

Lucille hurried away. A few paces along the boardwalk Bill Stoner cleared his throat. "Looks like every-thing's okay here," he said. "Guess I'll be moving along. Hunter, the sheriff wants a word before you leave town."

"Thanks, Deputy."

"No trouble." He touched his hat to Linda. "Ma'am."

"I guess we're on our own," Hunter said as Stoner withdrew. "May I buy you breakfast?"

"Breakfast! Oh, please! Then I want to start back."

Hunter really looked at her for the first time that morn-ing. She still wore the green dress he'd admired the night before, but she probably would never wear it again; the sleeves and skirt bore the reddish-brown stains of dried blood. Her face was pale, her eyes red-rimmed and bloodshot. A lock of hair fell down across her forehead, and she brushed at it ineffectively with the back of a hand.

"Have you had any sleep?" he asked.

"No. It doesn't matter. I don't want to sleep. Is there somewhere we can eat without—" She spread her hands before her skirt. "Like this?"

"We'll find someplace."

They ended up at the Suarez family's restaurant, eating Señora Suarez's *huevos rancheros* in the kitchen while she served strong coffee flavored with cinnamon. Linda ate ravenously, and Hunter found that oversleep-ing made him hungry, too.

"I'd understood you would be staying until the dress was finished," he said during the meal.

"That was before I knew about the wire." She put down her fork and frowned at him. "I wish you'd told me last night."

"There wasn't much time."

"No, when we went to dinner. Why didn't you say something then?"

I had one evening with you, he thought. I didn't want to spoil it. Hunter looked at the words in his mind and left them unspoken. "I didn't think it my place," he said instead.

She frowned again, as if that weren't the answer she had expected. After a pause she shook her head.

"No matter. I'm going back. I must talk to Edge and Uncle Morg—the more so if that was truly an ambush in the saloon. If Tom's in good hands, I want to leave at once."

"It will take some time to load the wire. We might wait until tomorrow morning."

"We don't need—" Linda began, then stopped herself. "No, you're right about the wire. But we'll go as soon as it's loaded and get as far as we can tonight."

"You're the boss."

She looked hard at Hunter's face, as though searching for hidden laughter. There was none. "That's right," she said.

Before noon they were on the river road, rolling westward toward the place they'd camped two nights before. The station agent, Higgins, had seen to the shipment of barbed wire, so Hunter had found time for a bath and a change of clothes before starting out. He felt almost human by the time they left. Linda was back in her traveling suit, looking much fresher and cleaner but no less tired. Even so, she refused all Hunter's urging that they delay their start.

"We can't move fast with the wagon loaded down. I doubt we'll make Dead Horse Canyon before dark."

"We'll get as far as we can." She smiled at him. "I'm giving the orders, remember."

For the first few miles Linda tried to keep up a conversation—about the wire and her misgivings, about Tom Banner and Lucille, about the valley and the ranch. Hunter answered in a quiet voice. Gradually Linda's voice slurred, her silences lengthened. Before they reached the river campsite she had fallen into an exhausted sleep. Fearful she might topple off the wagon seat—or using that for an excuse—Hunter put his arm about her shoulders. She murmured something without waking and burrowed against his chest.

The afternoon had started off fair, but soon clouds began to seep through the passes of the mountains, flowing together into a low, dark overcast. As the wagon climbed on the steep westward trail the clouds drew nearer. The sunlight faded into an odd blue twilight that grew dimmer as afternoon drew into evening. Except for boulders looming through the haze, Hunter could see little. He gave the horses their head, trusting them to hold to the road. Finally, as the last of the light was going, he recognized the sheer walls of Dead Horse Canyon just ahead.

Within the yawning mouth they were briefly under a clear sky again. Through the clouds a few stars glinted in patterns high over the sharp-edged velvet blackness of the canyon rim. Hunter set the brake and waited in unaccustomed stillness. His arm had long been cold and numb, but he was unwilling to shift position enough to wake Linda and let the time of closeness end. He knew he was stealing this time with her, taking something that could never belong to him. He knew, but still he made no move to end it.

After a moment she stirred against him. "Oh," she said drowsily. She blinked and raised her head. "We're here."

"Yes."

Gently Hunter disengaged his arm, then swung down from the high wagon seat and came around to help her. The northern wing of the clouds, silvered by moonlight, appeared above the canyon rim, promising to shut out the stars. Hunter reached up to Linda. His hands spanned her waist as he lifted her down from the seat, feeling the light pressure of her fingers resting on his shoulders. When her feet touched ground she held the pose for a moment, her face lifted toward his. Then Hunter slid his long arms around her, drew her to him, and kissed her.

To his surprise, she didn't push him away. Instead she put her arms around his neck. Her fingers touched the back of his head, tangled in his hair, tightened with sudden urgency as she pulled his mouth down on hers.

They parted at last, leaning backward to look at each other with their bodies still touching, each about to speak when the flat crack of a rifle shot filled the canyon with echoes. The bullet had already passed them to spend itself in the rocks. Hunter dragged Linda to the ground, covering her body with his. When a second shot didn't come immediately he lifted himself to one knee and snaked out an arm to get his rifle from the wagon seat.

The movement brought another shot. This time Hunter saw the muzzle flash high on the far wall of the canyon near the road. The bullet sizzled past close enough to hear, the echoing report of the rifle an instant behind it. Hunter fired at the flash, then dropped flat again, pushing Linda down as she tried to rise. Something smashed through the wooden seat of the wagon, and the sharp report came a third time. The team became spooked, throwing up their heads and straining against the brake. The saddle horse reared and kicked as it fought the rope holding it to the tailboard.

"Get over there," Hunter told Linda. "Toward the rocks. Stay low. I'll cover you."

"No!" she said at once. "I won't leave you here!"

"I'll come when you get there." He gave her a shove. "Hurry. We have to get away from this wagon!"

"Give me your pistol. No, don't argue. Give it to me." She took it, then raised herself to a crouch. "I'm ready."

Hunter rolled away from her and came to his knees. "Go!" The word was lost in the roar of the Winchester. He fired four shots as fast as he could work the lever, then dropped and rolled again. Answering fire came from a new place, higher up. At the first muzzle flash Hunter's Colt spoke from the rocks.

"Linda! Stay out of this," Hunter yelled. "Get down."

The pistol boomed again. Hunter pumped three more shots into the area where the rifleman had last shown himself. When he ducked back Linda fired again from a new position. No answering shots came. Working by feel, Hunter thumbed new loads into the rifle's magazine, his eyes probing the darkness of the canyon wall. He couldn't see anything, but in the distance he heard the clatter of hooves on rocky soil.

Then a single bolt of lightning split the sky over the canyon, throwing everything into vivid relief while a man might have counted to two. On the count of three blackness slammed down again, accompanied by a cold, pounding rain. The moment of light had been enough for Hunter to see a rider urging his mount up the trail, a big man in a flapping coat, his red hair flying behind him in the wind. The muzzle of Hunter's Winchester flared twice, but the sound was lost in a long rolling crash of thunder.

When the echoes died away Hunter rose to stand beside the wagon. After a moment he let the rifle's hammer down to half cock and turned toward the rocks where Linda had gone.

"Over here!"

Hunter followed her voice and found her crouched in the lee of a boulder, her head bowed against the driving rain.

"Did you get him?" she asked.

"I doubt it. We'll know for sure in the morning."

"It was Jack Harvey, wasn't it?"

Hunter knelt beside her, partially sheltering her from the rain. "What did you mean, popping away with that pistol?" he demanded. "I told you to stay down. He might've killed you!"

In the darkness he heard her laugh. "I scared him off, didn't I? He didn't want to face two guns."

"You should have kept out of it."

"Kept out of it?"

She turned toward Hunter in the rainy darkness, rising to her knees. Her body pressed hard into his, her arms clutching, her mouth seeking. Still holding the rifle, he got his free arm around her and bent toward her, tasting the fresh wetness of rain and the salty wetness of tears on her cheeks and her closed eyes and her mouth. They broke apart only when Linda began to shiver in his embrace.

"Kept out of it!" Her voice was something between a laugh and a sob. "Dear God, and I don't even know who you are!"

"We have to find shelter," Hunter said. "Come on, up to the base of the wall."

Clinging together, bent almost double against the strong cold wind that came down the canyon, they stumbled their way to the huge boulders lying along the base of the cliff. Linda was shivering uncontrollably now. Hunter half supported her along the slope until he found a crack between two of the boulders wide enough to admit the two of them.

"In here. Get back as far as you can."

A few feet back the crack opened out so Hunter could no longer touch both walls. He struck a match. In the seconds before the wind extinguished it he made out a shallow sheltered overhang beneath the cliff, a flat stone floor puddled with water, a tangle of driftwood and dead branches at the upper end. Scattered droppings showed that deer had bedded there. In fresh darkness Hunter helped Linda to the back of the shelter. Then he left her there and plunged back into the rain.

With fumbling hands he hobbled the frightened horses and turned them free of their harness. Carrying blankets and the provision bag and a tarp from the wagon, he made his way back to the shelter.

"Hunter—Adam?" Linda's voice was shaky. "I should have helped."

He wrapped a blanket around her shoulders over her wet clothing. She was still shivering, and her skin was cold to his touch. Hunter's own teeth were chattering. He spread the tarp across the opening between the boulders and tied it into place, shutting out the rain and much of the wind. Then he dug in the provision pouch until he found a candle.

"We'll have to make a fire," he said.

"He might come back. Harvey."

He might be dead, Hunter thought, but he didn't believe it. And it didn't matter. "We need the warmth. I'll keep it small. You get those wet clothes off and wrap yourself in the blanket."

Hunter broke branches from the dead brush, splitting the smaller ones with his knife to expose the dry core. Within a couple of minutes orange flames were licking at the pyramid of wood. The wind made a good draft through the gaps between rock and canvas, but occasional gusts spilled smoke back into the shelter. Linda coughed hard and rackingly.

Hunter had been hunched over the fire, drawing in its warmth. He hadn't realized how tired he was. Now he turned toward Linda.

"Linda, are you all right?"

She knelt with her back to him, still coughing. Her wet clothing lay in a pile beside her, and her bare back glistened in the firelight. Hunter reached her in two long strides, swathed her in the blanket, half carried her to a place beside the fire. Then he moved to the rear of the shelter and stripped off his soaked shirt.

It took him longer than he'd expected. The shelter was low and cramped. His fingers fumbled awkwardly, and his mind kept slipping away into hazy dreams. Minutes passed before he was able to wrestle free of the clinging garments and cover his damp skin with a blanket. By that time he could feel warmth spreading through the shelter. As he crawled to the fire the smell of boiling coffee came to meet him. Rain still drummed on the wet canvas, but it seemed very far away.

"I filled the pot with rainwater," Linda said. She pulled the blanket close about her, shivering from remembered cold. "What happened? It's not even freezing, but I couldn't stop shaking."

"Seen it in Wyoming," Hunter said. "You get wet, get in the wind, take a chill. Nothing helps but dry clothes and a fire." Men die from it else, he thought. Forcing a smile, he nodded toward the shelter wall. "We're not the first to camp here."

The wall was covered with pictures pecked into the smooth rock—handprints, spirals and concentric circles, sticklike figures of a mountain sheep, a man, a humpbacked god playing a flute. In the dancing firelight they seemed to move.

"They're in caves all through these hills," Linda said. "The Utes say they're from the Old People, before the world was made." She turned her eyes from the wall and looked into his. "Why did Jack Harvey try to kill you?"

"I don't know."

"Are you lying to me?"

"No. If he knew who I was, he'd have reason, but I don't think he does."

"I see. And who are you?"

Hunter drew a long breath. "It's something you need to know," he said. "I'm a drunkard. I'm a man who failed his best friend when he needed me." He stopped for a second, then said, "And now I'm a man who'd steal a woman promised to someone else."

"I won't believe that!" Linda's eyes were very large. "None of it! But what about Jack Harvey?"

"His name's Al 'Red' Converse. He and another man killed my partner. I followed them to Texas and lost them. Took me a while to track them here. Now I've found them."

"Your partner? Were you an—an outlaw?"

"I'm a deputy marshal where I come from." Hunter shrugged. "Red has reason to kill me, but he doesn't know it yet. This thing tonight, and in the saloon, was something else."

"Something to do with Pine Valley?" Linda asked. "Does Uncle Morg know about this?"

"Yes. And Sheriff Vargas now. And you." He paused. "Linda, what I said about myself—it's all true. The part about stealing another man's woman, too." He looked at her, then down into the fire. "Even though I've no right—a man like me."

Showing white against the folds of the blanket, the curve of Linda's throat seemed delicate and vulnerable. But her shoulders were squared against the night, against anything she might face. "Hush," she said softly. "I'm no one's woman." She closed her eyes for a moment. "I'll have to speak with Perry. If I loved him, I couldn't be here with you—as we are."

"Linda—" Hunter began.

"No." She reached out and put her fingers over his lips. "We'll have to get back to Pine Valley, then find our way from there. But that's enough talk for tonight. I know now who you are—maybe better than you do."

"Linda," Hunter said again. He caught her hand and pressed her fingers to his lips. Then, knowing the wrongness of it, he reached out and gathered her to him.

A dozen hard miles from Dead Horse Canyon Jack Harvey reined in his mount and scowled at the clearing sky ahead of him. For several minutes he sat there cursing his luck, cursing the name of Adam Hunter. Having scorned his own need for fire and a rest, he rode northwest along a trail that would lead him to the government graze that separated Pine Valley and Circle Eight. He was giving up his chance to pick Hunter off the wagon seat when morning broke, but he'd made his decision and was satisfied with it. He wasn't much given to reflection.

Two hours before daylight he topped a ridge on the southern tip of the open range, the corner nearest Pine Valley. Below him was the roof of Avery's most remote line cabin. Grinning in his beard, Harvey spurred the tired horse in that direction.

A horse nickered greeting or warning when Harvey approached the corral. He ignored it and rode straight to the cabin door, making plenty of noise.

"Inside there," he called.

The door rattled, then slipped open a crack. Harvey sensed rather than saw the rifle barrel that angled his way.

"Who's there?"

"Word from Avery."

"Yeah? Who in hell are you? What word?"

"Trouble at headquarters. The Circle Eight's riding against us. All the men's to get in quick to be ready for them. I'm passing the word."

"I don't believe you."

"Suit yourself, but it's old man Avery's orders hisself." Harvey turned his horse and let it begin walking away. "I got to spread the word."

The door creaked open. "Hold on a minute." A sleepy cowhand stepped out onto the porch, his rifle held loosely in one hand. "Am I supposed to ride with you?"

"No." Harvey turned crosswise in the saddle, looking back over his left shoulder. His right hand shielded by his body, he lifted his six-gun clear of its holster. "You ride straight in."

"Hell. All right, but it seems damned queer to me."

As the ranch hand, still muttering, turned to reenter the cabin, Harvey lifted the pistol and shot him three times in the back.

*　　*　　*

At first light Harvey lay in shelter along Circle Eight's boundary, his horse hidden in a defile behind him. Like a good hunter he dozed lightly until the morning breeze brought him the sound of a horse, one of Circle Eight's outriders sweeping for strays. Harvey waited, squinting along his rifle barrel, until the man was within forty yards. Then he shot him off his horse and put a second round into him as he lay. His work done, he rode away toward Sublette City.

Two hours into the morning Harvey reined in his horse in a stand of pines above town. He looked down on the shingled roofs for a time, then sat down with his back against a tree and began to roll himself a cigarette.

"You're late," a voice beside him said.

Harvey started violently, dropping paper and tobacco as he reached for his pistol. Halfway along he checked himself.

"Sid, you're going to get shot someday, sneaking around like a damn Apache."

"Not by you." Sid Tate stepped up beside him, tense and unsmiling. "Did you get it done?"

"Damn right I got it done! Handled it myself so's nobody knows but us."

"I heard it rained along the way from Antonito last night."

"Couldn't nobody have told you that."

"You did, seeing's you look like a drowned rat. Maybe you didn't think I'd hear Marvin Little and the Todd boys got themselves killed down there, bracing Hunter."

Harvey licked his lips. "I tried to stop them, Sid, but they were mean mad about Hunter killing Horse Webb." He spread his hands. "Nothing would do them but to try him."

"Don't lie to me, Red." Tate's voice was cold.

"You're not smart enough. If I didn't need you, I'd kill you where you sit."

"Listen!" Harvey started to rise.

Instantly a small, shiny pistol appeared in Tate's hand. The red-bearded man sank back, forcing a grin.

"No call for that, Sid," he said. "We're partners, remember?"

"You remember this: I need Hunter alive for now, and I'll see he's taken care of when I'm finished. If anything happens to him meanwhile, I'll mark it to your credit." The pistol vanished as quickly as it had come. For the first time Tate smiled. "In blood."

Chapter 15

Abel Carson spent much more time in careful thought than anyone might have judged from his fixed facial expression or his animal-instinct reactions. His apparent quickness was usually the result of long-calculated deliberation—tangling with Hunter had been an exception, and a costly one. His crew believed his fight with Edge Pardee grew directly from the confrontation in the Aces and Eights the day Pardee and Hunter had brought the body in. Carson and Pardee knew better; their quarrel was long-standing and would not be settled quickly.

Not so long as he nuzzles up to Miss Barbara! Carson thought blackly. But that wasn't the main thing on his mind that morning, and he let it slip away for future consideration.

As was his habit, he had awakened early, feeling a simple satisfaction at being the first soul moving on the place. Fifteen minutes later he'd led his horse away from the Circle Eight headquarters, leaving behind the breakfast and the belly-warming coffee he usually enjoyed.

It had been in his mind for weeks that Circle Eight's real trouble lay outside Pine Valley. As with all his thoughts, his idea had circled in his head like a dog settling itself for a nap, and he'd mentioned it to no one. His suspicion centered finally on the stretch of badlands where Circle Eight bounded the government graze. That was where he'd sent Ralph Mintner to have a look around, and that was where he was headed today.

Carson didn't hear the shots that killed Mintner, but he found the slain outrider before all the warmth had seeped from the body. He knelt beside the dead man, considering. He had liked and trusted Mintner, but he allowed himself no anger. Instead he mumbled a halting prayer for the man's soul, then rose and caught Mintner's horse. Having tied the stiffening body across the saddle, he tore a page from his tally book, licked the stub of a pencil, and wrote in a flowing scrawl: *Ralph shot by stealth at govt graze Im tracking killer send help my trail A. Carson.* Tucking the note securely into Mintner's belt, he whacked the horse across the rump with his leather gloves and shouted him away toward the distant ranch headquarters. Then he settled in to make his word good.

Like his thinking, Carson's tracking was neither anxious nor hasty. In less than five minutes he found the spot where the bushwhacker had waited. He bent to pick up an empty cartridge case. The powder smell was fresh. He saw that it had not been fired in a pistol but in a rifle. The action had made bright little scratches along the sides of the tarnished brass. Carson considered, frowning because the shell didn't fit his picture of things. It was a .44-40, a common caliber. He'd been sure he would find Hunter somewhere at the core of things, but this shell hadn't come from Hunter's bear gun. Leaving the puzzle to turn over in his mind, he dropped the cartridge into his pocket and went to find where the murderer had left his horse.

Two hours of dogged riding brought Abel Carson within distant sight of the stand of pines that leaned along the crest above Sublette City. He reined in and considered the trees, rubbing his chin. So far he had kept to the faint traces left by the killer's horse. He had moved cautiously, ever watchful of the rocks and ridges around him. Now he left the tracks and swung wide to the north out of rifle range to come at the woods from better cover.

Still a quarter mile from the trees, he left his horse to go in on foot. After some hesitation he pulled his rifle from its scabbard and took it along. Almost alone among the cowhands of that range, he carried a single-shot Remington rolling block. He'd always figured that a real man shouldn't need more than one shot to bring down a buck. He felt the same about bringing down a bushwhacker.

Soon he saw a horse, almost hidden by the trees, and then, in the deeper shadow, a man. He slowed his advance, moving ever more cautiously. He was close enough to recognize Jack Harvey, almost close enough for a rush, when the second man moved.

Carson sank into the deep grass, silent and still as a grizzly gone to cover. He hadn't seen Harvey's companion at all, and that shook him. Too, he was disappointed that neither of them was Hunter, but that might clear itself up. He'd come so close that now he could hear snatches of what they were saying. He thought they were quarreling.

"I tried to stop them, Sid," Harvey whined. "But they were mean mad about Hunter killing Horse Webb. Nothing would do them but to try him."

"Don't lie to me, Red. You're not smart enough. If I didn't need you, I'd kill you where you sit."

"Listen!"

Carson didn't understand. He knew both these men, but they were calling each other by names he'd never heard. He tensed as the pistol came into sight.

"I need Hunter alive for now," the one called Sid was saying, "I'll see he's taken care of when I'm finished. If anything happens to him meantime, I'll mark it to your credit. In blood."

"I told you, Sid. We're friends. Ain't I done what you said so far?"

"One more thing: You get with Kelly and tell him what to do. Once Avery's—" He broke off abruptly, reaching for the little gun again. "Somebody's coming."

Almost at the same moment Carson had sensed the rider approaching. He recognized horse and man immediately, saw that the cowhand was riding into a trap. Without thought he sprang up, leveling the rifle at the men under the trees.

"Stand where you are, both of you! Bob, look out, they're killers!"

Caught just as he'd started to dismount, Bob Golightly stared in frozen surprise at the men who'd been paying him, and at Abel Carson and his rifle. It took Carson only a moment to realize what that look meant, to understand why Golightly was so far from the ranch, to see how Circle Eight's enemies had gotten their information, to understand why even a real man might be wise to carry a magazine rifle.

"By Godfrey, you're one of them!"

Bob Golightly moved at last, grabbing for his pistol as Carson swung toward him. The Remington's single bullet took him cleanly out of the saddle, but Abel Carson didn't wait to see him fall. As he wheeled on the men beneath the trees he knew and didn't care that he'd never have time to reload. He'd never had much use for shooting, but he knew how to use his hands, and he meant to use them on Ralph Mintner's killers. His rifle held high, he bolted across the space between and fell upon them like Samson with his jawbone.

The afternoon shadows were long on the trail by the time Hunter and Linda Pardee crossed the last high saddle in the hills and started down into Pine Valley. They had made poor time because of the muddy roads and because Hunter insisted on riding ahead to scout the way, leaving the wagon to Linda until they were out of the canyons. Then, for a while, there was time to talk.

Before they were well inside the ranch boundary Morgan Avery's outriders had reported their return and Tom Banner's absence. When they rattled into the wagon yard at headquarters Avery and a half dozen armed men met them.

"Good to see you're safe," Avery said gruffly. "There's trouble. Jack Owen's been killed at Lone Mountain camp. I've sent word to Tobreen."

"Trouble in Antonito, too," Hunter said. With frequent additions from Linda he recounted the gunfight and its aftermath. "I didn't know the men," he finished, "but it's plain they were after Tom and me."

"Circle Eight?"

"They didn't say so. Nor had I seen them there." He glanced around at the circle of grim cowhands, then back to Avery. "Maybe we could talk in private."

"Kelly! Look after the wagon and Hunter's horse. Come inside, the two of you."

Morgan Avery led Hunter and Linda into the house. The rancher's face was as granite-calm as ever, but inside he was heartsick. He'd hoped the wire would be an answer, a barrier between Pine Valley and Circle Eight that would head off trouble for a time. But now the killing had started in earnest, and he feared he was too late to stop it.

Once inside Avery waved Hunter toward the study.

"You go along, Hunter. You know the way. Ask Anna to fix us some coffee." A quick, grim smile tugged his mouth. "We'll need the cups. I want a word with missy here."

"Uncle Morg, don't shut me out of this," Linda said quickly. "Adam—Mr. Hunter—has told me everything. And I'm worried about the wire." She lifted her head, her chin set. "Pine Valley's my home, too. If it's come to a fight—"

Avery shook his head. "I ain't meaning to cut you out, Linda," he said. "You're a woman grown, with as much of a stake in the ranch as me or Edge. But you're dead beat, and there's nothing you can do right now.

Clean up and get some rest. Edge will be back for supper. We'll talk then—honor bright."

Linda smiled at their old childhood promise. "Honor bright." She put out a hand to Avery. "After supper, then."

"I'll walk you a way," Avery said. "If you don't mind, that is."

They walked along the hallway to the door of the courtyard, neither speaking. Avery could see that Linda had something on her mind, something she hadn't mentioned yet. In the cool shade of the portico roof she turned and faced him.

"Uncle Morg—?"

"What is it, missy?"

"I can't—" She stopped, then shrugged and gave a quick, helpless shake of her head. "No. It can wait until after supper. I have to think something through first." She leaned to brush his cheek with a kiss. "Thanks—for everything."

Morgan Avery's throat tightened with the deep, helpless love he had felt for her ever since she'd been a freckle-faced yearling with a missing tooth. Her mother's daughter, he thought automatically, but it was more than that. She couldn't have been more his—nor Edge, either—if they'd been born of his own seed. He thought of trying to say so, but instead he put out one brown hand and touched her hair.

"Get along with you, missy," he growled. "You've earned your keep, same as Edge. No call to thank me."

She bent her head under his touch, then straightened. "I'll have to see Perry, too," she said. "There's something I have to tell him."

She smiled suddenly, with such a light in her eyes that he felt his heart clench like a fist, and then she turned away and ran lightly down the open portico. He stood watching, indifferent to the passing seconds.

Lord, I ain't ever bothered you much, he thought, but I'd take it kindly if you'd see after her—and the man she favors, too. Then he shook his head impatiently, turned away, and went to find Hunter.

Hunter was waiting in the study, sipping from a mug of steaming coffee. Another mug awaited Avery on the desk. The rancher swallowed a mouthful of coffee hot enough to take the skin off, then opened the desk drawer and took out the whiskey bottle, offering it first to his guest.

"I reckon not."

"What was it you didn't want to say outside?" the rancher asked. "Do you know more about those men that jumped you?"

Hunter shook his head. "Only guesses. Main thing is, the other side's started to move. However much I want to find my other man, I don't think we can afford to wait." He was silent a moment. "I've brought trouble on you—and on Miss Linda."

Over the rim of the cup Avery studied him sharply. "Linda's a woman grown," he said. "And the trouble's not of your making. Edge is out now with a couple of hands, bringing in the last of the line riders. By nightfall we'll be forted up and ready for anything. What then?"

"Then I'll—" Hunter broke off, staring at the window behind Avery. "I believe I'll need a drop of that whiskey after all," he said.

He rose as Avery reached for the bottle. With a nod he directed the rancher's attention to the window, where the shadow of a man's hat brim showed clearly on the shade. Avery got painfully to his feet and started for the door.

"Maybe you're right," he said. "Let me ponder that for a minute."

The two of them walked silently out of the office and around to the side door. By the time they got there the yard outside the office was deserted. Hunter led the way across to the barn where his gray stood at the feed trough, still saddled.

"Kelly!" Avery growled. "Even left the horses standing tight cinched."

They saddled Avery's horse and rode out the far end of the barn, Hunter keeping an eye out for anyone following. A ten-minute trot took them to a wide green pasture hidden from the house by a fold of ground. Cattle grazed at random, drifting slowly away as the riders approached. Avery reined his horse back to a walk and looked at Hunter.

"All right. Guess his ears ain't long enough to hear us now. What's your intentions?"

"I'm going straight after Converse—Jack Harvey, that is. Would have done so sooner had I been alone."

Avery eyed him narrowly. "Before you was hell-bent to use Harvey to get your other man. What changed your thinking?"

"He did." Unconsciously Hunter clenched the fist holding his reins. "His first shot last night could have killed Miss Linda as easily as me. I won't take that risk again."

"And the other man—this Tate?"

Hunter shrugged. "I'll deal with him somehow. We know he's a newcomer to the basin. Maybe I'll start from there." He almost grinned. "Or maybe Red will tell me."

"Hm!" Avery rubbed a hand across his mouth. "Well, I'll tell a half dozen men to ride with you. Harvey's got some real hardcases up there on his place."

"Appreciate the offer," Hunter began, "but—"

He stopped because Avery wasn't listening. The rancher was standing in his stirrups, shading his eyes as he peered toward the next ridge. "Look there," he said, pointing.

Silhouetted on the ridge line Hunter saw a horse with a familiar shape on his back. "It's Edge," he said. A moment later animal and rider were out of sight behind the ridge.

"Riding alone, too, against orders," Avery growled.

167

"And this ain't the first time. Hunter, that boy's up to something."

Hunter stared at him. "You don't think he's mixed up with Harvey, surely? I'd bet my life on him."

"I don't know what it is, but we better find out. You're younger, Hunter. Ride after him. Trail him down."

"But I don't question him."

"Keep him out of trouble, then." Avery snorted. "Seems like that's mostly what you've done anyway."

"What about you?"

Avery reined his horse around, drawing his rifle from its boot. "I'll head back in." Seeing Hunter's hesitation, he barked, "Boy, I been riding this range for thirty years and more! Go!"

Hunter took his horse north across the pasture at a gallop. From the top of the ridge he worked his way down a ravine, slowing his pace on the rocky soil to deaden the sound of his approach. Five minutes later he saw Edge Pardee's mount quietly cropping grass. He moved up slowly until he found Pardee himself, fifty yards farther along. The blond foreman stood beside a strong black pony, looking up into the face of Barbara Watkins.

The two seemed locked in serious conversation, the woman leaning down to speak with urgency. After a moment Pardee reached up and helped her out of the saddle. He folded her into a tight embrace, and she put up her face for his kiss.

Hunter didn't take any pleasure in spying on lovers, but this meeting explained a couple of things about Pine Valley and Circle Eight. He wondered if the pair recognized the danger of their position now that the shooting had started.

As he watched, uncertain whether to remain or withdraw, Pardee took the yellow scarf from around his own neck and tied it loosely about Barbara's throat. They kissed again, and Hunter began urging his horse back along the ravine. Rocks slid off the top and spilled down at his feet.

"Who's there?" he said.

He whispered the challenge, but his hand went to his pistol. A smothered giggle answered him, and then a small hand waved at him from the edge of the ravine.

"Annie Laurie! What are you—"

"Sh! They'll hear." She grinned boyishly at Hunter. "Told you I knew who Barbara was sweet on."

"Listen—"

Hunter's voice died in the deep, distant boom of a rifle from somewhere back the way he'd come. The rolling echoes didn't hide the flat stuttering sound of the bullet going home.

"Avery!"

Hunter didn't realize he'd spoken. Careless now of noise, he reined the horse around, then kicked it into a gallop. Annie Laurie shouted something, but he didn't hear. He was cursing himself savagely for disobeying his instinct and leaving the rancher alone. That was when he remembered the heavy round roar of the rifle, his rifle!

Bending low in the saddle, he reached for his scabbard. Instead of the familiar weight of the eighty-six he felt a shorter, lighter weapon, a .44-40 saddle gun. With a sudden sickness in his belly he spurred onward.

Halfway across the pasture Avery's horse stood riderless. Other men were coming from the direction of the ranch, but Hunter reached the spot first. As he leapt from the saddle the position of the rancher's body told him his haste was in vain. The bullet had caught Avery behind the shoulder and passed through, taking parts of three ribs and a quart of lungs with it.

"God *damn* a bushwhacker!" Hunter murmured as he knelt beside the body.

The others were there by then, crowding around, their faces slack with disbelief. Hunter scanned the ridge for any trace of the rifleman, then caught Billy Jackson's arm.

"Go back for a wagon," he said. "And head Miss Linda off. Make her stay with Anna until we're done."

"Who're you to be giving orders? Where's Edge?" somebody asked truculently, but Jackson went without protest. Before he reached the saddle Edge Pardee tore down to the group of men, his face filled with grim understanding even before he saw Avery's body.

"Where'd it come from?" he demanded.

"Back up that ridge you came over." That was Tag Kelly. "Only more off to the right. About where Hunter was."

"You bastard!" Hunter lunged for him, understanding everything. He landed one blow, but then half a dozen men were holding him. Given strength by his fury, he shook them off. "It was you!"

"My rifle's right here, mister," Kelly said coldly. He dabbed at the cut on his cheekbone where Hunter's fist had marked him. "Where's yours?"

"Look what the bullet done," somebody else muttered. "Just like that gunman Hunter shot."

Pardee was staring at him, his eyes filled with pain and doubt. "Hunter?" he said. "Hunter, I don't believe this of you." He put out his hand. "But I guess I better hold your six-gun until we sort it out."

Hunter hesitated. He'd liked Avery after a very brief acquaintance, and some of these men had worked for him for years. They might just hang him while they were sorting things out, whatever Pardee thought.

"I don't believe so," he said, but they were already upon him, angry hands striking him down and ripping his gun from its holster.

Chapter 16

Linda Pardee was unpacking her things when she heard the buggy approaching from the direction of the road. At first she was scarcely conscious of the sound. She had dawdled over the unpacking, studying each article carefully before putting it away or laying it aside to be washed. It was something to occupy her hands, to keep her from pacing or fretting until she could talk seriously with her uncle and brother.

Her mind had plenty to occupy it. The wire and the looming range war were, she knew, far and away the most important problems; but her thoughts kept returning unbidden to the question of her own behavior. She had been caught, tumbled headlong in an emotional flash flood she'd seemed helpless to escape.

She thought it had started with her half-innocent interest in Hunter, itself a reaction to her fear that she'd made a mistake in accepting Perry's proposal. Then had come the bloody horror of the saloon, the sleepless night beside Tom Banner's cot, the vision of Pine Valley fenced and choked with barbed wire, the ambush at Dead Horse Canyon, the storm—a trickle growing to a torrent, a woman she could hardly recognize as herself clinging fiercely to Adam Hunter while firelight made the carved figures dance and rain drummed on the canvas tarp. Looking back, the whole thing seemed a dream, though she had reason to know it was not.

Her hands were clenched on the bloodstained green dress. With conscious effort she relaxed them and let it fall to the floor. In Hunter's reassuring presence, through the long night with him and the long ride up the canyon, she had felt neither doubt nor fear. Now, surrounded by the familiar things of her life, she was reminded again how little she knew about him. She was finding she knew almost as little about herself.

I promised to marry Perry, she thought. She pushed the pile of clothing aside and sat down on her bed. I've betrayed him. Is that how I am, really? Is that what Adam thinks? *If* he's telling the truth about who he is and what he feels. And what will I tell—

"Mr. Bonham."

"What?" Linda sprang to her feet, her hand at her lips. "Oh, Anna! What—"

The cook stood in the open doorway of the room, surprise and concern in her face. Linda caught a deep breath and forced calm into her voice.

"I'm sorry, Anna. I was—thinking. What did you say?"

"Mr. Bonham. In the parlor he would see you."

"Thank you, Anna. Please tell Mr. Bonham I'll be in presently."

With a feeling of relief Linda sat down at the dressing table and began to brush her hair. She'd been dreading her talk with Perry Bonham, but the event could hardly be worse than the waiting. That's how Edge must feel now, or Hunter, she thought. No more waiting. For a second she almost smiled as she rose and went toward the parlor.

Perry Bonham heard her footsteps in the hall and met her at the door, catching her up in an embrace. She turned her face away when he would have kissed her, then stood quietly until he relaxed his hold.

"Tobreen told me about it—about the fight," he said. He took her hand, and she let him lead her to the sofa.

172

"The sheriff telegraphed. It must have been terrible for you. Is Tom all right?"

"Yes. Yes, it was, and yes, he is—or he will be."

Bonham clenched his fists. "Damn Hunter for exposing you to something like that. He'll hear from me."

"It wasn't his fault."

"Wasn't it?" Bonham asked. "Why would you want to take up for a stranger? For a gunhand?" Then he sank down beside her. Leaning forward intently, he clasped her hands between both of his. "I see," he said. "You were alone with him, weren't you? Last night, on the trail."

"Yes." She felt a vast relief at the word. "Perry—"

"Where?"

"Dead Horse Canyon. We—" She stopped. To put the moment off a little longer she said, "We'd hardly arrived when Jack Harvey fired on him—on us—from ambush."

"What?"

His reaction startled her. He jumped to his feet, his fists balled, his face flushing dangerously.

"Perry—I've never seen you so angry. What—"

"Of course I'm angry. He might have killed you!" He came back to her on the sofa. "You're sure it was Jack Harvey?" he asked. "The man from the Box H? Why could he possibly want to shoot Hunter?"

She started to answer, then hesitated again. She'd always been honest with him—until last night—but Hunter, too, had trusted her. "I don't know," she said finally. "But I'm sure. I saw him clearly in the lightning."

"Have you told Tobreen?"

"Not yet. Adam—Mr. Hunter—said he'd handle it."

"Hunter." Bonham clenched his fist again. Then his face changed, and he looked at her again. "You don't understand men like him, Linda. You trust too much."

"Perhaps I do." Linda looked at him, not sure how

to begin. With the feeling of diving into cold water she said, "Then there was a—a sort of cave. In the canyon. We went in to get out of the rain. I was so cold. And we built a fire. And—I—Perry, I can't marry you."

Outside, somewhere in the distance, a heavy rifle boomed. Linda jumped, but Bonham remained icily motionless, as if he hadn't even heard it.

"What was that?" she cried, relieved at the interruption.

"He's compromised you."

"What?" She looked at Perry Bonham. "Has he?" Linda mused. She felt a wild urge to laugh. She bit her lip. If she started, she feared she might not want to stop. "Is that what it's called?"

"You were tired. Overwrought. He took advantage."

"No."

Bonham moved from the sofa suddenly, dropping to one knee in front of her. Again he clasped her hands. His eyes holding hers, he said, "Linda, you don't realize what you've done—what you're doing. You don't know this man." When she started to protest he shook his head and went on urgently. "I know his kind, Linda. He's like Harvey, like the rest of them. He's a killer, an outlaw."

"No! He's a—"

"He's what?"

"Nothing." For a moment Linda saw Hunter's face, set and cold as it had been in the saloon, the rifle in his hands like a killing tool. Through her mind a hog ran squealing.

"He's not like that," she said. "He's helped us. He saved Edge, and Tom Banner. And me."

"Oh, yes! He certainly *saved you,* didn't he? He helped because it suited his purpose. How do you know what else he would—" He broke off. "Someone's coming." Then his voice was drummed out by the noise outside.

Getting to his feet, Bonham pulled her up, too.

"Linda, believe me, I'll never speak of this again. Don't make any decision now. You're infatuated with Hunter, but you'll learn what he's really like!"

A horse, ridden to a lather, clattered into the yard. In the sound of its hooves was an urgency they couldn't miss. Moments later angry voices sounded above the noise of more riders and the creak and rattle of wagon gear.

"Perry, I—" Linda began. But the words choked her, and she shook her head helplessly. "What's wrong out there?"

"I'll see." He stepped into the hallway and opened the front door, Linda following. "You, Dub Axtel," he called. "What's the commotion for?"

"It's that son of a bitch Hunter." Axtel's voice was thick with rage and sorrow. "He's killed Mr. Avery!" Then his face changed. "My God, Miss Linda, I didn't see you there."

Linda didn't hear the rest. Instead, over and over again, she heard his cry: *He's killed Mr. Avery!* She tried to speak, but the best she could manage was a wordless sound of denial. *You don't know this man. You trust too much.* She turned, reached out blindly for Perry Bonham. She saw that the floor was rising to meet her, and then she knew only a merciful darkness.

His mouth bleeding and his hands pinioned, Hunter stood quietly in the grasp of Avery's cowhands. He understood they were on the very brink of killing him outright, that any struggle might decide them. Then Edge Pardee shoved his way through to plant himself in front of Hunter.

"Hold him," Pardee grated. His round face wore an expression Hunter had never imagined there, a mixture of sorrow and anger that made him look a different man. "Just hold him. The wagon's coming."

A minute later a light spring wagon drew up, driven by Billy Jackson. Pardee and two others lifted Avery into the bed as gently as if he were a sick child, then covered the body with a blanket. The men holding Hunter wrestled him onto the seat, one standing behind him with a gun pressed to his neck as Jackson turned the wagon back toward headquarters. Halfway along they were met by Tag Kelly, who had gone off on a mission of his own. He returned riding hard, Hunter's rifle held in his upraised hand.

Jackson drew the wagon up in the yard before the front door. The other riders dismounted and clustered around while more men gathered from bunkhouse and barn. Hunter saw Linda on the porch, standing pale and motionless in Perry Bonham's arms. Her eyes touched his, but they were wide and vacant with shock. He didn't think she even saw him. When he made an involuntary move toward her the hand on his shoulder clamped more tightly and the gun's muzzle ground viciously into his flesh. A moment later Bonham turned Linda gently and led her inside.

Her departure was like a signal that loosed angry tongues. Tag Kelly was the first to speak.

"Hang him, that's what I say." He waved Hunter's rifle again, and the silver disk glinted in the sun. "No! No, I know what. Let's shoot the murdering bastard with his own rifle."

"Wait a minute!" Billy Jackson cried. He stopped, abashed, when all eyes turned his way, but then he swallowed and went on. "Now wait," he said, his voice gaining strength as he spoke. "I ain't so sure of this. Hunter saved Edge's life, and Tom Banner's, too. We got Miss Linda's word for that."

"Saved his own at the saloon," another cowhand said. "We don't know Miss Linda saw it right—she's just a woman. Might be Hunter shot Tom his own self."

"Billy's right," Dub Axtel put in. "Can't kill a man on what we think. We better send for Tobreen, have a trial, regular-like."

"There's no time," Tag Kelly cried. "Listen, he's

working for Watkins, plain as balls on a bull. We'll be standing here arguing it, like as not, when Circle Eight rides in and shoots us down." He levered a shell into Hunter's Winchester. "Stand clear, Will. I'll do it myself."

He started to level the rifle, but then Edge Pardee spurred his horse between Kelly and the wagon, shouldering the cowhand's mount aside.

"That'll do," he said. He held out his hand. "Give me the rifle, Tag."

Reluctantly Kelly handed it over. Pardee dismounted and stepped to face Hunter. "Get him down."

A dozen men jostled to drag Hunter off the seat. He landed hard on hands and knees and pushed himself up. As he came to his feet Pardee backhanded him hard across the mouth.

"Who *are* you working for?" he demanded. "Why in hell did you do this, and him treating you like you was a son?"

Hunter dabbed at his mouth with the back of his hand. "The neckcloth was yellow," he said quietly.

"What's that?"

"It'll come to you."

Pardee stepped into him and swung the rifle. The iron-shod butt caught Hunter at the arch of the ribs, and he went to his knees, fighting to breathe. Pardee clubbed him down.

"Won't matter much to you," he said. He looked at the men in the yard. "Dub, you're in charge. Take care of Mr. Avery. Help Bonham with him. Then be sure everybody's rounded up and ready to ride when I say." He raised his voice. "Not until then, understand?"

"You're the boss," Axtel said grimly. He nodded toward Hunter, on hands and knees again and shaking his head dazedly. "How about him?"

"Couple of you get him on a horse." He hefted the rifle. "Family business now. I'll attend to it."

He mounted and took the reins of Hunter's horse

close by the bit. Then he rode through the crowd and out toward the open range while they watched as silently as a jury.

Earlier, when the shot had come and Pardee left her at a gallop, Barbara Allen Watkins lingered a moment, stroking the yellow scarf at her throat. Then the brightness faded from her eyes, and she looked around in sudden uneasiness. Mounting her horse, she struck a trot away toward the Circle Eight boundary. Presently she reached a trail and set a faster pace so as to reach home before dark; that way she could more easily explain her absence. There was only one person on Circle Eight whom she could not easily deceive, and she already dreaded the scrutiny of Abel Carson.

That thought brought a cold fear into the pit of her stomach. After her minutes with Pardee she'd actually forgotten for a time that Carson was missing and Ralph Mintner dead. Edge had sworn to her that he knew nothing of Mintner's death and had told her about the murder of Jack Owen that same morning. After that they'd had only moments, time for a desperate kiss or two before the echoing shot had parted them.

Will it always be this way? she wondered. Will the sound of guns always be between us?

An hour's steady riding brought her near home, and she slowed her pace so as not to ride in with her horse lathered. As it turned out, she needn't have worried. No one was in sight around the ranch or its outbuildings, although angry voices rose from the bunkhouse. Hearing them, she left her mount unattended and stepped onto the bunkhouse porch.

"—telling you it's Hunter! Avery hired him for a killer, and he's doing his job! And the law ain't done a thing about it, so we got to handle it ourselves. I say we go against that Pine Valley bunch before they get us all!"

She didn't recognize the speaker. One of the new

men, probably, hired since the trouble began. She waited for her father's calm tones or Abel's bellowed command to silence the talk. Instead there was a confused clamor, mingled agreement and dissent. The first voice rose again.

" 'Not sure,' hell! We saw what Hunter did to Abel right here in the barn. Stands to reason he'd be the one to kill him!"

For a moment she simply didn't understand the words. When the meaning reached her Barbara Watkins brought clenched hands to her mouth, fighting the urge to break inside and start screaming at the men. *It isn't true! It's not! It can't be!* Turning, she raced across the courtyard and into the house. She had to find her father. He would tell her the truth.

Ellis Watkins was slumped in a chair in the big living room, staring into the cold fireplace. Barbara rushed to him.

"Daddy!" Then she was kneeling beside him, throwing her arms around him for comfort as she'd done when she was frightened as a child. "I'm so glad you're all right. What they're saying outside—about Abel—"

His hands on her shoulders, he pushed her away. "Where were you?" he asked.

She stared at him. His eyes were bloodshot, his voice harsh. He looked tired, older than she'd ever seen him.

"I—riding," she said. "Is Abel—"

"You're lying."

"Ellis."

Her mother's voice was crisp as always, still holding a trace of its New England accent. Barbara looked toward the stairs. Irene Watkins was descending slowly, holding the rail. Her dress was primly starched, and the rouge on her faded cheeks showed bravely as a flag. "Don't speak so to our daughter. Barbara, dear, wherever have you been?"

"Out running after that Pine Valley trash, likely," Watkins said. "While their pet killer was murdering

179

Abel." He shook Barbara hard. "Where were you? Tell the truth."

"She is telling the truth." None of them had heard the door open. Annie Laurie came over to stand beside Barbara, touching her lightly on the shoulder. "I was with her. We rode out to the overlook by Sublette's ridge." She smiled innocently. "Didn't we, Barbara?"

Barbara nodded, mystified by her younger sister's sudden interest. Before her father could speak again Irene Watkins's cool voice interposed.

"Ellis, is it your intention to sit idly by while newcomers rouse your riders to fury against Morgan Avery?"

"My God," Watkins said. "Will you speak his name in this house even now?"

"His name is not at issue."

"It ought to choke you."

"Nor is your belief about my past conduct an issue. You have a responsibility to those men—and to your daughters."

"Daddy," Barbara said, "did you send someone to Pine Valley? Did one of our men kill Jack Owen?"

"What?" Watkins stared at her.

"Jack Owen was murdered this morning at Lone Mountain. Did you—did we—have it done?"

"How do you know that?"

"Did we?"

"No! Not by my order, nor any man's on this ranch. What do you think of me?" His voice hardened. "And where did you hear about it? *Riding?*"

She gave back a little at the scorn in his tone, but she answered evenly. "That is my affair."

"My God," he said again. He looked at her, then at each of the others in turn. Then he put his face down and covered it with his hands. "Three of you," he said. "And one no better than the others."

Chapter 17

Ed Tobreen was tired. Over the years he'd found his badge getting heavier and heavier. Today its weight was so great he could barely lift it. Since midmorning, when an excited Circle Eight cowhand had summoned him, he had ridden more than thirty miles on three different horses. Now the sun was touching the tops of the western mountains, and Tobreen was nearing the end of a job he did not relish.

Within sight of the Pine Valley buildings he paused to have his look at the men gathered in the yard. The man he wanted wasn't in sight. Tobreen checked the loads in the long shotgun he carried, then angled in through the trees to keep the barn between himself and the men as long as possible. Heads turned, and a few hands hovered nervously near sidearms as he rode in. He paused at the edge of the yard and faced them all.

"I'm here for Hunter," he said.

They looked at one another, kicked the ground, fiddled with bits of rope or baling wire. One or two turned away as though returning to some job they'd left for a moment. None wanted to meet his eyes. He let the tension stretch tight, and finally it pulled Dub Axtel forward.

"He ain't here, nor ain't going to be."

"Where is he?"

Axtel studied the toes of his boots. "Don't know," he said.

"Mind if I look around?"

"Nope."

"Then I guess I don't need to. I'd better see Mr. Avery."

"Can't." For the first time Axtel really looked at him. Grief and anger showed in the cowhand's lined face. "He's murdered. Jack Owen, too, this morning."

"Lord God," Tobreen murmured, feeling the badge grow heavier still. Two murders, maybe three on Circle Eight, and now this. He'd known Morgan Avery for a dozen years, and he was diminished by Avery's death, but nothing showed in his face as he said, "Pardee, then. Where's Edge?"

"Don't know."

A lean gray-suited man had come out onto the porch. Tobreen shifted his eyes to him.

"Perry? What do you know about this?"

"It's an ugly business, Constable. I was visiting Miss Pardee when they brought Mr. Avery in. Shot from ambush, I'd say."

"Could I speak with Miss Linda?"

Bonham shook his head. "She's in no shape to talk, Ed," he said. "We've sent for the doctor."

"I see." Tobreen looked around him. "Anybody got anything to add?" Into the expected silence he said, "Hunter's wanted for murder. I have a warrant for him. If you're smart, you won't try to shield him." He reined his horse around. "I'll be back when Pardee's here."

He rode out, feeling their eyes follow him until he was screened again by the trees along the road. A hundred yards farther along a low whistle from a shallow gully stopped him. He swung the barrels of the shotgun that way.

"Who's there?"

"It's me, Billy Jackson."

"Billy?" Tobreen stared at the young cowhand scrambling up to the roadside. "What the mischief—"

"You gotta hurry, Constable!" Jackson pointed wildly toward the hills. "It's Edge. He's got Hunter, and they all think he shot Mr. Avery, but I bet he didn't because it was him saved Tom's life in the saloon, Miss Linda said, but he's gonna shoot him anyway, so I slipped off to tell you, and you gotta stop him!"

"Whoa, Billy! Who's going to shoot who?"

"Edge! Hunter!" Billy drew a deep breath and almost physically held himself back. "Edge thinks Hunter shot Mr. Avery. He took him up the ridge maybe twenty minutes ago. He's going to kill him with his own—"

He let his voice trail off because Tobreen was no longer there to listen. The weight on him forgotten, the constable was spurring up the slope, driving his tired horse desperately toward the distant ridge line.

As Pardee led the gray up the gentle slope toward the trees Hunter began slowly to gather his wits again. His head ached viciously, and pain stabbed through his chest each time he breathed, but he didn't think he'd suffered any permanent damage. Unless he could change Pardee's mind, though, it wouldn't matter how bad he was hurt. As soon as Hunter figured he could manage, he raised his head and focused on the Pine Valley foreman.

"You want to listen to me a minute before you shoot me?"

Pardee turned his head, shifting Hunter's Winchester at the same time so that its muzzle centered more directly on Hunter's belly.

"I imagine not," he said. There was no trace of his usual humor in his eyes or the grim set of his mouth. "I've done harm enough to Pine Valley on account of listening to you."

"The scarf was yellow," Hunter said again.

Pardee rocked the rifle's hammer back. "You don't

need leading," he said. "Ride ahead up the slope. You want to do me a favor, try and run for it."

They rode in silence for a hundred yards. Then Pardee said, "What scarf?"

Hunter nodded toward the ridge line. "Up over the crest, a little to the left, there's a ravine. Be a good place for what you have in mind."

"Yeah?" Pardee frowned a little and motioned with the rifle barrel. "All right. You show me where it is."

From the top of the ridge Hunter led them down into the ravine he'd followed before. Pardee seemed content to follow. Hunter decided the foreman really was hoping he'd make a run for it. Instead he reined up where the ravine began to open out.

"You were right out there," he said, motioning toward the open space ahead. "You—talked—with a friend, and then you gave her the scarf. It was yellow."

"Light down."

"You tied it around her throat. That's when I started backing off. I—"

"What were you doing there? Spying?"

"Yep. I was in the valley with Mr. Avery. We saw you heading this way. He sent me to see what you were up to."

Pardee leaned on the saddlehorn and looked down at Hunter. The rifle didn't waver.

"That's your story, that my own uncle sent you to spy on me?"

Hunter thought about the sound of it. "Part of it."

"Nothing that says he sent you at all. Might be you were already up here—waiting for a shot at him."

"The point is I *was* here then. You left your horse there. You and Miss Watkins stood not five feet from that old dead tree. There'll be tracks." He turned and pointed toward the edge of the ravine. "Annie Laurie was right up there, watching me watch you. We were looking at each other when the shot was fired."

Pardee's round face registered blank surprise. "Annie Laurie? She wasn't nowhere around!"

"You mean you didn't see her. But she was there. She told me early on that her sister liked somebody that would cause her trouble if their pa found out."

"That little devil," Pardee said. Then he looked at Hunter, still suspicious. "Still doesn't prove anything. You know she's not here to ask."

Hunter nodded. "That's so. But it'll be pretty embarrassing if you ask her later and find out I'm telling the truth," he said. "Especially after you've already shot me. But this is the thing: I was here watching you not a minute before that shot. How long would it take a man to ride from here to the place Kelly says he found my rifle?"

Pardee stared at him a minute longer. Then he dismounted carefully, keeping the rifle ready. "Hell's teeth, I knew I shouldn't've took this on," he said. "You'd talk the horns off Satan himself, and his pitchfork, too."

"You could give the job to Tag Kelly. He'd like it just fine."

"I noticed he don't seem partial to you." Pardee jerked his head. "Walk over to the dead tree and have a seat. I might as well hear what else you've got to say—like how somebody got hold of *your* rifle while you and Annie were having tea up here."

"My fault, and I'll always regret it. The rifle was in its scabbard when I rode in with Miss Linda. Later it wasn't. Somebody swapped it for a .44 saddle gun while the gray was in the barn, and I never noticed until I needed it."

Pardee squatted on his heels and considered Hunter thoughtfully. "Wouldn't nobody with any brains at all believe that," he said. "Don't suppose you noticed who took the horses to the barn."

"Tag Kelly."

"Hell."

"Kelly works for Jack Harvey. I saw the two of them together, along with a Circle Eight rider I can't put a name to. They're out to set Pine Valley and Circle Eight at each other's throats—doing pretty well at it, too."

"Kelly—one of my men—working for—" Pardee stopped and shook his head. "Hell," he said again. "You might' near had me going. But old Jack ain't half smart enough to be lead bull in this stampede. I'd sooner believe it was you."

Hunter nodded. "Can't blame you for that. As it happens, you're right about Harvey. He does have somebody behind him doing the thinking." He shifted position a little, easing his back against the tree. "The other thing you need to know is why I'm here."

He'd told the story often enough by now that he was getting pretty good at it. He touched on the high points for Pardee, ending up with Jack Harvey's attempted ambush in Dead Horse Canyon.

"I knew Tate and Converse—that is, Harvey—were making their move," he finished. "I'd meant to go right after Harvey soon as I knew Linda was safe. Harvey moved first. He had somebody kill Owen, or killed him himself, then sent word for Kelly to do his part." Hunter spread his hands. "That's all of it."

Pardee frowned at him without speaking. Hunter shifted his position.

"Want me to stand up?"

"I want you to *shut* up." Pardee thrust the rifle's muzzle at him viciously. "Just hold still and keep quiet and give a man a chance to think." He glared at Hunter. "That night after Harvey shot at you—what's between you and Linda?"

"Nothing that's any of your business. But you might want a word with her before you kill me."

"Hell." Pardee let the Winchester droop until its barrel was pointed at the ground. "I guess next you'll be saying—"

"Edge! Edge Pardee!"

The shout from the direction of the ravine sent Pardee down on his face, twisting so the rifle pointed that way.

"It's Tobreen, Edge. You just stand easy. I've got a warrant for Hunter, so don't you go shooting him before I can arrest him."

"It's always something," Pardee muttered. He got to his feet, brushing at his chaps. "Hell, no need to scare a man to death, Ed," he yelled back. "I ain't about to shoot him. What do you think I am, crazy? Come on up here, and let's talk a spell."

"I can't hardly believe it," Pardee said. "Abel Carson. I can't picture him dead."

"Well, he is," Tobreen said. He sat back against the stump and drew a cigar from his vest pocket. "But not by Hunter here. If you were in the lower canyon with Miss Pardee at daybreak, you couldn't very well have been out shooting Ralph or Abel." He looked at Pardee. "Nor Jack Owen, either."

"Sorry to disappoint you," Hunter said.

Tobreen bit viciously at the end of the cigar and spat out a fragment of tobacco. "You're a damned unlikely lawman," he said. "Sheriff Vargas couldn't say everything in his telegram—things like that have a way of getting around—but I understand it better now. And I still don't like it."

"It's going to take all of us to straighten this out without a war," Hunter said. "Tobreen, you're the only one can handle down Ellis Watkins and his men."

"If I can do that," Tobreen growled.

"Edge, you get your men under control. We'll need them later to deal with Harvey and his gang. But watch out for Kelly."

"Kelly's my problem."

"That leaves me to see if I can smoke out Sid Tate before we pour it on them."

Tobreen stroked his mustache. "Good way to get yourself killed," he observed.

"Good as any."

Edge Pardee rose and stretched. "All this thinking makes me tired," he said. "Tell you what, Hunter, lend me back that big rifle for a minute.

"What I'm thinking is I'll fire a couple of shots, then tell Kelly and the rest that Hunter's dead. That might quiet Ellis Watkins right smart, too, to think you're dead. Ed, if you'll just move away from that stump . . ."

Tobreen scrambled out of the way. Lifting the rifle to his shoulder, Pardee sent one bullet into the dead wood, waited for the echoes to die out, then fired twice more.

"Kicks a little," he said, passing the gun back to Hunter. "I figure I can find who killed Uncle Morg by looking for a blue-bruised shoulder." He went to his horse. "Luck," he said, and he rode off into the gathering dark.

Tobreen waited a moment longer. "You're a marked man, Hunter," he said. "Likely any rider from either ranch will shoot you on sight."

"Cheerful thought! I'll be careful."

"Sure." Tobreen swung into the saddle again. "I'll deal with Ellis—but it's no job for an old man. Luck."

"Luck."

The two of them rode together in silence for a time. At the trail that connected the two ranches they parted, with Tobreen taking the fork that led to Circle Eight. Hunter worked his way across the broad meadows into the more broken, rocky ground that marked the edge of Jack Harvey's Box H ranch. After an hour he found a sheltered hollow alongside a narrow, cold stream and dismounted. He unsaddled and picketed the gray, wrapped himself in a blanket, and settled back to consider his plan.

Instead he found the face of Linda Pardee coming between him and the stars. His mind pictured her, first laughing in the sun, then in the firelit shadows of the cave, then with blank face and shocked, empty eyes as she'd been the last time he'd seen her. He wished he could be with her now to offer comfort instead of half-way into nowhere with a pair of killers ahead. Later, if there was a later, he'd make it up to her. Until then there was nothing he could do but wait.

Around midnight he rose and ate hardtack and beef jerky from his saddlebags, then washed his face in the stream. The moon was high enough to light him on his way, and soon he was mounted and back on the trail to the Box H. He was beginning to think his memory for Avery's map had betrayed him when he came to the rim of a shallow rounded valley. Below, protected by rocky cliffs that he could never descend in the dark, lay the house and barn and outbuildings of Harvey's ranch.

The ranch itself lay in a pleasant spot scooped from the heart of the timber. Although the house was only a two-room cabin, twenty or more horses milled in the corral beside the dilapidated barn. The barn itself bled lantern light from every seam. Hunter marked the place and a route he hoped would take him there and turned his horse that way.

In the end he tied the gray a short two hundred yards from the barn and made his way in on foot, his rifle ready. At the edge of the timber he halted again. A hundred feet of open ground separated him from his goal. He could see occasional movement through the gaps around the double doors and hear the distant sound of voices. The realization that Sid Tate might be inside at that moment almost took him out into the open, but he held back. A few seconds later he heard the scuffing of leaves not far from where he crouched.

"Gabe?" The voice was a hoarse whisper. "That you?"

Hunter slid a little deeper into cover as the man's silhouette suddenly loomed up across the stars. In the waiting silence he heard the ratcheting click of a revolver being cocked.

"All right, I know somebody's here," the voice said. "Come out of there, or I start shooting."

Hunter didn't move, didn't breathe. Thinking about it, he doubted the guard would start shooting unless he had a definite target. Red and his boys in the barn likely wouldn't appreciate a sentry who cried wolf very often.

Surely enough, the man moved past, one careful pace and then another. Hunter came to his feet. One long step took him clear of the bushes. Startled, the guard started to turn, opening his mouth to shout. His mouth stayed open, but all that came out was an agonized gasp as the steel butt plate of Hunter's rifle slammed into his back just above the kidney. He dropped to his knees, and Hunter leaned across him to take the six-gun from his paralyzed fingers.

"That's good," Hunter whispered, ramming the Winchester's muzzle against the man's back. "Now as soon as you can talk you're going to tell me where we can find Gabe."

Chapter 18

Tag Kelly waited until the bunkhouse lights were out. Certain that Edge Pardee was inside the big house, Kelly slipped from the tack shed and made his way to the barn. His horse was ready, and he had only to lead it out the far end, continuing across the open space until he was among the trees. He paused to watch his back-trail; then, satisfied he hadn't been followed, he mounted and rode away. After a half mile he spurred his horse into a gallop. Speed, at the moment, was more important than caution.

He waved aside the guards at the narrow entrance to the Box H and rode toward the barn, where he expected to find Jack Harvey and his hired hands. As he turned his horse into the corral he grinned in anticipation. He had lived long enough to know that most people cared only for the news they wanted to hear. And he had good news indeed.

Inside the barn lanterns lighted the broad inner runway, casting deep, shifting shadows into the loft and among the rafters of the roof. Kelly strode past a couple of poker games, a group gathered around a man with a harmonica, a few men stretched out to doze on the hay in open stalls. Jack Harvey sat toward the back at a table brought in from the ranch house. The table held a few bottles, a clutter of dirty tin cups, and a general litter of cigar and cigarette butts spilling over from lids and boxes onto the stained wood. Kelly reached for one of the bottles.

"That damned cactus juice again. Jack, can't you find some decent whiskey?"

He splashed tequila into a cup and started to lift it to his mouth. Jack Harvey's big hand closed on his wrist.

"You've took time enough getting here. Speak your lesson before you take a drink."

Kelly made an effort to shake free but managed only to spill the liquor. He let the cup fall and took a step back.

"I done my part. Avery's dead, and I had the Pine Valley boys mad enough to go bobbing for rattlesnakes."

"You *had* them ready, did you? Well, why ain't they out there?"

"Pardee. He's not ready to fight."

Jack Harvey got slowly to his feet, towering over the smaller Kelly. "Little man," he said, "I think you just been leading me on."

"I done my part," Kelly repeated sullenly. "I can't figure it out. Pardee took and shot Hunter right away—"

"Hunter's dead?"

"I said so. But then he had a fit of cold feet. Sent the boys to bed like they was in delicate health and went off to the house."

"What about his sister? Didn't she have something to say about it?"

Kelly drew out a sack of Navy Cut and began rolling himself a cigarette. "Her and that undertaker feller stayed in the house no telling how long while we all stood around," he said. "Finally he come out looking like he'd been talking Choctaw to a pack mule. Didn't speak to none of us, just drove Avery's body off toward town while the Pardee gal took to her room." He stuck the twist of paper in his mouth and fumbled for a match. "We liked not to got any supper, because Anna was so busy—"

He stopped. Jack Harvey had risen, staring past him,

his beefy face flushing almost as red as his beard. Kelly suddenly realized that all sound in the barn had died as men turned to look at the open door. Blinking, Kelly also turned.

Two men came sheepishly up the runway, their holsters empty and their hands held at shoulder height. Behind them Adam Hunter stopped in the doorway, swinging the Winchester's barrel in a slow arc to command the space in front of him.

"Hello, Red," he said.

Kelly stared, the cigarette falling unheeded from his open mouth. His hand inched toward his pistol, but then Jack Harvey's big hand caught him by the coat and shook him as if he were a doll.

"Dead, is he?" Harvey roared. He shoved Kelly forward so that the cowhand sprawled in the dirt almost at Hunter's feet. "Well, you take that rifle away from his damned ghost, then." Still furious, he faced Hunter. "You can't fight the lot of us, Hunter. Let that Winchester fall."

Without shifting the rifle away from Harvey's middle Hunter raised his left hand, palm out. "Easy, Red," he said. "I don't mean fighting. Figured I'd better come in this way so's none of you would shoot me by mistake. Sid sent me."

"What?" Harvey's brow furrowed. "How do you—"

He broke off, frowning irresolutely at Hunter, then at the men to either side of the barn. A man with a blond beard that almost hid the long scar on his cheek stood up from one of the poker tables.

"Hunter, you say? This the one who killed the Todd boys?"

"That's right."

"Then he's killed his last man. Call and raise, Jack. I'll back your play."

"We can shoot it out if you're of a mind, Red," Hunter said. "But Sid won't like it, us killing each other off."

Harvey scowled fiercely. From where he crouched on the ground Tag Kelly could feel things poised on edge like a coin that might fall either way. He scrambled back toward the red-bearded man.

"Don't trust him, Jack. He's against us. It's a trick. Pardee said he'd killed him."

Hunter laughed. "Hell he did! I guess he didn't want to admit I'd foxed him." He grinned at Harvey. "Come on, Red. I shot to miss you when I had a clear sight in the canyon last night, which is more than you did for me. Who are you going to believe, Sid or this little weasel?"

The coin fell. Harvey waved at the blond man as if shooing flies. "Hold off, Joe, there's something funny here. Just sit down, all of you. There won't be no shooting until I say."

Reluctantly the men settled back into their places. The one called Joe was the last to sit, and he kept angry eyes on Hunter. Kelly started to get to his feet, and then Harvey grabbed him by the coat and yanked him upright.

"Dead! You get back down to Pine Valley. There's an easy way to get those rannies down there ready to fight. You just kill Pardee, same's as you did Avery. I tried to tell Sid— Anyway, I knew all along that's what we ought to do." He shoved Kelly away. "Get going! I want Pine Valley riding on Circle Eight by daybreak. I know my boys on Circle Eight will have them worked up enough to fight."

Kelly staggered back, cast a worried glance at Hunter, then rounded to Harvey. "Jack, I can't do that. They're on to me." He pointed at Hunter. "Listen, no matter what he says, Pardee knows something. If I go back, they're apt to kill me."

"Oh?" With speed surprising for his bulk, Harvey drew his right-hand pistol. "Well, if'n you don't, *I'm* apt to kill you right where you stand." Rocking back the hammer, he pointed the gun at Kelly's chest. "I got twenty good men here waiting to clean up after those spreads tangle. That means they're waiting on you— unless you want me to send Hunter here."

"All right by me, Red," Hunter put in. "I owe Pardee one."

"Of course, then I wouldn't need *you*," Harvey told Tag Kelly. "Do what you're paid for, or we'll part company right here."

Kelly looked from the red-bearded man to Hunter and back. In some way that he didn't understand, things had changed. He couldn't figure Hunter out, but he understood Harvey well enough. Unless he put on a show the big man was likely to drop him then and there.

"All right, Jack, all right," Kelly said. "If you say so. But I was only just paid for one, not two. Pardee's going to cost you extra."

"Hell." Again the coin stood on edge for a moment, and then Harvey laughed and holstered the pistol. "I might've known. It's always money with you, ain't it, Tag?" He drew a handful of bills from his pocket and tossed them at Kelly's feet. "Take this and get on with it."

A few of the men laughed, but Kelly paid them no mind. He knelt and scrambled in the dirt for the money, never looking away from Harvey. When he rose he turned without another word and left the barn.

Hunter stepped aside for Kelly to pass, then moved a few steps to his left, out of line with the doors, just in case his back should prove too much temptation for the Pine Valley cowhand. In a few moments they all heard Kelly's horse heading out toward the mouth of the valley.

Jack Harvey barked a loud laugh. "Struts just like one of them banty roosters, don't he?" he roared, and the men hooted with laughter. Then Harvey's watery eyes fastened on Hunter. "You going to stand there all night with that cannon pointed at us? Give these two

195

fellers their irons and let them get back to guarding—
for whatever that's worth. We got to talk."

"Sure, Red." Hunter dropped the Winchester's hammer to half cock. "Just wanted to be sure you were
over the idea of shooting me. Getting pretty tired of
that."

He drew one six-gun from his belt and then the other,
laying them carefully on the barn floor. The pair of sen-
tries stepped toward him, then hesitated until Harvey
bellowed again.

"Get moving, you two! Don't no blame attach to
Hunter 'cause you're dumb enough to give him your
guns. Get out there and see if you can keep somebody
else out!"

They went in sullen silence. The blond man who had
spoken before rose from his place, laying the deck of
cards in front of him. He was still watching Hunter.

"By rights he's mine, Jack," he said without looking
away.

"Not tonight, Joe. Maybe when this is over you'll get
your chance, but not now. I got a friend who's got plans
for Hunter."

"Your friend willing to die over it?"

Hunter rocked the rifle's hammer back again. "Are
you?" he asked.

Joe looked at him, then cut his eyes back to Harvey,
whose hand was on his own pistol.

"Sit easy, Joe," Harvey said. "Plenty of chance to
get killed tomorrow, when you're being paid for it.
Don't waste it for nothing."

"Right," Joe said.

He squatted against a post, but a dark anger showed
in his face. Joe looked like a man with a grudge, Hunter
decided, and one who wasn't likely to forget it. It
wouldn't do to turn his back on him, Hunter thought,
but that didn't distinguish Joe from any other man on
the Box H.

Harvey dropped back onto his seat and waved to

Hunter. "Let's hear your story, Hunter," he said. "Come on over and have a seat."

"I guess not. If it's all the same, I'd just as soon go somewhere with less of a crowd."

Jack Harvey chuckled and heaved himself to his feet again. "All right," he said. "Let's us just go on up to the house and have our little chat. But you'd better know something that'll be worth my time."

Tag Kelly passed through the unguarded entrance to the Box H at a walk, but as soon as he reached the wider trail he kicked the horse into the fastest pace he could manage by moonlight. He would have to sneak back into the Pine Valley headquarters without waking anyone. Then there was the problem of Pardee. He'd never thought the foreman was right bright, but now he wasn't so sure. There was something funny about the business with Pardee and Hunter, something Harvey was too dull-witted to see.

Kelly's wits were sharp enough. He thought of ways to get to Pardee, rejecting each in turn as too risky or not certain enough. He was far away from the Box H, near the spot where the trail forked to go down to Sublette City or on to Pine Valley, when he realized he'd made his decision already. He turned it in his mind and smiled. For the first time in months he felt satisfied with himself.

He wasn't going near Pine Valley. That was a fool's game, worse than drawing to an inside straight. All the logic, all the caution he could muster spoke against it. He was betting now that things would go against Jack Harvey, but even if they didn't, Jack would be about finished with him.

No. He was in line for a hanging from one side or a bullet in the back from the other. Time to toss in his hand. He would take the money he had already and what Jack had given him tonight and ride for New Mexico. Then Jack and Pardee and all the rest of them could go to hell at their own pace.

"Whoa back. Easy, there, girl."

His mind at rest, he reined back to an easier pace. He had a long ride in front of him now. Best to save his mount.

Ahead of him a stand of pines loomed black against the moon-bright sky. Kelly glanced at them, then reined his horse in sharply. The shadows beneath the pines moved, thickened, became the shape of a man on horseback moving out to block the trail. The long barrels of a shotgun jutted Kelly's way.

"Tag Kelly."

The voice belonged to Edge Pardee. There was no way out of it. Pardee had let Hunter go because the two of them knew something. Now Pardee had trailed him to Box H. There was no way out at all.

"Kelly! Throw up your hands," Pardee ordered, but Kelly was past listening. His six-gun was already in his hand as he turned sideways for the best advantage.

Chapter 19

"It's that son of a bitch Hunter. He's killed Mr. Avery!"

Dub Axtel's despairing shout was still in Linda's ears when she opened her eyes onto darkness less black than the place her mind had been.

"No. No, he didn't," she murmured, clenching her fists with the effort of speaking. Her fingers tightened on someone else's hand, a hand that returned a strong, reassuring grip. "He couldn't have," she said more confidently.

"What?"

Perry Bonham leaned close to her. Even in the half dark, she read the concern in his lean face.

"Is it true?" she asked, sure Perry would tell her the truth. "Is Uncle Morg really"—she had to swallow, but the word still choked her—"dead? Is he really dead?"

"I'm afraid so. It happened very quickly. He was in the saddle, where he would've wanted to be."

His voice was low, somber, reassuring. Of course it is, she thought. He's the undertaker. Again she felt the wild urge to giggle. Impatiently she shook off her weakness.

Bonham misunderstood. "It's true, Linda," he insisted softly. "You'll have to accept it. He's gone." He paused a moment, then said, "You can't stay here."

That brought her awake, her eyes wide. "What?" She struggled to sit up, but Bonham pressed her back gently.

She was lying on the sofa in the parlor, she realized, with a pillow behind her head and a down comforter covering her. The windows were dark, and no one had lit the parlor lamps, though light streamed in from the hallway. Bonham knelt beside her, holding her hand, while Anna hovered by the door.

For a moment she wondered how she'd gotten there. She remembered Dub Axtel's voice, the sensation of falling, a distant, unreal vision of men gathered around a wagon in the yard, of Hunter—

"Hunter," she said, and a sudden fear filled her. "Perry, where's Hunter?"

Bonham hesitated. "I don't know," he said at last.

She couldn't read his face. "What do you mean?" She gripped his hand. "Where is he?"

"He—went off—with Edge," Bonham said slowly. "Linda, listen—"

Linda let herself sink back, relaxing her hold on Bonham's hand. "That's all right, then," she said with a sigh. "Edge will do the right thing."

"Yes. Edge will take care of it." He paused again, seeming uncertain. "Linda, you can't stay here."

"You said that before. I don't understand. I've always lived here—nearly always."

"Now it's different. There's going to be a war here, Linda. Come daylight there'll be more killing between Pine Valley and Circle Eight. It's not safe for you here."

"No!" Linda cried. "We have to stop it. We'll go to Ed Tobreen."

"You can't stop it. Nor can Tobreen. Ellis Watkins was behind your uncle's murder. Hunter is working for him. You can't wait here until his men ride in on you."

"But Edge won't let them ride in. He'll—"

"He'll fight," Bonham said. "And your ranch hands will back him. That's the war I'm talking about, and I won't have you in the middle of it." He caught her up in his arms. "Linda, come into town with me. Once you're my wife I can hold Pine Valley for you. Then I'll have the right."

"No." Linda shook her head in confusion. Too many things were crowding in on her. "We can't. Uncle Morg—and Hunter—"

"It's not lack of respect, Linda. Your uncle would understand. He'd want to know you were protected."

"I don't need to be—"

"And now you see what Hunter is. He killed your uncle."

"No."

"He's working for Watkins. That's the only explanation. That makes his—his conduct—with you even more shameful."

"No," Linda said again. She sat up suddenly. "Anna! Anna, bring some tea."

"Anna, wait," Bonham said, but the cook had already gone. Quickly he turned back to Linda. "Dearest, you're not yourself. Come with me. We'll find the Reverend Walker and be married. Then I can help you. It'll be my duty, my natural place."

"Perry, please listen. I need time—"

"There is no time."

"—to think. I need to talk to Edge—and to Adam."

"God have mercy," Bonham said. "Even now you won't believe the truth about a man who . . ."

"The truth." Linda closed her eyes. What if she were mistaken? What if Hunter had betrayed her? She didn't believe it, but was her judgment sound? "Maybe not," she said aloud, "but Tom Banner's is. Uncle Morg's was."

Bonham frowned. "What? I don't—"

"No, Perry." She felt herself growing stronger as she answered, as though she was drawing strength from those others. "I won't marry you tonight. And I won't leave Pine Valley tonight—not if there's trouble coming."

Bonham rose slowly to his feet. His face was shadowed, but his voice was cool and level. "I've tried, Linda," he said. "I've been as fair as a man can be. If you shut me out now, I'll not be responsible for what happens."

"I don't mean to shut you out, Perry. I still—care for you—just as before. But I can't do what you ask. Please understand."

"I understand."

Anna came back in carrying a tray with a teapot and a single porcelain cup. She set the tray down on a low table, then went to the fireplace to light the lamps on the mantel. By their glow Linda looked at Bonham's set face.

"I have to go now, Linda," he said. "I have work to do, and likely I'll have more. I'll see you tomorrow—if there's time."

"Perry!" She put a hand out toward him, hesitated, and slowly drew it back. "All right, Perry," she said. "Good night."

She heard the front door close, and then the sound of Bonham's wagon moving away. She didn't look. Weariness lay on her like a shroud. Now, with Bonham gone, she felt more bleakly alone than ever, but she knew Pine Valley was in danger. She had to act.

Crooning softly in German, Anna poured the tea. It was hot and strong, scented with dried mint leaves, and Linda drank it greedily, then poured herself a second cup.

"Anna," she said. "Anna, where's Edge? And Mr. Hunter?"

Anna looked at her strangely. "Together they left, before it grew dark. Mr. Pardee came back alone and talked to the men. Then he rode out again."

"I see." Linda thought a moment. "Are the men—all right? Is everything quiet?"

"Two men watch. The rest sleep. Mr. Pardee later will give them their orders."

Linda almost smiled. "It's *Mister* Pardee now?" she asked.

Anna nodded, expressionless.

"I understand." She rose and picked up the tray. "When Mr. Pardee comes back, tell him Miss Pardee wants to see him. I'll be in Uncle—in the office."

Ellis Watkins came to his front door still tucking his nightshirt into his jeans. Behind him his wife was poised uncertainly but still primly on the stairs.

"God Almighty," Watkins roared as he stumbled along the hallway. "Stop that pounding! I'm coming."

The pounding didn't stop. Watkins set aside the lamp he carried and drew a pistol from his waistband, cocking it as he swung the door wide.

"What in Tophet—Ed! You'd as well have spent the night. You've woke the dogs, and likely everything else on the place." He tucked the Colt in his waistband and put out his hand. "Come in. Irene will hot us up some coffee."

"That's good," Tobreen said, heading straight for the study. "Ellis, there's some things you got to know."

He closed the door behind them and began to explain. He was only halfway through when Irene Watkins brought in the coffeepot.

"—can't picture Avery dead," Watkins was saying as she entered. He broke off and stared at her, but her expression didn't change. Unbidden, she took a seat and watched them with unblinking eyes. Tobreen waited a moment, then went on.

"Harvey's got a spy on your place, too—maybe more than one. I'm afraid he's had your trust."

"It can't be," Watkins protested. "Not on Circle Eight."

"Robert Golightly," his wife said in the same breath.

"And you're sure Hunter didn't shoot Abel Carson?"

"I'm sure. He was driving out of Dead Horse Canyon when Abel was killed."

"Who says so?"

"Linda Pardee." Tobreen tugged his mustache. "I'd like a word with Golightly."

"He's missing. Even so, I can't think it of him."

"That's hardly surprising," Irene Watkins said in her cool, precise voice. "Belief in the obvious has always come hard for you."

Tobreen sipped from his cup and said nothing. Scowling, Watkins rose and slapped his hand down on the desk. "All right," he growled. "Let's uncover those other spies you spoke of. And then we'll go burn out that snake den at Box H."

Irene Watkins followed her husband up the stairs pace for pace, silenced her curious daughters with an upraised hand, and closed herself in the bedroom with Watkins. As he began to pull on his boots she placed herself in front of him and crossed her slender arms.

"Ellis, I've something to say to you."

He glanced up at her. "If you've set yourself to talk me to death, never mind," he said. "If you're lucky, one of Harvey's men may do the job for you."

"Yes. I know you're determined to go, although you needn't. And I wish you well."

"You—"

"But you'll not go without hearing this. Morgan Avery has stood between us for twenty years. You've hated him that long; worse, you've hated me because he wasn't here to fight face to face."

Watkins stripped the nightshirt off over his head and reached for a shirt. "I was never afraid to face him," he said.

"No. But you never did. Now he's dead, and that should satisfy you."

"Should it?"

"Yes. It's true Morgan courted me twenty years ago, just as you did. But it was obvious to him that *you* were my choice. It was obvious to everyone but you." She shook her head. "But you've never gotten it fixed in your mind that I love you—always have."

When he started to speak she raised her hand. "Now you go and get yourself killed if you must. But understand that if you do, it will leave a space in my life nothing can fill. And if you don't believe that, then when you do come back I'll be on my way to the train."

"Irene." Watkins stared into his wife's pale, clear eyes. He didn't expect to find tears or pleading there. That would not be her way.

"I believe you," he said. He rose and clasped his gun belt around his waist. "And I will be back."

Linda Pardee lifted her head from the thick ledger book that lay on the polished desk. She remembered opening it and starting to work. After a few minutes, reassured by the familiar musty smell of the office and the warmth of her uncle's big leather desk chair, she'd closed her eyes for a moment—only for a moment, she was sure.

Drowsily she ran her fingers over the smooth surface of the chair arm. Often when she was a little girl she would slip into the office at night and sit in that chair, pretending she was running the ranch. More than once she'd fallen asleep there, only to awaken safely in her own bed.

I won't tonight, she thought. There's no one to carry me there. With that she came fully awake. Her cup still sat by her elbow, the tea in it grown cold and thick. The only sound in the house was the steady, hollow ticking of the wall clock. She frowned at the clock. The night had gone by, dawn was near, and she had no idea what had happened while she slept.

Edge, she thought. He was supposed to be here. And as if her thought had brought him, Edge knocked lightly at the oak-paneled door, then came inside. He held a shotgun in the crook of his elbow, the barrels slanting over his arm, the action open. He snapped the gun closed and stood it in the corner of the room, then settled heavily into a chair across from her.

"It looks like you've been hunting," Linda said.

He didn't smile. "I sort of have," he said. "I just killed Tag Kelly."

"Kelly! Why?"

"Because he was trying to kill me, mostly. Because he was a spy for Jack Harvey, or whatever his name really is." Pardee closed his eyes for a second. "Because he's the one shot Uncle Morg."

Linda tried to take in all the parts of what he'd said, but it was too much for her. There were too many things she didn't understand. She fastened onto the one point she knew about.

"They said Adam killed Uncle Morg. Dub said so, and Perry. But I knew he didn't."

"They thought he had. Me, too." Pardee gave her a lopsided grin. "Hunter said he didn't reckon you'd believe it. Figured you'd know better, for some reason."

She felt her face burn and knew how guilty she must look. But her brother was carefully not watching her. He rubbed a weary hand across his eyes.

"Anyhow, it's more than *I* knew. I came within an ace of shooting him down, just like that."

Linda caught her breath quickly, fear welling up inside her as deep and cold as water from a spring. "Edge, no—you didn't." She looked hard at him, then said, "You didn't."

"Hell, no. I might've managed it if I hadn't started listening to him. He's gone after Harvey."

"Oh!" She put her hand to her mouth. "I should have known. After Harvey shot at us—"

"What?" Pardee stared at her, no longer looking tired. "Shot at you, hell. When was that?"

Linda started to recount Harvey's ambush in the canyon, then backed up because Pardee hadn't heard about the wounding of Tom Banner. She found it easier to think about the fight in Antonito now that the initial horror was past. Pardee frowned and muttered during her account but didn't interrupt, not even when she told about shooting at Harvey with Hunter's pistol. When she finished he launched into an account of his meeting with Hunter and Tobreen on the ridge. Linda listened with mounting impatience.

"And you let Adam go into Harvey's nest *alone?*" she demanded. The fear had flowed back, making a deep pool inside her. "Edge, how could you do that?"

"In case you ain't noticed, it's middling hard to stop Hunter doing about whatever he wants to," he said with some annoyance. "I wasn't any too keen on the idea either, Sis, but he was set on one more go at that Sid Tate yahoo. And we had to give Tobreen time to get Watkins lined up so's he don't come after us while we're going after Harvey." He pulled himself to his feet and reached for the shotgun. "Dub's getting the men up and ready right now. I figure we'll go get Hunter out of there."

Linda jumped to her feet. "Have them saddle my mare. I'll be ready as soon as I can change out of this dress."

"You ain't going."

"Like hell." She raised a hand to cut off his outraged protest. "Listen, Edge, it's middling hard to stop me doing whatever I want, too. Uncle Morg couldn't, and don't you start trying."

"Linda, it ain't ladylike—"

Someone tapped on the door. Pardee broke off what he was saying and reached for the knob. Anna came into the room with a tray bearing a coffeepot and three cups. The smell of fresh-boiled coffee filled the room.

"Pastor Walker is here," she said, setting the tray on the desk. "He asks to see you. Breakfast is ready when you wish it."

Linda looked at Pardee. "Bring him in here, Anna," she said. "See that the men get fed. We'll be with you directly."

"Early to come calling," Pardee observed. He returned the shotgun to its corner and sat down again, reaching for the coffeepot. "Better have some if we're going to get a sermon."

"Sh!" Linda hissed impatiently. A moment later she smiled as the minister came in from the hall. "Reverend Walker, it's so good to see you. Please sit down."

In the crowded room Wendell Walker looked even taller and wider than usual. He smiled gravely at Linda and Pardee and took a seat holding his Bible across his lap.

"Thank you," he said. "I know it's early, but I came as soon as I learned of your uncle's death. I was afraid there would be violence between the ranches." He glanced toward the shuttered window. "I suspected you'd be up. There seems to be a lot of activity this morning."

"We're glad you came," Linda said, ignoring the implied question. "Please have some coffee."

"Thanks, I will. No, Edge, I take it black." He took a sip and set the cup down. "Your uncle was a good man and a pillar of our church. I'll miss him, as I'm sure you will. If you'd like to talk about the service for him—"

"Tell you the truth, Preacher, we haven't had much time to think on it," Pardee said. He hesitated. "Looks like today's going to be pretty busy, too."

Walker considered him thoughtfully. "I see," he said. "You know, of course, about the other killings—the one on your land, and Ralph Mintner and Abel Carson—"

"No!" Linda cried. Pardee nodded.

"It's true. Didn't get the chance to mention it."

"Damn them!" Linda was on her feet again. The two men looked at her in surprise. "Brother Walker, you're a man of God. Why are there men like that—men like Jack Harvey and—"

"Linda!" Pardee warned.

"Jack Harvey?" Walker asked, frowning.

"I mean—we're not certain how things lie. But we'll know quite soon."

"I see," Walker said again. He drank more coffee, studying Linda over the rim of the cup. "It seems a poor time to mention it, but Perry Bonham suggested the two of you might be moving up your wedding date."

Linda felt Pardee's questioning glance but kept her face expressionless. "I'm not ready to discuss that," she said. "Not until Uncle Morg is"—paid for, she thought—"is buried."

"Not meaning to be inhospitable, Preacher," Pardee said, rising, "but we've got some things to take care of, and not a hell of—not a lot of time. Maybe we could finish this talk later."

Walker drained his cup and stood also. Linda saw his eyes pause for a moment on Pardee's shotgun and then return to her.

"I'd hoped I could be an instrument in keeping the peace. If that's not the case, perhaps you'll join me in a prayer before I go."

"Yes," Linda said.

"Praying's fine," Pardee added. "That's good. But for the rest, it ain't a time for preachers."

"Yes," Walker said, his long face sad. "It may not be a time for preachers. A man wants to choose what sort of instrument he will be. But all he gets the choice of is whether he's willing to be used. God chooses how to use him." He folded his arms, holding the Bible to his chest in such a way that Linda saw the heavy black gun belt beneath his coat. "Now if you'll bow your heads . . ."

Chapter 20

Adam Hunter walked ahead of Jack Harvey out through the open barn door. The moon had set, and the stars burned hard and bright overhead. A wind blew gently out of the east, stirring the tops of the pines so that the barren yard between the house and barn was filled with a sound like running water.

"That way." Harvey jerked his head. "Inside the house, so's we're out of this wind."

"Just a minute. I need to get something from my saddlebags."

"Well, hurry it up." Harvey wrapped his thick arms around his body, muttering a curse. "Be glad when this is all done with. I'm halfway minded to sell out and head back for Sonora, where it's warm."

Holding his rifle easily in the crook of his arm, Hunter walked slowly and tried not to shiver. The wind had a cold edge, but the idea of Harvey—Red Bull Converse—armed and behind him was the thing that made him cold. He caught the gray and untied his saddlebags from their place.

"Sonora, huh? Were you there before you came to the Nations?"

"Oh, sure, that was years—" Harvey stopped suddenly. "What do you know about me and the Nations?"

"Ease back, Bull," Hunter said. "I told you, Sid sent me. We go back a long way, Sid and me."

"Huh! Seems like he could've told me. I might have saved myself a heap of worry had I known you were in with us—and a couple of tolerable good men." He pulled open the cabin's door and waved Hunter through. "Go on. Ought to be a pot of coffee on the stove. Help yourself."

The first room of the cabin was kitchen and parlor all in one. A black iron Windsor cookstove squatted near the center of the room, its stovepipe extending upward almost to the rafters, then angling out through the back wall. A table with four rickety chairs stood in front of the stove. The near wall was taken up by a tall oak icebox and a heavy sideboard. The room was cluttered but surprisingly clean, and there were curtains at the one window. Hunter looked at the curtains, then at the closed door in the far wall.

"Is your woman around?"

"Myra? Nah, I sent her away until the shooting's done. We can talk straight." He picked up a tin cup, dashed its contents into the slops crock, and poured coffee from the blue enameled pot on the stove. "Now what's your message from Sid?"

Hunter dumped his saddlebags on the table. He picked up an empty cup and turned it in his hands, taking the moment to think. Too much romancing would be risky. Best to keep his story simple.

"Nothing all so special. I was to come to you for orders as soon as I was sure Avery was killed. Sid says you're to be in charge from here on out."

Harvey grunted. "He would. Leave it to him to be holed up safe while we're out getting shot at." He poured a dollop of whiskey into his cup from a bottle on the table, then offered the bottle to Hunter. "Here, good for what ails you."

"Not tonight. I want to keep a clear head.".

"I think you better have one," Harvey said, scowling. "I don't rightly trust a feller that won't drink with me."

"Does Sid drink with you?"

"Who says I trust him?"

"All right." Hunter moved to the stove and poured half a cup of strong black coffee. He held out the cup to Harvey. "Here you go. Pour me a shot." Swirling the mixture of coffee and whiskey, he looked at Harvey. "Where do we meet Sid when we're finished?"

"The usual place." Harvey shrugged. "That hogback up above town. You ought to know that."

"Lots of things I don't know. How'd Sid happen onto this valley? He must've been planning his play for a long time, the way he's got himself set up in town."

"Don't know," Harvey muttered. "I expect he ain't hardly as smart as you think. But he's had the notion for a while. All the time he was down in the Nations he kept talking about it." He frowned. "You ain't drinking."

Hunter swirled the dark liquid in his cup again. Just one won't hurt, he told himself. I've got to keep him talking. Better have a drink and work into it. And then he knew that he could have just one. He was certainly strong enough for that. But he would choose the person he drank with. He set the cup down and laid his hand on his rifle.

"No," he said. "Don't do that, Bull. Keep your hands on the table."

Harvey grinned. "Know what I think, Hunter?" he asked. "I think you're playing me. Everybody figures they're smarter than old Red, and you're another one."

"I've got something for you in my saddlebags." Hunter lifted the rifle. "Open that one."

Still grinning, Harvey unbuckled the flap. Hunter leaned across the table, keeping the rifle steady. Cautiously he reached inside the saddlebag and withdrew a pair of shiny nickeled handcuffs.

"So," Harvey said. "A goddam lawman."

"All the way from Arkansas." Hunter tossed the handcuffs on the table. "Put these on. Then I'll have your pistols. After that you can tell me who Sid Tate really is."

"Not likely."

"I don't want to shoot you, Red. I'd rather take you back to Judge Parker."

"Not neither one likely. Myra!"

Hunter took it for a trick, and an instant later he knew he'd been wrong. The woman's voice came from behind him, level and deadly cold, from the other doorway.

"Put down the rifle, mister. I'll shoot if you don't."

Had the voice belonged to a man, Hunter would have swung around and fired instantly. The odds were on his side. A quick enough move would certainly catch the other by surprise—people pointing guns didn't ordinarily expect an argument—long enough for him to get off a shot. And even taking a bullet in return was likely to be better than what Harvey could think up for him. As it was, though, he hesitated an instant, weighing the idea of killing a possibly innocent woman.

Before he could decide to act Harvey moved with surprising speed. The big man darted out a hand and grabbed the Winchester's barrel, yanking it down and away. Thrown off balance, Hunter fired automatically. The bullet plowed through the plank floor, and Harvey lunged upward. His heavy fist smashed into the side of Hunter's head, whirling him backward.

He held on to the rifle even when the force of the blow slammed him against the iron stove. The impact lanced pain through his right arm and side, and his hand wouldn't obey as he tried to work the rifle's lever. The rickety stovepipe shuddered, bleeding smoke from its joints. Hunter slid to the floor and rolled desperately, expecting a bullet, trying to shift the rifle to his left hand. Then a booted foot came down on his wrist. Grinning, Jack Harvey leaned over and thrust his pistol into Hunter's face.

"Now then, lawman, let's hear what *you* have to say."

Slowly Hunter released the rifle and lay back. "Your play, Red," he said.

"You got aces and eights," Harvey said sharply.

"Jack! Don't you do it!"

Harvey looked up in surprise. The gaunt woman Hunter had seen before came forward. He saw his hesitation had been justified; she held a shotgun that would certainly have cut him in two.

"Jack Harvey!" she said. "You'd up and kill a man right in front of me?"

Harvey shrugged, looking at the floor. "If it bothers you, I'll take him outside," he said. "But I got to kill him. He'll hang me else."

"No."

"Hell. You would've shot him just now."

"That's different. He was threatening you."

"Listen, Myra, he's still threatening me. He knows enough to wreck everything."

"Worse than that, Red," Hunter said, "I've already wrecked everything. If you want to get out of this alive, you'll need me before morning."

"You!" Harvey shifted the pistol to his left hand. With his right he belted Hunter across the mouth. "Why would I need you?"

"You guess," Hunter said. "Sid knows. He knows when to make a deal."

"Sid wouldn't do that. He wouldn't sell me out."

"Wouldn't he? There's a couple of your gang buried in the Nations that know better." Hunter managed to laugh, tasting blood from his split lip. "I hope you got your share from those banks, Bull. I hope Sid wasn't holding the money for you."

"Sid wouldn't do that," Harvey repeated, but with less conviction in his voice.

Somebody pounded on the cabin door. "Jack? Hey, Jack, what's the shooting for?"

"Nothing to worry over!"

"All right. Shake a leg, the men's ready to ride."

"In a minute!"

"Hell, you're the one as set the time. How long you want us to wait while you're pulling your pants up?"

With a muttered curse Harvey sprang up and jerked open the door. Before the startled gunman outside could react Harvey snatched him off his feet and shook him, then shoved him back into the cabin wall. Hunter tensed and started to rise, but Myra was right there with the shotgun.

"That's my wife in here," Harvey snarled. "You talk with a little respect next time. Now get out to the barn and wait until I tell you different, hear?"

Harvey shoved the man away and turned back to Hunter and Myra. "I got to go," he said. He jerked the pistol barrel Hunter's way. "You. Get up and come along."

"Wait, Jack," Myra said. "What if he's telling the truth?"

"Won't matter none," Harvey said.

"It might."

Harvey pushed out his lower lip, scowling irresolutely at Hunter. Then his eye fell on the shiny handcuffs. With a low growl of laughter he picked them up.

"Tell you what," he said. "We'll just hang on to him until we see how it comes out. If everything goes good, Sid can have him to play with."

Grabbing Hunter's right arm, he snapped one shackle around the wrist. Then he half dragged Hunter across to the stove and threaded the other through its iron grillwork.

"Reckon that'll hold you." He dropped the key into his vest pocket, then leaned to pick up Hunter's rifle. "I'll carry this with me. You're not likely to need it again." To Myra he said, "You're so concerned, you see he stays here safe. I'll deal with him when we're done with them ranchers."

"Yes, Jack."

He pulled on his coat and started for the door, Myra

trailing behind. Hunter sat up. His arm hurt where Harvey had used it for a handle, his head rang, he was chained to a quarter ton of scrap iron, and he still didn't know who Sid Tate was. But he was alive, at least for a little while longer.

"You take care, now, Jack," Myra said.

She stood on tiptoe to kiss his bearded cheek. He gave Hunter a last venomous scowl and went out, slamming the door behind him. Myra came across the room to sit in one of the kitchen chairs, not looking at Hunter.

"He'll kill me when he comes back," Hunter told her.

"Your own fault." She still didn't look at him. "Somebody's always dogging him. Why can't you let him be?"

"His partner killed a friend of mine."

"That wasn't Jack! It was that Sid. It's his doing. It's always him getting Jack into trouble. Like now."

Hunter nodded. "It was surely that way in the Nations," he agreed. "Sid was the one. I expect Jack—Al Converse, they called him there—would have been just fine if it hadn't been for Sid." He paused, twisting uncomfortably to get farther from the stove. "I guess he would've been in a tight spot about the bigamy, but—"

"What?"

"The bigamy. That's what we meant to arrest him for." Hunter rubbed his manacled wrist. "Ma'am, could you get me a dishcloth or something? This steel is downright warm."

"You're lying."

"No, ma'am. It's because of the other end being tied to the stove, see. The metal carries the heat—"

She stood up, gripping the shotgun. "Don't sass me," she snapped. "You know what I mean. You're trying to turn me against my husband."

"No, ma'am," Hunter said again. "It's all in the warrant." He nodded toward his saddlebags. "There's an oilskin pouch in the left one. You can see for yourself."

"Liar."

She walked into the other room, closing the door behind her. Hunter immediately twisted around and braced his feet against the stove. Gripping the handcuff chain with both hands, he pulled until the metal edges of the shackle cut into his wrist. He'd hoped he might bend or break the stove's grillwork, but it was solid. Solid as iron, he thought without humor as he eased his straining muscles.

There had to be another way. He had begun a slow survey of the cabin when the bedroom door opened and Myra Harvey came out. Again she stood looking down at him.

"Why would you do a thing like that? Why would you try to make me believe it?"

As best he could, Hunter shrugged. "A man who'd lie about a thing like that ought to be shot," he said. "You have the gun. If the warrant's not what I say, you can shoot me." At the moment he thought death would be as easy as having his hand burned off.

She glared at him, her face white and strained. He tried to meet her eyes but finally broke off from her stare and looked at the floor. Damn you, Hunter, he thought. Maybe next you can find a puppy to kick. He sat still until she turned away from him. Then he spat on his wrist and tried to save the skin before the brand took.

"Don't think I won't," she said, and she began to unstrap the saddlebag.

She went through the contents hurriedly, scattering his belongings on the floor. Outside Hunter heard voices, then the sound of many horses moving away toward the entrance to the valley. He tried to guess at the time, but he'd lost track of things. If all had gone well, Pardee and Tobreen should be ready for the Box H riders. If.

Finally the woman held up a thin packet tied with twine. She looked at it, then at Hunter. For a moment she hesitated and started to lay it on the table. Then with angry vehemence she took a kitchen knife and slashed through its bindings.

Hunter knew the contents as she scanned them: his commission as deputy, letters of introduction from Judge Parker and the chief marshal, a reward poster for the Claremore bank job, the warrant he and Barney had meant to serve on Albert Converse. She studied the warrant for a long time.

"Can you read it?" Hunter asked.

"I can read." Her voice was thick with unshed tears. "Probably better than you." She drew in her breath. "This was really him? You ain't lying?"

The plea in her face was so obvious that he looked away. "It's him," he said softly. "He was living with two women. Sisters. From the Choctaw tribe."

"I wish I'd let him kill you," she said. She sat heavily in the chair, laying the shotgun beside her. "I got no way to set you loose."

"Is there a saw?"

The door rattled, swung open. A man came in, the scarred man who had challenged Harvey in the barn. He had his pistol drawn, but when he saw Hunter he laughed and holstered it.

"That's nice," he said. "Jack left me behind on guard, so I thought I'd look in on you. This is even better than I expected."

"You get out of here," Myra Harvey said.

He ignored her. "I owe a score to you, mister," he told Hunter. Grinning, he bent and drew a long, thin knife from his boot. "You can sit right there until I get it paid off."

"Joe, get out of here," the woman said again. This time he glanced her way.

"You better get out yourself, lady, less'n you like to watch things being skinned and gutted alive."

Hunter braced again, dragging desperately against the handcuffs. The stove shifted, and the stovepipe fell in a clattering tangle, filling the room with smoke and soot.

Joe took an involuntary step backward, and Myra Harvey snatched up the shotgun.

"I'm warning you—"

It happened just as Hunter had pictured it. He guessed what was coming and made a lunge for Joe's ankle, hoping to throw him off balance. He was too late. All in one motion the gunman dropped the knife, pivoted as he made his draw, fired. An instant later the shotgun boomed, lancing flame through the smoky dimness. Joe crashed to the floor. The ankle in Hunter's grip kicked wildly once, twitched, was still.

"Myra?" Hunter choked on the smoke and began to cough. "Myra, are you all right?"

Nobody answered. Hunter's right arm, still at full stretch, ached viciously, and he could feel blood from his wrist trickling over his hand. Joe's pistol had fallen a few feet away. It was out of arm's reach, but he worked around until he could hook it with the toe of his boot and draw it in. Awkwardly, with his left hand, he cocked the revolver, pressed its muzzle against the shackle where it looped over the stove, and pulled the trigger. The bullet spanged off the stove and sang like a hornet up into the rafters, and Hunter was free.

He needed only a moment bending over Joe to see that he'd been right about the shotgun cutting a man in two. He knelt longer over Myra Harvey, but there was nothing he could do. The gunman's bullet had taken her full in the chest. Her eyes, open and empty, still held the hint of tears.

The smoke was getting thicker. One section of stovepipe had fallen among some rags, and a sullen red glow came from them. Keeping low and trying not to breathe, Hunter gathered up his papers and snaked to the door, then out into the darkness. Apparently Joe had been the only guard; at least nobody else had come to investigate the shooting. Satisfied the yard was empty, Hunter pulled himself upright and staggered toward the corral.

He was surprised to find the gray still there. He

caught the horse, then stood still, holding the reins and thinking. The only way he knew out of the valley was the route Harvey and his men had taken. The gunshots might draw them back, but even if they didn't, he wouldn't want to ride into them along the trail. He glanced at the sky. No more than a couple of hours of darkness were left. Maybe his best move was to lie up in cover until he saw how things were going, although that would mean giving up his chance at Sid Tate.

The thought of Tate decided him. He struggled into the gray's saddle and turned toward the road. Whatever else happened, he didn't mean to lose Tate again.

A fierce crackling grew up in front of him. He thought the house must have caught fire after all. Flames were leaping up from its roof as he rounded the barn, but the crackling seemed to come from another direction. Hunter shook his head in weary puzzlement, and then his mind began to work, and he reined in hard. The crackling was gunfire, distant but clearer now, a confusion of rifles and pistols with no apparent pattern. As Hunter hesitated a rider came tearing into the yard from the direction of the entrance.

"Joe, Joe, they're laying for us! Get—"

He recognized Hunter and hesitated. Hunter drew Joe's pistol, the handcuff chain dragging at his wrist, and shot the man. Then he turned the gray and galloped for the shelter of the trees.

As he reined in and dismounted the rolling echoes of gunfire moved closer. More riders came into the open, dismounting and taking cover around the house and barn. Hunter held his place and waited. The broken shackle, shattered by his bullet and gaping open, bothered him, but he could find no way to secure it. He settled for working a handkerchief under the cuff that still held his wrist. Satisfied it was the best he could do, he watched Harvey's men digging in for their stand.

He didn't see Harvey himself until the red-bearded man was already at the door of the burning house. The outlaw flung off his horse and plunged inside. A moment later he was out and mounted again, spurring off into the trees at the far side of the clearing. Behind him muzzle flashes flared from the hillside and guns answered from the barn and the yard, but Hunter was no longer watching. His weariness forgotten, he was pushing the gray through the trees to get onto Harvey's trail.

Chapter 21

Since he didn't know the woods, Hunter made poor time until he got clear of the trees and onto the rocky stretch below the cliffs. He'd circled wide of the fight, and by the time he reached the spot where Harvey had disappeared the redheaded outlaw was far ahead. Once Hunter heard the sounds of a horse ahead of him, but he never regained sight of Harvey.

His path led him through a dark valley where he had to allow the gray time to choose its own way, but above him to the east the sky was already aglow. He used the light to pick a narrow cut rising toward the east. Along the way he noted traces that another horse had recently passed, and at the top he found a regular highway toward Sublette City.

"That's fine, Red," he murmured, putting the gray into a long lope. "Let's us pay a little visit to Sid."

At the top of the ridge above the town he paused and looked down. One or two early lamps winked from windows below, but as yet no light showed in the shops. Although he saw nothing that resembled a trail, the distant slide and rattle of small stones told him the steep slope could be traversed. Hunter rode slowly along the rim until at last, near a grove of pines, he found a narrow track that switched downward as far as he could follow it with his eye. Without hesitating he pointed the gray down it and concentrated on holding onto his saddle while the horse found a precarious path.

When he reached the level of the darkened buildings he dismounted and left the horse standing. He could neither see nor hear any sign of Jack Harvey. The streets and alleys seemed deserted. Hunter waited, listening, then cut behind the hotel for a look at Hanover's livery barn. One of the back doors was ajar. Hunter slipped through the fence and raced across the feed lot, holding the dangling handcuff to silence its rattling. Inside, the sound of heavy breathing led him to a horse that stood saddled and unattended in the drive-through. Lamplight spilled from the doorway of Hanover's little office, its yellow stain a suggestion at last of the identity of Sid Tate.

Hunter paused at Hanover's door, listening for voices. Then he stepped through, pistol in hand. Hanover sat at his desk in the light of a shaded lamp. His head was bent over an open book. His big yellow dog rose from its bed in the corner and bared its fangs. Its low growl was a clear warning.

But Hunter was scanning the room for any possible place of concealment. He thrust aside the hanging blanket covering a doorway but found only another room furnished with a single bunk, a mirrored washstand, and a chair. Still growling, the dog met him as he returned.

"Make your sign to him," Hunter told the liveryman. "Call him off."

"I can't. It's the gun. He don't like guns."

"Make your sign or I'll kill him."

Hanover said, "Gen'ral Houston." At once the dog settled on its haunches and began to sweep the floor with its tail.

"I take it you're after Jack Harvey," Hanover said. "You'll not find him here."

"Where, then?"

"Around somewhere. Rode in like Old Nick was two lengths behind him and gaining. Off his horse and gone without even a word." Hanover considered him sleepily. "Course, he didn't point any guns at me, either— Wait!"

Hunter heard boards scrape as the front door opened. Hanover waved a hand his way.

"Back behind the curtain. Hurry."

Heavy steps clumped toward the office. Hunter let the curtain fall, keeping an eye to the gap between the cloth and the door frame. Jack Harvey stuck his head inside the office, bringing another growl from General Houston. Harvey glared at the animal but stopped in the doorway.

"I need a team and wagon, old man." The outlaw's breath came in deep gasps, as if he'd been running. "That delivery rig will do. Be quick."

"Pretty early for hauling," Hanover said.

"Be quick. Five minutes. I'll be back for it."

He pulled back and stomped away, out through the front doors again. Hanover looked toward the curtains, mild exasperation in his heavy-lidded eyes.

"Well, there he was, big as a cow in the parlor. Why'd you let him go?"

Hunter stepped back into the office. "Get up," he told Hanover. "Walk ahead of me."

Hanover laid his book aside carefully and pushed himself erect. "Who put the handcuffs on you?" he asked.

"Walk ahead."

"Come over to the anvil. I can cut through the chain. Be easier on your hand."

"No time. Leave the dog."

The liveryman nodded to General Houston. The dog curled itself in a corner as if for a nap, and Hanover ambled out into the hay-scented runway of the barn. Hunter paused in the doorway, then followed. The big front doors stood half open, and Jack Harvey was gone.

"Better hitch up a team like he said."

"Working with him, are you?" Hanover went toward the stalls where a pair of big Percherons stood dozing.

"Surprises me. Gen'ral Houston likes you. He's most often a good judge."

Hunter looked at him thoughtfully. He knew Sid Tate was clever enough to play a part well. Tate could as easily be hidden inside Hanover as anywhere else. But there was something about the combination of Hanover and his dog that didn't fit with what Hunter expected of Tate.

"You don't care for Harvey, then?"

"Me nor the Gen'ral neither." Hanover went about leading the horses out and harnessing them as he talked. "Seen his kind in Texas—one reason I left. Big ideas and a big mouth and two big pistols. Sits on his ranch with as many men as he has cattle. Gets his money on the sly. Gen'ral Houston growls at him."

"Who does his thinking?"

Hanover opened his eyes a little wider. "I was suspecting it might be you," he said. "If not, I don't know. Best-kept secret in these parts."

"Thanks," Hunter said. "Finish hitching up the team for him. Then get out of here. Find Constable Tobreen and tell him Harvey's in town. I'll manage it from there."

"You bet." Hanover led the horses to a light delivery wagon, backed them into position flanking the tongue, and hooked up the lines and traces. Then he turned and whistled. "Gen'ral! Come, boy. We're taking us a walk."

Hunter peered through the front doors to check the street. Finding it empty, he went out the back and circled until he had a clear view of the livery. He hadn't been watching for long when Harvey's squat shape reappeared. The outlaw was moving quickly, keeping to the shadows, so that Hunter couldn't tell which building he'd come out of. He was alone. Hunter fought down his disappointment. Maybe he'd been wrong about Tate. Maybe—

"No," Hunter murmured. He wouldn't consider that

possibility yet. Obviously Harvey had a reason for wanting the wagon. Tate was around someplace. Given enough time, Harvey would lead the way to him.

As Hunter watched, the red-bearded man drove the wagon out through the back doors and down the alley in the direction from which he'd come. Hunter started to follow, then changed his mind. There was a good chance he'd be spotted in the open, and he didn't want to give the wagon free passage out of town. The loose handcuff clattering, he ran along the street parallel to the course the wagon had taken. The alley was too narrow for Harvey to turn around, so eventually he would have to come out the other end. Hunter touched the holster that held Joe's pistol and wished for a shotgun, or for his lost rifle, still in Jack Harvey's hands.

When Harvey had first left his horse at the livery stable he'd slipped along the backs of the buildings until he reached Sid Tate's door. He banged loudly on it, waited a moment, then kicked it in with a crash. Inside he almost walked straight into Tate's leveled gun.

"If I don't kill you on purpose, Bull, you'll make me do it by accident," Tate greeted him coldly. "What's the idea of waking the whole town?"

"Myra's killed," Harvey said. "Everything's blowed up on us. They ambushed me at my own gate, and I didn't but just barely get out ahead of them."

"Who? Who ambushed you?"

Harvey was breathing in ragged gasps. He caught his wind and glared. "How in hell should I know? Men with guns, a big bunch of them." He walked past Tate and into the room that held the stairway to the cellar. "Help me with the box, Sid. It's time we hauled our freight."

Slowly Tate lifted the revolver and pointed it at Harvey's back. "Time to haul *your* freight, you mean. You're the one they're on to. I've worked too hard on this deal to let you spoil it all."

"You ain't as smart as you think," Harvey said, turning to face the gun. He didn't seem surprised. "We both of us have to get out, and quick. Hunter's a law dog from Fort Smith. He knows about you."

"Hunter's dead."

"Like hell. I had him at the Box H, but he got away. Wouldn't surprise me if he's on our track right now." He shook his head sadly. "But Myra's killed. Be hard to find another woman as good as Myra."

"How did Hunter get away from Pardee? Pardee, hell, how'd he get away from *you?*"

Harvey shifted his eyes away. "Too long to tell," he mumbled. "We got to hurry." He turned toward the hidden stairs. "Come on, Sid. Put up your iron. You'll never lift that box without me."

Sid Tate hesitated for a minute, thinking. Then he spun his pistol back into the holster beneath his left shoulder.

"Go get a wagon and team from Hanover," he said. "When you come back I'll be ready."

When Harvey returned, Tate was just strapping a black gun belt over a well-worn suit of trail clothes. The red-bearded man looked at him and grinned.

"Now that looks like the real Sid Tate. I'd about forgot, seeing you in that town getup so long."

"Shut up." Tate lighted a candle and nodded toward the stairs. "Let's get the money."

Together they sweated the long box with its rattling padlocks up the stairway and out to the back door.

"That's good," Tate said. "Bring the wagon. I'll stand watch."

He waited in the doorway, scanning the alley in both directions. Full daylight was near, but no townsmen were stirring yet, at least not at this end of town. After a couple of minutes Harvey drew the wagon up at the door. Together the two of them hoisted the box aboard, and Harvey lashed it down with a length of rope.

"Got it. Let's get gone."

"You go ahead. I'm going to have a look out front.

Pull up at the end of the alley, and I'll meet you there.'' Tate looked up at him. "You know better than to try shaking me off.''

"I know better. We'd best be watching each other's back for a while.''

At the corner of the last building Hunter paused. No wagon showed at the end of the alley. He went swiftly down the side of the building and peered around the corner, unaware that one citizen of Sublette City was watching him from the boardwalk.

The wagon stood midway down the alley. As Hunter looked on, Jack Harvey emerged from a building there and climbed up onto the wagon seat. Hunter waited for Tate to join the big man, but Harvey was already calling softly to the team, starting them at a walk up the alley.

Hunter drew his six-gun. He had a choice. If he waited longer for Tate, he risked allowing Harvey to get away. It came to him suddenly that Harvey might no longer have a partner, that he could have killed Tate himself. The thought made up Hunter's mind for him, and he stepped into the mouth of the alley, raising his pistol.

"Hold up! Stop where you are!''

Harvey never hesitated. He let out a whoop and lashed the horses viciously with the reins. They broke into a run straight at Hunter. He leveled his Colt, but Harvey was already shooting. Standing in the wagon box to see over the tossing manes of the horses, the outlaw held the lines in one hand and his revolver in the other, firing steadily at Hunter.

The reports of gunfire rocked the peaceful morning and sent the horses into ever greater terror, but Hunter judged that Harvey had little hope of hitting anything from his swaying perch. Hunter held his ground, taking careful aim at the outlaw's broad chest. When the angle of arm and gun barrel had the right feel, he fired.

Harvey lurched heavily back against the wagon seat,

fell over the back rail, and tumbled into the wagon's bed. Their reins dragging free, the horses plunged onward. Hunter waved his arms at them. Unable to get around him in the narrow alley, they broke stride and began to slow as Hunter stepped aside and caught at the harness of the near horse. He dragged along for another twenty feet before his trailing weight brought the team to a stop in the open space past the mouth of the alley.

Cautiously Hunter moved along the side of the wagon until he could see into the bed. Red Jack Harvey lay on his back, sprawled across the lid of a polished wooden coffin, his eyes and mouth open to the sky, the front of his coat drenched with blood. Hunter put away his gun and tore at the big man's coat, hoping to find the handcuff key still in his vest. As he fumbled with the slippery buttons his eye fell on the two shiny padlocks that held the coffin closed. He saw that the locks were not alike. It took a moment for him to realize their significance. Tate! he thought. He's here after all.

He drew back and started to turn but was stopped by the unusually loud click of a revolver's hammer coming back to cock. He had heard that one before.

In that second Hunter knew the man he'd tracked so far stood behind him holding all the cards. Swift and bright as flash powder in a photographer's studio, fear blew through him. It flashed and was gone. He'd lived a long time for this moment, and now it was here. If it cost him his life, he would see the man whom he'd hated without knowing.

"Put down your gun." The voice, deep and clear, belonged to the Reverend Wendell Walker. "You don't think it, but I'll kill you if I must."

Hunter turned. Walker stood by the corner of the building thirty feet away, holding the cocked American. Halfway between them another man pointed a shiny little Colt pocket pistol at Hunter. He was dressed for a long ride, and his gun belt rode at his waist like a part of his body. A longer, heavier pistol was holstered on the belt. So complete was the transformation that it took Hunter a moment to recognize Perry Bonham. Very slowly Bonham lowered the little pistol and allowed it to drop in the dust.

"You've forgotten your promise, Dell," he said, still looking at Hunter.

"No. It's you who's forgotten. You were supposed to be through with guns and killing."

"I have to kill him. It's come to that or hanging. I tell you what I'll do to soothe your conscience. *You* kill him for me."

"No." Walker's voice was like a death sentence. "It's not him I mean. It's the others—Owen, Mintner, Abel Carson. And Morgan Avery."

"That was Harvey, not me."

"It was you who shot down my partner in Rocky Comfort," Hunter said. "I'll lay odds it was you doing Harvey's thinking. I know it was you who meant to inherit Pine Valley when you'd married Linda and seen Edge killed."

Bonham stared into Hunter's eyes, but neither his face nor his voice changed. "You can see he's out to get me, Dell," he said. "It's him or me."

"No," Walker said.

"Then hold him here while I ride out. Give me a head start, and you and me'll each keep our secrets to the grave."

"No," Walker said.

"No," Hunter said.

"You've got no choice," Bonham snapped. "Dell will shoot you. I'm his blood, and he promised Pa. Didn't you, Dell? Hunter, drop your gun belt and stand clear."

The chain on Hunter's wrist rattled as he lowered his hand to the butt of the Colt. "I can't do that," he said. "I'm arresting you for robbery and murder." He turned slowly as Bonham moved to the side, keeping his entire attention on the outlaw, paying Walker no heed.

"He's my blood, Hunter," Bonham said. "He's got

the drop on you, and you've seen how he can shoot. Drop your gun belt, and we'll let you live."

Hunter shook his head slowly. "He can shoot me or not. It's his choice. But you're stopping here."

He saw the slight shift in Bonham's stance and knew it was all the warning he would get. He brought his hand up sharply, three fingers wrapped around the butt of the Colt, thumb rocking back the hammer, index finger already closing on the trigger. And then the trailing shackle of the handcuff snagged at the bottom of his holster, and his shot went into the dirt.

Bonham's gun barked. Hunter saw that it, too, was a long American—probably the mate of Walker's. Bonham had drawn and swung smoothly past Hunter to fire first at Wendell Walker. Without a pause he pivoted back to send the second bullet toward Hunter. Hunter frantically shook free of the holster and brought the Colt up as Bonham turned. The reports of the two guns merged into a single roar.

Hunter felt a hard blow to his chest. He staggered back against the wagon, throwing his left arm over the sideboard to hold himself erect. Bonham swayed backward like an aspen in the wind. He put a foot behind him to keep his balance. The muzzle of his gun sagged downward, but he dragged the hammer back and jerked the big pistol up to center on Hunter.

Hunter had one round left, and he fired it at the figure that wavered before his eyes. The bullet sledged Bonham straight back and off his feet. Then Hunter's pistol was too heavy to hold anymore, so he let it fall. With a great effort he turned his head toward the place where his death—and Wendell Walker—waited.

The minister sat against the wall of the building, his head down. The cocked pistol lay beside his open hand, its muzzle still pointed toward Perry Bonham. After a moment he raised his head and looked at Hunter.

"I couldn't do it," he said huskily. "God knows I'm

a weak man. I couldn't drop the hammer on him." He shivered as though he were cold. "I'm sorry."

"No—need."

Hunter found it hard to talk. Nothing hurt, but the taste of blood was in his mouth. He eased his arm from the wagon box and took two steps toward Walker before his legs failed him and he fell.

He twisted his face in the dirt until he could see the minister. "I—wasn't—quick enough," he said.

"No man was, except me. And I didn't have the sand." Walker was still looking at the place where Hunter had stood. "We rode together once. Long ago. He kept on after I left it."

"Don't—talk."

"For the stone. His name's Walker. Sidney. See they get it right."

Ed Tobreen pelted around the corner from the board-walk, a shotgun in his hands. He stopped abruptly, staring at the three bodies. Behind him Adrian Hanover peered cautiously past the edge of the building. A dozen more townsfolk jostled for a look.

"Help's—here—doctor—don't talk."

"Tried to be his conscience. Didn't work. Guilt's a poor medicine. For you, too." He moved his eyes then, looking higher, past the wagon, toward the sunlit green hills. "Funny. That guilt's gone. Free! And I didn't have a thing to do with it."

"Don't—"

Within a minute the doctor was there, bending over the men one after another.

"Well?" Tobreen asked.

"Two's dead. Help me with this other one."

Chapter 22

Constable Ed Tobreen finished his breakfast and took a quiet half minute with the last of his coffee. Nodding to the proprietor of the restaurant, he went out on the boardwalk, drew a cigar from his pocket, and bit down solidly on its end. For a few moments he studied the locked doors of the deserted funeral parlor. Then he strode easily down toward the hotel, casually taking note of the horses tied along the rails. From the door of the livery stable Adrian Hanover hailed him.

"Hey, Ed, how's the patient?"

Tobreen lifted a hand toward the liveryman. General Houston, sitting in a pool of sunlight beside the open door, woofed once, his wide tongue lolling.

"On my way to check," the lawman called. "He didn't know anything last night."

Tobreen turned into the hotel, crossed the lobby, and went down the hall to number six. Finding the door closed, he knocked gently.

The sound awakened Adam Hunter, although at first he didn't realize he'd been asleep. He looked around the unfamiliar room, wondering where he was. Near his bed was a ladderback chair and a small table. Beneath a lamp on the table were several small bottles, a glass of water, and a damp cloth. Thin, frilly curtains fluttered at the window, letting in sunlight and a fresh breeze. Beyond the open doorway voices buzzed busily, but

Hunter couldn't make out the words. He felt sick and cold and dizzy, but none of that seemed to matter much just then.

After a while Ed Tobreen stepped into the room, closing the door behind him and hanging his hat on a peg. Hunter frowned and rubbed at his eyes with one hand, trying to clear his vision.

"Constable? That you?"

Tobreen faced about quickly. Hunter wasn't sure, but he thought he caught a smile beneath the dun mustache.

"Morning, Hunter. I've just sent your nurse off for breakfast. Said you hadn't come out of it yet. How do you feel?"

"Awful."

"Well, I shouldn't doubt it." Tobreen came closer and inspected Hunter with a professional eye. "We've had to bury people who looked a lot more pert than you. But I reckon you'll make it, now you've finally decided to wake up."

"How long—"

"Couple of days. You talked enough for a couple of months, but nothing that made a lick of sense. You're at the hotel, being treated more like a hero than a shot-up lawman. You remember the rest?"

Hunter wrinkled his forehead. It all seemed far away in the past and of little importance. "Most of it, I guess. It was Bonham, after all." He looked up quickly. "Is Pardee all right? And Linda?"

"Fine. They cleaned out Harvey's bunch pretty good, with Circle Eight's help. Killed six. Sheriff Vargas came and gathered up the rest, though the judge likely can't do much more than run them out of the county. You saved us trials for Bonham and Harvey, though—the preacher, too, I guess. Was he in with them?"

"No." Hunter closed his eyes. "He saved my life."

"So." Tobreen stroked his mustache. "I'll see that word gets around." He held up a hand, ticking things off on his fingers. "That coffinload of loot is in the bank, waiting for somebody to come up from Arkansas. Melvin Cox has your Colt and Winchester. Tuning them for you, he says. But I think he's engraving them with that high country scene you were so taken with."

"Really?"

"No charge. We've all chipped in to have a part in it."

"That's more than nice."

"Not nearly enough. Here's what you'll want to know: Your sorrel's healthy again. Reckon you can ride out soon as you've a mind to, once you're walking. Pardee"—he glanced toward the door—"I'll bet that's Pardee right now."

Tobreen went to open the door. Edge Pardee stuck his blond head in, grinning when he saw Hunter awake.

"Hey, Hunter, I told them you were too mean to die." He sidled in, holding his hat awkwardly in both hands. "Tobreen caught you up on the news?"

"Pretty much, I guess. How's—" He stopped. "How are things at Pine Valley?"

Pardee sobered. "We buried Uncle Morg yesterday. Up in the high pasture. Pretty place." He was silent a moment. "Ellis Watkins and his wife were there."

Tobreen looked as surprised as Hunter. "Watkins," the constable said. "Now that beats all."

"I thought so. He come right up and told me he'd been a nickel-plated jackass for years, and he was just sorry he couldn't say so to Uncle Morg. Said he wanted our ranches to be closer." Pardee grinned. "I told him that would be right nice, since I meant to marry his oldest daughter soon's she'd say yes."

Tobreen laughed. "How'd he take that?"

"Pretty well, once he got over swallowing his tongue. Invited me to dinner tonight. If I don't come back, you'll know where to look."

"I expect you'll be all right," Hunter said.

"Still a damn shame," Pardee said. "About Uncle Morg, I mean. Seems like it's about half my fault."

"Or mine," Hunter said. "Or nobody's. Things happen, good and bad. I was blind drunk when my partner was killed. My fault, and it brought me here." He shook his head. "But he was caught by surprise, and Tate was too fast for any of us. If I'd been with my partner where I belonged, why, the chances are we'd both be buried in Arkansas."

Pardee started on an answer to that, but a clear voice from the doorway beat him to it.

"Are you already talking about going back to Arkansas?"

"Linda!"

She came swiftly across the room to his bed. "That's about all Arkansas is good for, is to be buried in!" Bright tears had sprung to her eyes.

Hunter tried to sit up, but dizziness and the spreading pain in his chest defeated him. Linda Pardee pushed him back against the pillows. She was dressed all in black, but her golden hair caught the sun in a celebration of light.

"Don't try to move," she said. "There'll be plenty of time for that before we bury you in Arkansas."

"She's mostly been here ever since you went down, Hunter," Edge Pardee said. "If I didn't know better, I'd think she wanted to be sure what you were saying while you were out."

Linda blushed but turned on Pardee and Tobreen. "Him just awake, and here you are tiring him out." She made a shooing motion at them. "Go on. You come back when Doc Richards says, and not before."

"I guess we ain't wanted, Edge," Tobreen drawled. He stroked his mustache. "Why don't we step on over to the Aces and shoot some pool with your future in-laws?"

"Sounds good. So long, Hunter. Look after yourself."

They went out, Pardee shutting the door noiselessly behind them. Bright moisture glinted in Linda's eyes. She bent and pressed her lips to Hunter's forehead.

"Your fever's less," she said.

"Yes."

"Does your chest hurt you?"

"No."

"Liar," Linda said. She sat in the chair beside the bed, took his hand, kissed it.

"You're looking serious again," she said. "You have something to say."

"I want to tell you. I'm sorry it had to be Bonham. I know how you felt about him. But I hope you'll believe I didn't do it because of the way I feel about you."

She looked down. "I don't know how you feel," she said quietly. "You haven't told me. I only know what we did." Her eyes rose to meet his. "And you don't know how I felt about Perry, only what I said when he proposed."

"You knew I was there?"

"I knew." She almost smiled. "What were you thinking then?"

"That he was the luckiest man I'd ever heard of, and I the biggest fool."

He recognized the irony as he spoke, but he didn't dwell on it. Linda nodded gravely.

"If you had come earlier—" she said.

"Yes?"

"But you're here now."

"Yes."

"For as long as you care to stay." She looked at him steadily. "I know my mind, Adam. But you'll have to tell me about yours."

With the hand that she still held, Hunter drew her toward him until he could press his mouth to hers. Her hands went to the sides of his face, holding him while they kissed. After a time he drew back a little.

"I'd care to stay," he said.

"Till you're able to ride?"

He shook his head. " 'Till death do us part,' " he

said. "Then I want to be buried here in the high country."

"Do you mean it?"

"I can't figure how it is I've ever come to deserve so much luck."

He felt her lips curve in a smile. "I think you'll work out the answer," she murmured. "Given time."

About the Authors

2 Midland Men Hitch Wagon to a Literary Star

Duo cooperate in successful sideline career in Western fiction

By Elizabeth Edwin

Midland Reporter-Telegram

MIDLAND—Midlanders Wayne Barton and Stan Williams may have their homes firmly established in modern West Texas, but they each spend many hours "living in the wild, wild West."

But that doesn't mean they play cowboys and Indians. They write about the Old West days. In fact, the trail they have blazed in Western fiction writing has earned them several awards as well as the distinction of being billed as "Today's hot new Western action team!"

"One thing we've discovered is we really enjoy speaking together almost as much as writing together," Mr. Williams said.

Both men have what others would term normal lives. Mr. Barton is an engineer with Atlantic Richfield Co., and Mr. Williams is an assistant professor of English at Odessa College. But they have a dream they share: a dream to write.

After meeting each other about 15 years ago at a meeting at the University of Texas of the Permian Basin, the two didn't see each other again until they ended up serving on the same jury.

"We got acquainted and discovered we were both writers, and we became friends," Mr. Williams said. "We were both working on our own things. I don't know how exactly it came about for us to write together."

But many readers of the Western genre say it's a good thing they did hitch up. To date, the duo has three books published by Pocket Books—*Manhunt, Warhorse* and *Live by the Gun*—and Mr. Barton's two previous individual books titled *Ride Down the Wind* and *Return to Phantom Hill*. They were published in hardback and reissued as part of the four-book deal with Pocket. They also have several short stories published in magazines, both as individual writers and as a team. In fact, they joke that they put one magazine out of business.

Warhorse, their first collaborated book, was a project the men worked on during 1986–87, and it was published in April 1988.

"It took about six to nine months for it to go through the process [of being published]," Mr. Barton said.

On the back cover of *Warhorse*, Mr. Barton and Mr. Williams are described this way: "Writers in the classic Western tradition, award-winner Wayne Barton and partner Stan Williams are today's most exciting Western storytellers. Wayne Barton has received the Golden Spur award and the Medicine Pipe Bearer's award from the Western Writers of America."

Their second Western fiction, *Live by the Gun*, was published in spring 1989. The book was a finalist for the 1989 Spur Awards.

"We've been very lucky," Mr. Barton said.

As for their formula for success, the recipe seems simple.

"We brainstorm a plot and the characters. Then Stan does the first draft. I follow up with a final draft, and we meet periodically," Mr. Barton said. "We've asked a lot of teams how they do their writing, and they all seem to do it in different ways. You should just do whatever works. We have a good balance."

Mr. Barton said he had always been interested in writing. "It was something I had always wanted to do, but

I knew nobody made any money writing, so I became an engineer," he said.

After settling into his career, he found that his desire to write had not dimmed. He started writing short stories and sold the first two he attempted to sell.

"I got lucky," Mr. Barton said. "I thought, 'Hey, there's nothing to this.' But it was almost two years before I sold another one."

His first book, *Ride Down the Wind,* was really more an accident than a plan. "I started writing a short story, and it kept getting longer," he said. "I worked on it off and on. With the first one [first book], at the beginning, I really learned a lot."

Mr. Williams, who has been a professor of English for 20 years (17 of which have been at Odessa), had always been interested in writing and had several published works before hooking up with Mr. Barton.

"The hardest part of writing is dealing with the disappointment of getting one back in the mail. You never get used to the rejection," Mr. Williams said.

Although both men had written about topics outside the Western genre, "I kept coming back to this area and the people I know," Mr. Barton said.

To write accurately about the period of time in a manuscript, many writers spend months doing nothing but research, however, "research implies a lot more organization than we have," Mr. Barton said. "We read a lot and explore a lot of the area [the book's setting]. The people we write about are not all that different from those we know today; their attitudes, their dreams, their desires."

Mr. Barton and Mr. Williams said it's important for the proper hardware to be used in their books, not only in the guns used by their good guys and bad guys, but the farm equipment and other utensils.

"If you convince people you know what you're talking about in certain areas, then they'll believe what you're talking about," Mr. Barton said.

"And if you get the background right, it makes it easier for people to believe in your characters," Mr. Williams said.

For those who are interested in becoming writers, "Take two aspirin and lie down until it goes away," Mr. Barton advised jokingly.

"But probably the advice that everybody gives and nobody listens to is to set aside some time and space every day and write. And don't stop when you get discouraged. Work on writing like you would work on anything else," Mr. Barton said.

Although both writers think that writing every day is good advice, they admit that it doesn't always work that way with their schedules.

"You should also read what you want to write," Mr. Williams added.

For the Western genre, Mr. Barton and Mr. Williams selected Elmer Kelton of San Angelo as the best living Western writer.

"Anyone who doesn't write does not realize how much work it is," Mr. Barton said, adding that it helps to have an understanding family as well if you want to be a writer.

"When it's going well, it's a tremendous amount of fun," Williams said.

As for projected completion dates, the team said they set a time limit for the finish of their projects. "But we never conform," Mr. Barton said.

WAYNE BARTON
& STAN WILLIAMS

In a town full
of liars, there's only
one way to get the truth

MANHUNT

"Plenty of action and suspense...combines
the best elements of the classic Western
and the classic detective yarn."
—T.V. Olsen, author of *The Burning Sky*